BLOOD EVIDENCE

A Cass Leary Legal Thriller

ROBIN JAMES

For all the latest on my new releases and exclusive content, sign up for my newsletter at:

http://www.robinjamesbooks.com/newsletter/

Chapter 1

"You OPEN that oven one more time and I'm sticking this meat thermometer up your rear end!"

My brother Matty froze, his hand on the oven door. He slowly turned to see me brandishing the business end of the thermometer and he knew I wasn't kidding.

"I'm hungry!" he said.

"We eat in an hour," I said. "Have a roll." I tossed him one from the wooden basket on the table.

Well, it wasn't really a table. It was two tables, shoved together. We'd pulled every chair we could find and stuck them around the thing.

My sister Vangie's house was barely big enough to hold us all, but we were making the best of it. Matty gave me a sour look, but retreated from the kitchen, taking a wolfish bite out of the roll he'd caught. He joined the others in the living room. A cheer went up followed by a chorus of cursing as the Lions' kicker missed an extra point.

I stood with my hands on my hips and surveyed the table settings one more time. Sixteen. We'd made room for sixteen.

We'd cobbled together some mismatched table settings.

Vangie had only moved into the house a few months ago. It was small. Only two bedrooms. But it was big enough for her and my seven-year-old niece Jessa. Plus, it was supposed to be conveniently down the street from me. It would have been, until faulty wiring burned my lake house to the ground a couple of months ago. So this Thanksgiving, we were making the best of it here on Finn Lake.

"Relax," my brother Joe said. He had come from the hallway. One bathroom for sixteen people with half of them drinking beer had also been a challenge.

"Did you bring the cranberry sauce?" I asked.

He scrunched his nose up. "Nobody likes that crap Cass. Grandpa Leary was the only one and he's been dead for a billion years."

"We have to have cranberry sauce," I said. "It's a thing, Joe. It'd be like forgetting the gravy."

"Who forgot the gravy?" Matty yelled from the living room.

"No one!" Joe and I yelled back together.

"You need a drink," Joe said.

"Try this." Jeanie Mills, my law partner, came out of the kitchen and handed me a freshly poured glass of apple Riesling. Making it was her new hobby. Jeanie wasn't related by blood, but she was as close to me as everyone else in this room. She put an arm around me.

"I'm glad you're here," I said. Jeanie usually traveled to Fort Wayne for the holidays. She had a sister out there. This year, she and her brother-in-law had taken a European cruise for their anniversary so I happily inherited Jeanie for the day.

Tough, short, no-nonsense, Jeanie had always been able to help me keep my brothers in line growing up. She'd been one of the only responsible adults in our lives after we lost our mother. Our father was ... well ... absent.

2

"Maddy, sit!"

Jessa held a biscuit in her hand. She'd been trying to teach my dog Madison some basic commands.

Matty turned around. "You're gonna have to come up with a different name for that damn dog." I hadn't thought it through when I named her, but Maddy and Matty sounded the same.

I held a hand over my mouth to cover my giggle. "Mads," I said. "Remember, Jessa? We call her Mads when Uncle Matty's around."

"Wouldn't hurt you to learn to heel either," Jeanie said, ruffling my brother's hair as she passed by him.

I took a sip of my wine. The doorbell rang. Vangie was closest and answered. Matty's wife Tina stood there with a tentative smile on her face.

I held my breath for a moment. Matty and Tina had been off and on again for the last year and a half. When Matty stayed on the wagon, Tina stayed around. When he didn't, it got ugly for everyone.

Matty rose. Tina held up two cans of cranberry sauce.

"To the rescue," Joe said. He stepped around me and gave our sister-in-law a hug.

"Hey, Vangie," Tina said.

The two of them had a frosty relationship. Despite Matty's shortcomings, Vangie would defend him to the death against anyone for anything. And my sister wasn't one to hold her tongue for diplomacy's sake.

"Hey, Tina!" I called out. Her shoulders sank with relief for the diversion from Vangie's withering stare. Matty shot her a look aimed to get her to back off.

"Good luck gettin' that to work," I muttered under my breath as Tina came closer. Jessa was at my side ready to take her coat to the back bedroom.

"Full house, huh?" Tina asked.

It really was. Joe's daughter Emma was here with her new boyfriend. Joe's wife Katy brought her brother and sister in from out of town. Their house would have been better for this particular shindig, but for the Leary family, holidays at the lake was a tradition going back eighty years, come hell or high water. It felt like bad juju to break it.

"Everything smells great," Tina said. She really was a sweet girl. Dark-brown hair, she had apples in her cheeks when she smiled. Her hug felt genuine as she wrapped her arms around me.

"It's good to have you here," I said. "You're good for Matty."

"Don't start," Joe said through gritted teeth.

"Turkey's done!"

My sister-in-law Katy called out from the kitchen. It caused a mad scramble to the tables.

"Perfect timing," Matty said. "It's half-time anyway."

Marbury, my other dog, opened a lazy eye from the end of the couch. He was far more laid back than his mother. Jessa held Madison in her arms as she took her seat next to Vangie.

"No dogs at the table," Vangie told her daughter.

"Guess that leaves you out too," Joe said to our little brother. Matty slugged him in the arm. Tina gave Matty some side-eye. He cleared his throat and took a seat beside her.

"They're brothers," Vangie said in a sharp tone to Tina. "They don't need you to mediate."

"Vangie," I whispered.

Joe went to the head of the table as Katy brought the turkey out for him to carve. Emma and her boyfriend, Ian, scooted past little Jessa. Katy and Joe didn't really approve of Ian, but I wondered if it was always like that with teenage daughters.

4

"Come, you heathens," Katy said. "See if you can manage to get through grace."

"Technically we're papists," Joe said. I bit my lip past the mention that very few of us at this table had actually been to Mass in a while. Still, our Irish-Catholic blood ran strong.

"Balls," Matty said. "The gravy's still on the stove."

"You owe me a dollar, Uncle Matty," Jessa said. "No swearing at the dinner table."

"How about no swearing anywhere?" I waved a ladle at my brother. He stuck his tongue out at me and dodged around Joe's knife for the kitchen.

"I'm missing a fork," Jeanie called out.

"I've got two," Ian said, handing her one.

Matty came back from the kitchen and deposited two gravy boats, one at each end of the table.

"You mongrels all situated now?" I said, exasperated. And yet, a warm glow filled me. I couldn't remember the last time we'd all been together like this. In the past few years, other things had always gotten in the way. First I left Delphi. Then Vangie did. Matty and Tina had been separated as much as they were together.

This was good. Familiar chaos that made this house feel like home, despite how tiny and temporary it all was. After dinner, I had a surprise for my brothers and sister.

"Grace, Joe," Katy said. He froze, holding his carving knife in one hand, a serving fork in the other.

"Cass, you do it," he said. "I always forget the words she used."

He put down the utensils and everyone around the table joined hands.

I missed my mother today. She was here in spirit though. I pretended I could see the room through her eyes and knew I could through her heart. We were all her babies. We were all in one piece.

I cleared my throat. "I think I remember how this goes. May there always be work for your hands to do. May your pockets always hold a coin or two. May the sun shine bright on your windowpane. May the rainbow be certain to follow each rain. May the hand of a friend always be near you. And may God fill your heart with gladness to cheer you."

I think I saw Jeanie wipe a tear from her eye. I wondered if she felt my mother's spirit too.

"What about the other part?" Jessa asked. "The food part."

"Right," I said. We linked hands again. "Bless us oh Lord, for these thy gifts which we are about to receive from thy bounty, through Christ, Our Lord, Amen."

The amens wound their way around the table and Jessa looked to Matty and mimicked his proper sign of the cross. I scooted my chair back in.

"Rub a dub dub, bless this grub," Joe said, winking. That was Grandpa Leary's favorite blessing. He plopped the first slab of turkey on his plate and passed the platter around.

"Save some for the rest of us, fatass," Matty called out.

"That's *two* dollars," Jessa said.

Matty winked at her. "Can I just give you a twenty and call it even?"

"Stop," Tina said. She was blushing though. They were holding hands under the table. Lord, that's how it was with those two. There was no middle ground. They were either living in separate houses, or all over each other. We prayed over the food, but I had secretly prayed for Matty to keep himself straight through the coming year. Tina deserved that from him. And he deserved it for himself. He'd be twenty-seven in a few weeks. Far past time to grow up and settle.

As the food made its way around the table, the conversation died down as everyone stuffed their mouths. Jeanie caught my eye. Of course she was thinking of my mom too.

Later, with my brothers' bellies full and the Lions hopelessly behind in points, I figured now was as good a time as any to do the other big thing I had planned for the day.

I pulled the rusted, partially charred lockbox out from the bottom of the front closet along with a set of bolt cutters I borrowed from my brother for the occasion. A few months ago, one of the demolition crew members had found it in the ashes of my former home. It had been buried near the foundation of the house our great-grandfather had built. The faded lettering on the side of the box read: "Clan Leary – April 14, 1922."

"Turn the television off," Vangie said, eyeing the box. I took a seat on the floor in the middle of the living room. My brothers, their wives, my sister, various in-laws, and Jeanie all sat up straighter in their seats.

"We're never all together like this these days," I said. "I figured today would be the perfect day to see what's inside this thing."

"Let me," Joe said.

He took the bolt cutter and sat on the floor beside me. The brittle lock broke easily and fell away. I hesitated before opening the lid. I didn't expect to find anything of monetary value inside the thing. Still, as far as we knew, this box hadn't been opened in nearly a century. I felt the ghosts of my family's past whispering in my ear.

The lid creaked as I opened it. Inside, there were yellowed stacks of folded paper. I took them out one by one. At the bottom of the box was a mountain of old photographs. Joe took some of them and began to spread them on the coffee table in front of the couch.

"Wow," Vangie said, kneeling beside the table. "Look at all of them."

The largest of the pictures was a group shot with the lake itself as the backdrop. The caption written on the front in white chalk read: "Clan Leary, 1921." On the back of the photo were written all the first names. We read them together.

A handsome fellow stood in front, one hand on his hip, the other on a shovel that he'd just planted in the earth.

"That's Great-Grandpa," Joe said. "Patrick. I think he's breaking ground on the original lake house."

"You're right," I said. The man in the photo had an opaque right eye. We'd always been told he'd gone blind in it after a battlefield injury suffered in the waning days of World War I. The lake view behind him hadn't changed much in a hundred years. I stared at it every morning in the year and a half since I came back to Delphi and moved into the house. I missed it.

From the group photo, we were able to recognize most of the rest of the people in the other images. They depicted various stages of construction of the old house. We'd always heard Great-Grandpa built the place with his bare hands, but it was another thing to see it actually happening. He worked alongside his brothers, our great-uncles. He'd hung a tire swing on the giant weeping willow tree that hadn't survived the fire. In one shot, a little boy sat in it, ready to get launched straight into the lake.

I picked up the folded, yellow pages that I'd found on the top of the box. My heart tripped as I carefully spread them out. They were sketches, done in Great-Grandpa Leary's hand. House plans drawn in painstaking detail, floor by floor. At the top of each page, he'd written "My Someday House."

It was beautiful. He'd dreamt of a home with tall windows

on each floor facing the lake. It had a huge, wrap-around porch and a stable beside it.

"That's not what the old house looked like at all," Matty observed.

"It never would have fit on that lot," I said. "He says it's the Someday House. Maybe he was planning to upgrade someday."

"Just like you," Vangie said, smiling.

I folded the pages and tucked them against my chest. There were tears in my eyes. I turned away so my brothers and sister wouldn't see. Jeanie did though. She reached around and patted my shoulder.

I hadn't yet told any of them except for Jeanie that I'd bought a double lot from the township earlier this fall after a tense negotiation. This house my great-grandfather conceived, almost a hundred years ago? It looked uncannily similar to what I'd discussed with my contractor. While the rest of my family pored over the photos, I put Grandpa's plans in my leather bag. I wanted to study them in more detail when I was alone.

"Dad should see these," Matty whispered to Vangie. I don't think he knew I was close enough to hear. She shot him a nervous glance and nodded quickly. My stomach dropped. I knew that look. My youngest brother and sister were hiding a secret.

Matty looked up and caught my glance. He swallowed hard.

"Matty," I said. "Can I talk to you for a second?"

Joe froze on the other side of the room.

"Matty," Vangie said. "You might as well just tell them."

Tina moved closer to her husband. "Tell us what?" she asked.

Matty let out a hard sigh. "Don't freak out," he said. "But ... Dad's back in town."

The earth shifted beneath me. Joe rose with the force of a volcano.

"What do you mean, Dad's back in town?" His voice thundered. The dogs scrambled for cover.

"He wanted to come today," Vangie said. "We didn't think that would be such a good idea."

"When were you going to tell us?" I asked.

My father, Joe Leary, Sr. had been the single, most significant destructive force within my family. He was volatile when drunk and that had been most of my childhood. Then, when my mother passed away, he all but disappeared, leaving Joe and me to practically raise Matty and Vangie alone.

"We're telling you now," Matty said, his voice taking a hard edge. Tina's eyes caught mine. I tried to force a smile. She of all people knew what this meant. My father's presence had been one of Matty's biggest triggers as he struggled with his own alcoholism. She was near tears, which told me this bombshell was news to her too.

"You've been talking to him?" Joe said. "Both of you?"

"A little," Vangie said. "We told him now wasn't the best time to come back into the family. We were going to talk to you guys first."

"He's different this time," Matty said. "He's got his drinking under control. He told me he's been seeing Sheila Brewer."

"The town librarian?" Joe said, incredulous. "You mean that sweet little lady who wears the cat sweatshirts?"

"Yeah," Vangie said.

"Christ," Joe said. "She's lived in Delphi her whole life. What the hell is she thinking of getting mixed up with him? And if Dad's drinking at all, it's not under control, Matty."

"He's happy," Matty said. "And he's changed. If you'd just give him a chance ..."

Joe's bitter laugh sent a flash of fear through me. Of all of us, he'd suffered the most at our father's hands. The last day we all lived under the same roof together, my brother had finally chased him off with a shotgun after Dad threatened to hit Matty in a drunken rage. Matty had been maybe twelve years old.

"You listen to me," Joe said. He pointed a finger at our younger brother. "You stay away from that man. He's nothing but trouble. He'll drag you down. How many times has he done it before? Huh? What's it going to take for you to learn?"

"Joe," Matty started. Tina was full-on crying now. She feared the same thing Joe and I did.

He was back. My father was back. By the look on Matty's face, I knew it was already too late. Matty had probably already let him all the way back into his life. I heard a sound then in my imagination as if a fuse had been lit.

Tick. Tick. Boom.

Chapter 2

THE MONDAY AFTER THANKSGIVING, I'd never been so happy to head back to the relative calm of my office. My secretary, Miranda, greeted me with a smile and a warm cup of coffee. For nearly two years I'd chided her not to do that. But making my coffee served her mothering instincts and I'd learned not to argue with or cross Miranda Sulier, or else.

"So," she said, sipping from her own mug. "Old Joe's back in town, huh?"

It didn't surprise me that the news had already reached her.

"It appears," I said.

"Hmm," Miranda snorted. "You want to tell me how that's going?"

"Not really," I said. Despite the tornado that was Joe Leary Sr., my weekend had been relatively calm. "I haven't actually seen him yet. I think he's too scared of Joe Jr. and me to show his face. Though I did hear a rumor. Is he really shacking up with the town librarian?"

Miranda's face turned sour and it was enough of an answer. "I don't get that at all. Sheila Brewer has always struck me as pretty sensible. I think she's spent too much time alone over the years. Anyway, I wasn't going to say anything, but I think you should know, he was at Mickey's bar last night."

Acid flooded my chest. Mickey's had been my father's old haunt since before I was born. Most of the explosions at home came after Dad had spent a night there. For the longest time, the smell of that place filled me with dread.

"Well that didn't take him long," I said. With bitterness, I recalled Matty's comment that our father had his drinking *under control.*

"You know I'm good friends with Serena," Miranda said. Serena Cox was married to Mickey Junior. He inherited the bar from his old man, Mickey Sr., another legendary town drunk, though he'd turned his life around in the end.

I sat down hard on one of the waiting room chairs. It was early still, just past seven. Miranda wouldn't unlock the office doors until eight. I put my feet up on the coffee table, dislodging some magazines Miranda had carefully fanned out.

"It's okay," she said. "For now, anyway. Serena said he didn't order anything harder than a Sprite."

"You're kidding," I said.

"Nope," Miranda answered. "And he gave Mickey Jr. a hundred-dollar bill to cover a long-standing tab. From what I hear, he had a great old time playing pool in the back with some of the old-timers."

"Thanks for letting me know," I said.

I left my coffee on the table. I didn't have the stomach for it. I made my way upstairs. I tried to distract myself by organizing the mess of papers on my desk. I'd just finished a civil trial on a personal injury case. We won, but the insurance company planned an appeal. It was a ploy to force settlement even after a victory. I had a sobering conversation ahead of me with my clients.

Sometime past eight, there was a soft knock at the door. Jeanie poked her head in.

"You holding up okay?" she asked.

No doubt Miranda had already filled her in on the gossip from Mickey's. Jeanie had been cool with the news on Thanksgiving.

"I'm just peachy," I said.

She waved a hand. "Give me a break. I just don't like seeing how your dad riles you and Joey up. Don't give him that kind of power over you. You haven't even seen him yet."

"I'm not worried about Joey or me," I said. "I'm worried about Matty. He spirals when Dad's around."

Jeanie's smile turned grim. "Yeah. We'll keep an eye on that."

I wanted to thank her for not saying everything would be okay like most people would. She more than anyone knew how *not* okay things could get when my dad was involved.

"Listen," she said. "I only partially knocked on your door to ask about Joe Sr. More than that, I wanted to pick your brain. I need help with a client."

"You need *my* help?" I asked. Jeanie specialized in family law. I dragged her out of retirement a while back. She started out just acting as counsel and second chair on some of my more complicated cases. Recently, she'd started taking a few of her own again. Word was getting out and Jeanie Mills was in demand.

"Come on," she said, opening the door wider and jerking her chin. "Come meet with her."

"Her?" I asked, rising from my chair.

"You'll like her," Jeanie said.

I walked with Jeanie down to her office. I'd given her the

big one on the first floor. It actually took up half that part of the building. She had a sitting area in front of a non-functional fireplace. We used it as a conference room for new clients.

A young couple sat holding hands on the leather couch in front of the mantel. The woman was pretty. Chocolate-brown hair that she wore in a pixie cut. Big brown eyes that darted over me. Her skin was pale and smooth. She had expertly applied eyeshadow that I envied. Her husband was tall, broad, formidable. They complemented each other. His skin was dark, his head shaved bald. He kept a protective arm around his wife as he reached out to shake my hand.

"These are the Romaines," Jeanie said. "Terrence and Alicia."

"Nice to meet you," I said. I took a seat beside Jeanie on the other couch opposite the Romaines. Mrs. Romaine held a thin file folder under her arm. She put it on her lap and fidgeted with the tab, nearly fraying it.

"Alicia," Jeanie said. "This is Cass, my partner."

"I've heard of you," Alicia said. She cast a nervous glance at her husband. There was something a little familiar about him, but I couldn't quite place it.

"I read about the Drazdowski case," she said.

I nodded. That told me right away that Alicia Romaine wasn't from Delphi. I'd been the public defender in one of the town's most notorious crimes, the murder of Coach Larry Drazdowski. Even with that, Delphi regulars knew me from my family name better. We were from the "wrong" side of the lake and my law degree seemed as implausible to most townies as if I'd married the Prince of Monaco.

"Would you mind repeating to Cass what you told me?" Jeanie asked.

Alicia kept playing with that file tab. "An adoption," she said.

I looked at Jeanie. Adoptions were firmly in her wheelhouse, not mine. My primary exposure to them was representing my sister in her guardianship proceedings for Jessa. What in the world did Jeanie think I could bring to this particular table?

"My wife has been looking for her birth parents," Terrence Romaine chimed in. "Your firm came highly recommended."

I shot a look at Jeanie. Yeah. This was definitely *not* in my wheelhouse.

"I've tried a lot of different things over the years," Alicia said. "I mean, on my own. It's just lately ..."

Her voice trailed off. Terrence cleared his throat. "Alicia lost her parents ... her, uh ... adoptive parents last year. They were good people, my in-laws. The very best. First her mom passed away from breast cancer. Her dad had a heart attack two months after that. He really just lost the will to live without Caroline. I guess it happens that way sometimes."

"I'm so sorry," I said.

Alicia's eyes fluttered. "It would have hurt their feelings if I'd pursued this when they were alive. I mean, they never told me not to. And they shared with me what they could. But I knew they found it threatening no matter how many times I tried to explain. Nick and Caroline Merrit *were* my parents. It's just now ... I'm a mother too. Our son Corey just turned one. We've got another one on the way."

She put a hand over her as-yet flat stomach. I smiled. "Congratulations."

I shot another look to Jeanie. What in the world did she expect me to do with this one? At my core, I was a litigator. If anything, the Romaines needed a private investigator. No sooner had I thought it than I recognized that look in Jeanie's eyes.

Dammit. Jeanie Mills was one of the toughest lawyers in the county. In the state. She'd come up at a time when there weren't that many women lawyers, never mind ones that owned their own practices. I'd seen her shred judges, opposing counsel, dead-beat parents, and hostile witnesses with little more than a look and a word. But at her core, she was a teddy bear. Though I didn't yet know why, Terrence and Alicia Romaine had gotten under her skin.

The moment they left, I could give her my spiel about the conservation of firm resources, but I knew I'd lose. If Jeanie wanted to take this case, nothing I could say would stop her.

Alicia handed me the tattered file folder. I opened it. There wasn't much to it. I flipped through the yellowed pages of a thirty-year-old adoption order, a birth certificate, and a letter from the Precious Gifts Adoption Agency. Alicia had been identified only as Jane Doe. There were a few bits of non-identifying information about her birth mother. In essence, she'd just handed me the haystack. She was hiring us to find the needle.

"You know," I said. "Sometimes, for a variety of reasons, birth parents don't want to be found."

I had my own sister in mind. She'd given Jessa up for adoption all those years ago. My niece had been the product of a rape. When her adoptive parents died, Vangie was the only person Jessa had left.

"I know that," Alicia said. "And whatever happens, I just want to know. I can handle whatever it is. It's just ... it's a lot. The not knowing. I didn't mind so much before my own baby came. And if you can't find out, I'll understand. I just ... I know how good you are. I've asked around. You and Ms.

Mills. If you can't get to the bottom of this, then I'll know nobody can. I can live with that."

"It's okay. We'll do whatever we can for you. No matter what," Jeanie said. She had a tear in her eye. Yep. It would be a waste of my breath to try and talk her out of this one. The freight train that was Jeanie Mills had left the station long before I walked into her office.

Alicia Romaine let out a strangled cry. Her husband tightened his arms around her. He kissed her head. They were a team, that was easy to see. I wondered what that would be like.

Terrence Romaine rose to his considerable height, taking Alicia with him.

"Talk it over," he said. "That's your copy. Just let us know what you decide."

We shook hands. Miranda was at the door, ready to usher the Romaines out to the lobby. She shut the door behind her and gave me a knowing smile. Oh, she'd clearly already been flattened by the Jeanie Mills freight train.

I waited until I heard the front door open and shut before turning back to Jeanie.

She already had a hand up. "Don't say it," she said.

"I didn't say anything," I said.

"They're willing to pay," she said. "And it might be fun."

"Fun," I said. "Man, I've spent my entire life trying to get out from under my real parents. I can't imagine what it's like trying to find them."

"See," she said. "Then this is just what you need. Something lower key. Simple. Non-confrontational. We've had more than enough excitement around here to last a lifetime. I'm doing you a favor."

"Quick," I said. "Give me five Glory Bes before you jinx us."

There wasn't enough time to even explain myself before Miranda opened the door again. She held my cell phone in her hand and a severe expression on her face.

I knew before she said it. The jinx was already unfolding. "It's your dad, honey," she said. "It's trouble. The really bad kind."

I shut my eyes and let out a breath. Of course it was. It always was. As I took the phone from her, I swear I could once again hear that time bomb go off.

Chapter 3

How many more times in my life would I have to pull up to one of my family member's houses and see flashing lights and cop cars in the driveway?

I steeled myself for what I knew would happen as I slammed my car in park and headed toward Vangie's. I did a mental checklist of the most immediate problems. Jessa wasn't here. She was safely at school today. That turned out to be the only bright spot on the horizon. As I got to Vangie's back door, my brother Matty came stumbling out, followed by two massive Delphi cops.

"Stop it!" I yelled, not sure if I meant Matty or the officers. Matty's face was purple with rage. I saw him clench his fists and covered my face with my hands. He reeked of alcohol.

No. Not again.

"Cass!" he yelled, seeing me. "What took you so long?"

"Is he under arrest?" I asked the officers. They passed a look.

"Not yet," the bigger of the two said. He was new. I think

his name was Bart or Burt or something. He couldn't be more than a couple of years out of high school, that one.

I took the opportunity to grab my brother by the arm. "Shut up," I said through clenched teeth.

"It's not me," he said. "I didn't do a damn thing. I'm trying to keep these assholes from messing with Dad."

I looked back toward the road. In addition to the two patrol cars, I saw another gray sedan. My heart sank as I recognized it as an unmarked cop car. There was already a detective on scene.

"I've got this," I said to the cops. "My brother isn't going to get in your way."

"He needs to watch his mouth," one of the cops said.

"Don't I know it." I pulled Matty away from the house. His nostrils flared and I swore I could see steam coming out of his ears.

"What the hell is going on?" I asked him, whispering so we wouldn't be overheard. "One of the neighbors is friends with my secretary. She called saying there was trouble here. Where's Dad?"

Matty jerked out of my grasp. "I was gonna call you myself until *that* one decided to play tough guy."

"Matty, shut up," I said.

"They've got Dad inside," he said. "You need to get in there."

I covered my face with my hand. God knew what my father had done this time. It was bad enough my brother was clearly off the wagon again.

"I'm going," I said. "But you stay here. Better yet. Go home, Matty. You'll only make things worse being here."

"I'm not moving," he said.

I let out a sigh. If he would just make good on that statement, I could work with that. Only I knew my little brother far too well. He had a lot of fight in him he'd inherited from our father. I just hoped he'd have the good sense not to get himself in further trouble on top of whatever I had waiting for me inside that house.

"Where's Vangie?" I asked. My sister's temper was even worse than Matty's.

"At work," he said. Vangie had gotten a waitressing job working mornings and lunches.

"So what the hell are the two of you doing here?" I asked.

"Dad and I met for breakfast at that new coffee place in town. I told Vangie I'd stop over today to put the plastic up on her windows to keep the cold air out. Dad came to help."

I heard yelling coming from inside. "Just ... just stay put. And stay quiet," I said, shaking my head.

I marched up my sister's back porch and let myself inside. Two more uniformed officers tried to stop me. I saw my father seated at Vangie's kitchen table smoking a cigarette. He had a sly smile on his face as he watched me come in.

"That's my daughter," he said. "And she's my lawyer."

Lord. At the moment, I wasn't sure which thing I hated worse.

The detective sitting with my father had his back turned to me. I recognized him anyway from that thick, dark hair, broad shoulders, and slightly wrinkled gray suit.

Detective Eric Wray straightened and rose from his seat. His face was grim as he turned toward me.

"Cass ..."

"Is he under arrest?" I asked.

"No," Eric said. "I just have some questions for your father. He knows he's been free to leave this entire time."

"Questioning him about what?" I said.

I don't know if it made me feel better or worse, but Eric looked positively nauseous. It occurred to me for the first time that he probably wanted to be anywhere else but here too. But, here we were. When Joe Leary Sr. came to town, it was a given trouble would follow him. I just didn't yet know how deep. "Can we talk?" I asked Eric.

His nostrils flared. He looked from my father to me.

"Better listen to her," my father said, his smug smile widening.

Eric rapped his knuckles on the table. "I'm not done with you," he said.

I crossed my arms in front of me and walked into Vangie's front room. Eric followed. I turned on him.

"What's going on?"

"Cass ..." he started.

"What is it you think he's done?"

"Do you know Sheila Brewer?" he asked.

A cold pit formed in my stomach. Sheila Brewer. The quiet librarian with the cat sweatshirts.

Eric pursed his lips. "Why do I feel like you already know where this is going?"

That cold pit turned into a ball of ice. "I really don't. Go on."

"There's been a missing person's report filed on her," Eric said.

"What do you mean?" I asked.

"Just what I said. She didn't show up for work today. She's got a cousin she's close to who says she hasn't been returning her calls or texts for over forty-eight hours. She wasn't home when the cousin checked early this morning. I'm following up on some information I received that your father has been seen with her recently."

"Right. The minute you heard my father was peripherally involved, you raced right over. What's he told you?" I asked, looking over Eric's shoulder. My father snuffed out his cigarette on a plate.

"Cass," he said. "This is an ongoing investigation. If this woman is in trouble ... if your dad can give us any help in how to find her ..."

"He's a person of interest," I said.

Eric looked down. "Cass."

"Eric, my father's under suspicion. That's why you're here. You know what I'm going to tell you."

"Dammit, Cass," he said. "I'm trying to do my job."

"And I have to do mine. If you want to question my dad, I'll come down to the station with him. If you're planning on arresting him ..."

"You need to be careful," Eric said. "One of these days your old man is going to try to get you to cross a line, Cass."

Oh, he already had, more times than I could count.

"I'll ask again. Is he under suspicion?"

"No," Eric spat. "Not yet anyway."

"Fine. Then what are two patrol cars and four uniformed officers doing outside my sister's house?"

Eric dropped his chin. "Your brother doesn't make things easy. And your dad doesn't have the most docile reputation. I wanted to make sure everything was done by the book. I know how the two of them get."

"So why didn't you call me first?" I asked. "If you'd told me what you were after, I would have brought my father down to the station to talk to you. All of this wasn't necessary."

"Right," he said. "Exactly when was the last time a Leary man came willingly down to the police station to answer questions?"

"Eric ..."

"Don't. You know I'm right."

"This is my sister's house," I said. "Jessa lives here. What if she'd been home?"

Eric at least had the decency to look chagrined. "I made sure she wasn't."

Jessa had witnessed the murder of her adoptive parents just last year. It had taken her months to come out of her shell. She was only now settling into a regular routine and accepting Vangie as her mom.

"Eric, I need you to leave," I said. "I meant what I said. If my father has anything useful to say in your missing person's investigation, I'll be in touch."

"Cass, he's already made some statements ... willingly."

"What statements?" I asked. I felt like I was already in the death spiral of whatever family crisis my father had brought on. I hadn't even had an official conversation with him yet.

"If you coach him ..."

My blood boiled. "You're accusing me of obstructing justice now?"

Matty picked that time to completely ignore what I told him. He walked into the kitchen and stood at my father's side. My brother looked positively murderous. I'd be lucky if I could get Eric and his men out of here without Matty racking up an assault charge. This mess was growing bigger by the second.

"Either arrest my father or leave," I said. "Please. It's bad enough all the neighbors saw this little show."

Eric let out a hot breath through his nostrils. As he passed by my father, he paused and shook a finger at him. "Don't leave town."

It was an empty threat. If my dad weren't under arrest, Eric had no legal right to restrict his movements. I, on the other hand, felt ready to kick his ass straight out of Michigan.

I stood frozen, waiting until I heard Eric's car start up and drive away. A few seconds later, the patrol cars followed suit. I let out a breath I hadn't meant to hold and joined my father and brother in the kitchen.

"Son of a bitch," Matty said.

"Don't start," I said to him, my voice sharp. "You're only making things worse."

"Dad hasn't done anything wrong," Matty said.

"I need you to get out of here," I said. "I want to talk to Dad alone."

Matty opened his mouth to argue. My father stopped him with a hand on his chest. "It's okay, son. I'm not afraid of your sister. Head on home. I'll meet you there later and we can take a look at that truck engine of yours. You're leaking oil."

Matty threw a hard look my way, but did as my father ordered. I saw Matty's keys on the kitchen counter and grabbed them. Matty flipped me the bird and charged out the front door on foot.

I stared hard at my father. I hadn't seen him in years. His deeply lined face was so much like my brother Joe's. He leveled those cold eyes at me and calmly sipped from a chipped mug. It looked like coffee, but I wondered if he'd spiked it.

"Good to see you again, daughter," he said. "Come here and give your old man a proper hug."

I shook my head. He could sit there and pretend like nothing whatsoever was wrong. I wasn't having it.

"Come on," I said. "I want you out of here before Vangie and Jessa get here. Where have you been staying?"

"Here and there," he said. "With Davy Monroe some. But I've got a room at the Harmon off U.S. 12."

Davy Monroe was one of my father's oldest friends and drinking buddies. Davy had always idolized my dad for reasons I never understood.

"I'll take you back to the Harmon," I said.

"I wanna stay here and meet my granddaughter."

"Not a chance," I said. "Not today. Get in my car. We're gonna track down Matty and drive his ass home. Then I'll deal with whatever the hell else this is."

For once, my father didn't protest. He grabbed his pack of cigarettes and followed me out to my Jeep. I drove slowly, scanning the streets for Matty. He was nowhere to be found. I pulled down a side street and parked the car.

"You want to tell me what the hell all that was about?"

He shrugged. "Your boyfriend seems to think I know something about a missing woman."

"Sheila Brewer," I said. "And he's not my boyfriend. Don't start that crap. What's the deal with the two of you? Matty and Vangie said you've been seeing her. Since when?"

He rested his arm on the side of the door. "We went out a couple of times. Wasn't serious."

"When was the last time you saw her?" I asked.

He narrowed his eyes and took a longer beat than I thought necessary. "A few weeks ago."

"Is that what you told Eric?"

He raised a brow. "It's Eric now? I saw the way he looks at you, sweetheart. That's a good thing. It could come in handy."

I didn't like his tone. He was smarmy, acting like he was smarter than I was. If he'd done that with Eric, no wonder he wasn't satisfied.

"Eric said you gave a statement. I need to know everything you told him."

"I told him I haven't seen Sheila in a couple of weeks. I have no idea where she's gotten off to. It wasn't serious between us. She's just a nice gal who needed somebody to talk to sometimes."

A car honked behind me. I waved them off then put the

car back in gear. We sat in silence as I combed all the side streets looking for my brother. Then I drove around the lake. He'd vanished. More than likely, someone he knew had seen him walking and picked him up. I just prayed he didn't get himself in any further trouble while I figured out what to do with my dad.

"Just take me back to my hotel," he said. "We've been driving around for almost an hour. I've got things to do."

I didn't dare ask what. I turned down Porter Street heading toward the expressway. It only took another fifteen minutes to get to the Harmon Arms Hotel from this side of the lake. It was really just a strip motel with about a dozen rooms. Clean, but cheap. He was probably waiting for one of us to invite him to stay. For the first time since it happened, I was glad my house burned down.

"Sheila Brewer," I said. "Is somebody telling the cops you were the last person seen with her? Did you have an argument? Anything that would make someone suspicious?"

He shook his head. "Just minding my own business, like always."

He was full of it. But I knew it was all I would get. He made me so tired. I needed to know a hell of a lot more about Sheila Brewer and what was going on with her. I only knew her a little. Like my father described, she was just a nice, lonely lady. Quiet. Always smiling. I knew she ran storytime for kids on Monday afternoons because Jessa sometimes went. I'd ask around once I got my father off my hands. For now, if I could just get my old man to stop pissing off the cops.

"Have you been drinking?" I asked him.

"No," he spat back. "I don't care for your insinuation."

"Dad," I said. "I haven't seen you in years. I pull up and you're being questioned about some woman's disappearance and Matty reeks of beer. I need to go check on him."

"Fine," he said. "Just drop me off and go save the world."

I pulled into the motel parking lot. I was about to ask my father which room was his.

"Son of a bitch," he muttered. I wouldn't need his answer on the room number.

There were three more Delphi P.D. patrol cars parked in front of one at the end of the row. I pulled up just as two cops closed off room number seven with crime scene tape.

Chapter 4

"STAY IN THE CAR," I said to my father.

"Like hell I will. They can't do that. I have a right to privacy. Doesn't matter it's a hotel."

He was weirdly calm. It could mean nothing good. I turned to him.

"Listen. You and I are going to have to have a serious conversation. For now, you need to keep your trap shut and let me figure out how deep a hole you've already dug for yourself."

He sneered at me. "I know my rights, Cass."

"I know them better. And if I find out you had anything to do with whatever's going on with that woman ..."

"You'll what?"

It wasn't a threat, exactly, but I'd seen that hard look in his eyes so many times. In some ways, it took me right back to being ten years old. The man got downright mean when he drank. He was stone-cold sober now. No matter what else happened, I needed him to stay that way.

I left his question unanswered, and got out of the car. I

slammed the door behind me and walked up to the crime scene tape.

Detective Megan Lewis stood in front of number seven just as I approached. She startled when she saw me.

"Can you show me your warrant?" I asked.

"Cass ..."

Where Megan Lewis was, Eric Wray would soon follow. A few months ago, she'd been reassigned to partner with him. Megan was a good egg. A few years younger than me, she'd had her work cut out for her being the only female detective in Delphi. It was some small consolation that she looked as miserable to be here as I was.

"It's on the way," she said. "Is that your dad in the car?"

"Yes," I said. "But unless you're charging him ..."

"Save it," she said. "Eric's already given me the rundown."

"Great. Now give it to me. What's going on, Megan?" Had Eric known they were planning to search my dad's hotel room? He had to have. My blood simmered. Had he been stalling us the entire time? If so, it was unethical as hell.

Megan cast a furtive glance at the man standing on the other side of her unmarked patrol car. He was wearing a bleached-out tank top and pajama pants with leather slippers. He twirled a keyring in his right hand. I could only assume he was the hotel manager and for whatever reason, had seen fit to open my dad's room.

"Cass," Megan said. "This isn't what you think."

"Really? Did you or did you not just tell me you don't have a warrant yet? That door's been opened. There's crime scene tape up."

She took my arm and pulled me aside. As we stepped around Megan's car, I caught a glimpse of one of the maids sitting in the back seat of a black and white. She was crying and one of the uniformed cops handed her a cup of coffee and a tissue.

"There was a 911 call," she said. "The maid came in and said she'd heard some screaming coming from room number seven late last night. She was too scared to report it until now. One of the field ops officers came out here on a welfare check. The manager keyed him in. He ... uh ... he called for a detective right after. I got here about an hour and a half ago and wrote up the warrant based on what he saw. No one has set foot inside that room since. But my warrant's been signed and it'll be here any second."

The air felt thick in my lungs. What the hell had they found in that room?

"I was in the area," she said. "The patrolman saw signs of a struggle when the manager opened the door and called it in. I'm here. Nobody has searched anything. I told you, we're waiting on that warrant. In the meantime, nobody's going in or out of that room. That's why I'm here."

The hole my father was in kept getting deeper. Signs of a struggle. What the actual hell had he gotten himself into? The sooner I got him away from the cops, the better. At the same time, if he really was involved with Sheila Brewer's disappearance, I didn't want to touch him with a ten-foot cattle prod.

Just then, another patrol car pulled up. The uniformed officer was out of breath and carrying a piece of paper as he ran up to us. He handed the paper to Detective Lewis. She scanned it, nodded, then gave it to me.

I took a breath and read it. Judge Castor had granted their search warrant for my father's room just fifteen minutes ago. The particulars matched what Megan had just told me. The night maid said she'd heard disturbing sounds coming from room seven late last night, or rather early this morning. She'd been too scared to knock, but worried all night about what might have happened. She reported her story to the manager when he showed up at eight and he called the cops.

I moved past Megan and went to the open doorway of my father's room. I saw immediately what prompted the warrant and my heart dropped to the floor.

The chair near the television set was overturned. The bathroom mirror was cracked. I couldn't see all the way into the bathroom, but my vantage point told me plenty. There was blood splattered all over the walls.

I stood frozen as Megan took over and directed two patrolmen into the room with her. She immediately picked something up off the floor. It was a woman's wallet. Lewis's mouth turned down.

She pointed toward my father still sitting in the back of my car. I didn't have to ask what that meant. I turned on my heel and walked back to my car with Detective Lewis.

"Mr. Leary?" she said. "I'm going to need you to step out of the car."

My father gave me a cold look as he did what he was told. Megan didn't even have to say anything else. My father turned his back to Megan and flipped his wrists behind his back, ready for cuffs.

Megan at least had the decency to look apologetic as she read my father his rights and slapped the metal bracelets around his wrists.

"Don't worry, cupcake," he said to me, winking. "I know the drill."

Christ, I thought. The trouble was, so did I.

Chapter 5

"I wasn't even in that room last night," my father told me. We sat in an interrogation room at the Delphi police station.

"Can you prove that?" I asked. "Who saw you? Who were you with?"

"I went to Mickey's last night same as I've done every night since Thanksgiving. Ask Mickey Jr. Ask Scotty behind the bar. Ask the seven or eight waitresses who work every night. Mickey's got security cameras installed. I was there."

"This maid said she heard screaming coming from your hotel room this morning. Mickey's closes at two, Dad," I pointed out.

"I didn't come back last night," he said. "Davy Monroe came in. I told you I've been staying with him off and on. You know we go way back. We got to talking. Davy just lives a couple blocks down from Mickey's. After we closed the bar down, we went over to his place."

"Were you drinking?" I asked.

"Sprite," he said. "I haven't had a drop of anything harder in over a year. I'm sober."

I wanted to believe him. The truth was, I did. At least about

ROBIN JAMES

the drinking. Despite not having seen the man in years, he actually looked younger to me. His eyes were clear. His skin tone even. I only remembered one other time in my life where I'd seen him like that. It was during the summer when I was eleven years old. I only recently found out he'd tried to get sober because my mother had been struggling with pills that year.

"I didn't come here to louse things up for you," he said.

"Why *did* you come here, Dad? And if this is you *not* trying to mess up our lives, God knows what you would have done if you'd been trying," I said.

I could almost hear my mother's voice in my head telling me to give him the benefit of the doubt. She'd always done that. No matter how awful my father was to her or me or my brother Joe, Lynn Leary always turned the other cheek. Even if half a dozen times, he'd smacked her for it.

It was just a throwaway thought. But a cold shudder went through me. Had my father put down one bad habit only to pick up another?

"Tell me about Sheila Brewer again," I said.

"I already did. She was a friend. I've known her since high school. We dated a few times recently. But I haven't seen her in weeks. I got nothing to do with whatever might have happened to her."

"Davy Monroe," I said. "Your alibi is Davy Monroe."

"Yep," he said. "Ironclad. I was with him all last night until I left to go pick up Matty this morning."

"Was Sheila in a fight with anyone?" I asked. "Did she have enemies, exes?"

"I dunno," he answered. "She was a nice girl. Kinda clingy though. Not real smart. Stacked though."

I rolled my eyes. "Spare me. And you just said she *was* a nice girl."

"Was, is. Whatever."

I sat back hard in my chair. "Do you understand what's going on here, Dad? This woman is missing. Your hotel room was turned upside down. There was blood everywhere. How do you explain that?"

"I don't," he said. "I told you. I wasn't in that room last night. I haven't been there since Saturday morning. Ask that busybody maid. She saw me leaving it. I handed her a twenty-dollar bill for the week."

I pulled up the notes app on my phone and wrote that down. I also made a note to check in with Davy Monroe. There was a harsh knock on the door. Eric Wray didn't wait to step inside.

"You either charge me or cut me loose," my father said.

Eric narrowed his eyes at him. "Oh, don't worry, Joe. We're charging you." He saved his next hard glance for me. I straightened my back and followed him outside.

"You gonna keep me from questioning him?" he asked.

"No. I'm not. I'm just as interested in finding out what happened to that Brewer woman as you are. As far as he's concerned, you need to have a conversation with Davy Monroe."

Eric nodded. "Yeah. Your dad told me that line too."

"Well," I said. "What did he say?"

"This is an ongoing investigation," Eric said. "You know better than to ask me that."

"Fine."

"Your dad's being charged with obstruction."

"On what grounds?" I asked.

"On the grounds that he's been lying since the get-go, Cass. He's sworn up and down that he hasn't seen Sheila Brewer for weeks. I've got credible witnesses who have put him with her more recently. Lewis found *her* wallet and ID inside his hotel room."

My heart plummeted. This was getting worse and worse.

"None of those things prove he had anything to do with whatever happened to her," I said.

"Not yet," he said. "But what are you going to say to me when that blood comes back as a match for Sheila Brewer's?"

I had no answer. Eric knew that too.

"She's probably dead, Cass," he said. "You get that, right?"

I had to be careful what I said. I'd walked into about ten different conflicts of interest as it was. As it stood, Eric would probably need to question me as a witness if he was tracking my dad's movements since he came back to town. Only Eric actually saw him today before I did.

"He's willing to cooperate," I said.

"Right," Eric said. "I've already gotten a taste of Joe Sr.'s brand of cooperation."

I hated this. On all levels. I wanted to murder my father myself. He'd brought his shit storm right to my front door. Again. He was the main reason I left Delphi in the first place after law school.

There was a commotion behind me. I closed my eyes and took a breath as I recognized my brother Matty's voice as he yelled at the desk sergeant.

Eric's face went purple. "Perfect," he said. "Just want I need."

I put a hand on his chest. "Eric, I'll deal with my brother too."

He shook his head. "Cass, you're going to let them drag you down with them. I know you."

"Just stop," I said.

"You and your lost causes," he said. "One of these days

you'll get yourself in so deep I won't be able to save you. No one will."

I took my hand off him. "In case you haven't noticed, I'm capable of saving my own damn self, Eric."

He pursed his lips and looked skyward. He put his hands up as almost a gesture of surrender. Then he turned on his heel and walked away from me.

I dropped my chin and steeled myself as I went to my brother to put out yet another family fire.

Chapter 6

"You feel like talking about it?"

The following Monday morning, I sat at my desk with my forehead resting on my arms. I hadn't slept all weekend. They'd charged my father with obstruction but I doubted it would stick. It was just a ploy to keep him from skipping town while they tried to figure out what really happened to Sheila Brewer. I'd had to more or less beat my brother over the head to keep him from pissing off any more cops before I dumped him off at his place.

Jeanie stood in the doorway holding two cups of coffee. She walked in, plopped down in a chair on the other side of my desk, and slid one steaming mug in my direction.

"Not really," I answered.

"Fine. So why don't you tell me what the hell you're doing?"

I lifted my head. So much for not talking about it. It's not like I thought that would work with Jeanie for more than five seconds anyway.

"My father's out on bail," I said.

"Small miracle, that," she said. "How the hell did you swing it?"

"He's staying with Matty. Tina threw a fit, told Matty she's gonna change the locks on their place and get a P.P.O. if he tried to come back."

Jeanie got comfortable, swinging one leg over the other. "Judge Tucker granted bail?" she asked.

I nodded. Kent Tucker was Woodbridge County's newest District Court judge. He'd just been appointed by the governor when the last judge retired for personal reasons. There was a scandal there, I just didn't know the details and didn't want to.

"Well, old Joe's lucky," Jeanie said. "If he'd have drawn any of our old-timers, they'd have taken one look at his last name and let him rot."

"Yep," I said.

"You know," Jeanie said. "Don't take this the wrong way, but I'm thinking it's a small blessing your house burned down otherwise he'd be staying with you."

I couldn't help it, her words brought a bitter laugh out of me. I'd thought the same thing about a dozen times.

"You think he did it?" Jeanie asked.

"He's not being charged with murder," I said. "They don't have the elements on that. No body yet. Too many unanswered questions. LaForge signed off on obstruction of justice."

"What?" Jeanie shouted. "How?"

"They think they can prove he lied about when he saw her last. They'll circle back to a murder charge if they can, don't you worry."

Jeanie shook her head. "Well, that's thin as paper right now. Christ almighty on a stick."

I choked a little on my coffee. It was one of her more

colorful expressions and it had been a while since I'd heard her utter it. There was still enough Catholic girl in me to cringe.

"Do you think he did it?" she asked.

I puffed my cheeks out then exhaled. "Jeanie, I can't imagine it. My dad's a lot of things. A son of a bitch? A narcissistic asshole? A drunk? A deadbeat? Yeah. He's all that. But there's a lot about this that makes no sense. He comes all the way back to Delphi to date some woman he's known from high school. He offs her in his hotel room and leaves her there for the cops to find? Then he just goes about his business with Matty the next morning?"

Jeanie raised a brow. "It's perplexing, I'll give you that. But he *did* lie about being with the woman. Right?"

"He still insists he hasn't seen her in weeks. And as far as the hotel room, Davy Monroe's backing up his story about where he was that night."

Jeanie took a sip of her coffee. "Well, that's a thin shred of hope. LaForge will slaughter him on cross if this gets that far."

"Maybe," I said.

"What's your instinct telling you?"

I pressed my thumb and forefinger to the bridge of my nose. I'd had a migraine coming on since last night.

"I just wish he'd never come back to town."

"Cass," she said, putting her mug on my desk. "I could pretend this is none of my business. I suppose on paper it's not. But you're family to me. So why the hell are you getting knee-deep into this? You don't owe Joseph anything. Need I remind you that every time you've ever needed something from him in your life, he wasn't there. Not for you, for Joey, and most of all not for Vangie. You don't have to take this on."

I folded my hands in my lap. "You sound like Eric."

Jeanie cracked a smile. "That man makes sense every once in a while. I'm guessing he's fit to be tied over all of this."

I took a beat. Jeanie said all the things I'd mulled over in my brain for over a week now. Joe Sr.'s mess didn't have to be mine, no matter how much DNA I shared with him. "It's not about him," I finally said. "I'm worried about Matty."

Jeanie tightened her lips into a grim smile. "I feel like he was hanging on to his sobriety by a thread as it was. He's out of his mind worried about Dad. As messed up as it all is, Matty loves him deeply. I don't know, he's always viewed my dad as some kind of canary in his addiction coal mine. Like if my dad can't get his act together, how can he?"

"That's not healthy for him," Jeanie said.

"I know. Believe me. So, for my brother's peace of mind, I'll at least make sure my father's rights are protected."

"For how long?" she asked. "What if they do end up charging him with something more serious? You planning on going all the way with that? Through trial?"

I hoped like hell it didn't come to that.

"I don't know," I said. "Probably not. It was different when it was Vangie. Or if it were one of my brothers. It's like you said, I know I don't owe this to my dad. But for Matty, I'll do what I can for as long as I can. Beyond that? Well, I can hand it off. Plus, his alibi might be pretty solid. This will go away. It's not going to go very far."

Jeanie nodded. "You know what you need?"

I braced for her answer.

"A distraction."

I blinked. Then a smile warmed my face. Jeanie picked up a file that had been sitting on the corner of my desk. She opened it and pulled out a photocopied letter.

"The Romaines?" I asked. With all the family excitement,

44

I hadn't given much thought to Alicia Romaine's birth family search.

I took the letter from Jeanie. There wasn't much to it. The thing was thirty years old, written within a few weeks of Alicia's birth. She was identified as baby Jane Doe. It was a very generic accounting of the circumstances that brought her to the adoption agency.

Alicia's mother was listed as being twenty-one years old at the time of Alicia's birth. No information was provided about her father.

"There's not much to go on here," I said. "The adoption was finalized in Wayne County. She was born in Kent County but it doesn't say that's where the mother lived. I mean, we can assume, but that's Grand Rapids area. It's huge."

"It's a start," Jeanie said. She took the letter from me and kept reading. "Says here the mother was a gymnast. No college education, at least as of the time, though she'd been offered an athletic scholarship. And it says she came from a big family of all girls."

"It's a needle in a haystack if we can't get some of those adoption records unsealed," I said.

"Maybe. Maybe not."

She had a wistful look on her face. It wasn't like Jeanie. I'd always known her to be no-nonsense and practical. She wasn't one to give in to flights of fancy or pipe dreams. Also, she liked being paid.

"Jeanie, why this girl?" I asked. "Why this case?"

She put the paper down and stared out the front window.

"They're the ones who just opened that coffee and pastry shop two blocks over on Clancy Street. Sweet Delights?"

I followed her line of sight. "They are? I've been meaning to stop by. That's a risk though. That space has been what, ten different businesses over the last twenty years or so? You ask me, it's cursed."

Jeanie smirked at me. "Right. You don't believe in that crap any more than I do. And you should stop in. And tell as many people as you can to do the same. There are enough jerks in this town to make things that much harder for them."

"Did something happen?" I asked. Jeanie wasn't wrong. Delphi wasn't the most welcoming town to outsiders.

Jeanie scratched her chin. "I saw some rough comments on the town Facebook page, is all. People just try to tear others down for no good reason other than being bored."

I rolled my eyes. "Well, that's just plain awful. Screw those people. Why the hell do you even go on there? It's a viper pit. Nothing but a bunch of narrow-minded assholes with internet muscles stirring up trouble."

"I know," she said. "It's fun to watch sometimes. And it's even more fun to blast them when I'm of a mind."

Lord. I'd seen some of Jeanie's online takedowns. They were brilliant and blistering, but it was like playing whack-a-mole as far as I was concerned. Any victories were short-lived.

"So anyway," she said. "Alicia and Terrence and I all got to talking. I want to do this for her. Help her if I can."

"You're a good noodle, Jeanie Mills," I said. "So let's help."

She slid the letter back to me. "Got any brilliant ideas as to how?"

I sighed as I picked up the paper and read through it again. "Well, we have the mother's birth year. We know where she gave birth and we know she was a gymnast. It's not glamorous, but I'd say we need to start making lists of the schools in Kent County and let's say the three or four neighboring counties. Let's look for reports of gymnastics scholarship winners for the school years, say, four and five years before Alicia was born? Bonus points if we find any that came from big families with all girls. That ought to help narrow it down."

"Then we what, cold call?" she asked.

"You got a better idea?"

Jeanie smiled. "I do not. And this might be fun. This is old-fashioned gumshoe detective work."

"Right. Well, you said I needed a distraction."

"I'll get Miranda and Tori on it too. They'll love this," Jeanie said.

I shook my head. "I half wonder if maybe Alicia Romaine is better off not borrowing trouble by looking for these people."

Jeanie had her hand on the doorknob. "Maybe. I mean, I see your point. You can't choose your family."

I smiled up at her. "Except you chose mine."

Jeanie paused. Her eyes got a little misty. Then she waved me off. "Oh, shut it. Don't go getting all sappy on me. It's too early in the day for that."

I was about to do just that. Then the intercom went off. I pressed the button.

"Hey, Miranda," I said.

"Hey, kiddo," she said. "You've got a message from Jack LaForge I think you're going to want to return."

My heart turned ice-cold yet again.

"What now?"

"He wouldn't give me the details. But it's to do with the security footage they finally pulled from the Harmon Arms."

"Great," I muttered. Jeanie took her cue and quietly left the room.

"Thanks, Miranda," I said. I clicked off with her then took a deep breath as I picked up the phone to call Jack LaForge.

Chapter 7

JACK SAT BEHIND HIS DESK, his fingers looped behind his head as he regarded me. Behind him, fat snowflakes started to fall outside the window.

"Well," he said. "I guess you can't pick your family."

It was an odd opener and one I'd just used on Jeanie. I gave him a tight-lipped smile. Jack leaned forward, grabbed a packet of papers off the corner of his desk and handed them to me.

"You can pick your clients, though, Cass."

"So can you," I said. "It's called prosecutorial discretion."

I read fast. Let Jack think I wasn't the slightest bit worried about what I'd find in this report. As my eyes darted over the page, it stopped being an act.

"Jack," I said. "You've got no solid proof that my dad was anywhere near that hotel room between November 30th and December 2nd."

The police report had one addendum since the last time I saw it. The security cameras at the Harmon Arms weren't aimed at that part of the building. They only showed the main entrance to the parking lot. There were no cameras at the side entrance to the parking lot so it was impossible to tell who else came or went with any certainty. No one saw my dad going in or out after eight o'clock in the morning on Saturday the 30th when his car was shown leaving the main entrance to the parking lot. Security cameras at Mickey's picked him up there from nine o'clock in the evening until closing. Davy Monroe gave an affidavit saying Dad was with him until eight the next morning. The motel maid testified she heard the commotion coming from room number seven at approximately four a.m.

"He wasn't there," I said, putting the police report down.

"We're not charging him in connection with anything that happened with the hotel room. At least, not yet," he said. "But we've got him on obstruction. He told Delphi P.D. he hasn't seen Sheila Brewer for weeks. Your dad is lying, Cass," Jack said.

He picked up another file and handed it to me. "This just came in."

I took it and leafed through it. It was more security footage, this time from the House of Waffles on Blanchard Street. It was dated November twenty-ninth. The day after Thanksgiving. He was shown holding the door for a pretty blonde woman. Then the two of them took a booth near the door.

They were smiling in the grainy, still photos. Holding hands. At one point, the woman leaned in and kissed my father on the cheek. Though I didn't know her well, I recognized her.

"That's Sheila Brewer," LaForge confirmed it. I felt sick.

I tried to keep my personal feelings out of this. I tried to think like a lawyer. I wanted to murder him myself. Why couldn't criminal clients ever figure out that lying always made things worse?

"Is this fun for you?"

Jack's eyes narrowed. I knew I was a thorn in his side. Last year, he'd been the lead counsel in the Coach Drazdowski murder trial. Losing to me had severely damaged his credibility and career. He'd been angling to take over the County Prosecutor's job in the election we just had. But the powers that be withdrew support from him after Drazdowski. In January, he'd have a new boss and a badly weakened position in the office. Rumor had it, Jack was in shit-or-get-off-the-pot mode. His best move might be to go into private practice and leave the politics behind.

I just couldn't believe he'd use my father's latest troubles as a way to get back at me. Jack was smarmy, but I'd always pegged him as a straight shooter.

"We're moving forward," he said. "I brought you in out of professional courtesy. I like you, Cass. I'll be honest, I didn't at first."

"Last year was tough for both of us," I said. Even though I'd proven my client's innocence in the Drazdowski trial, there were plenty of people in this town who hated me for even getting involved. Coach Drazdowski's sins didn't matter to them. He would always be their beloved home-town hero. And I would always be the trailer trash who dragged his name through the mud and spoke ill of the dead.

"Go to your boss, Jack," I said. "Spending county resources going after my father when you've got a real bad guy out there isn't a good look for you. He's got an alibi."

Jack folded his hands on his desk. "Cass," he said. "I like you. That's the truth. You need to know I don't hold you personally responsible for anything that happened in the Drazdowski case, despite whatever rumors you may have heard."

My mouth dropped. "Hold me responsible? Jack, you had

the wrong girl then. You've got the wrong man now. Aren't you getting sick of me being the one to call you on it?"

His nostrils flared and he sucked air through his teeth. "There's no need to get smug."

"Jack," I said, sighing. "I appreciate the appended police report. But you could have sent a runner over with it. Was there anything else you wanted to talk to me about?"

"I just wanted to make sure you knew ... this thing with your dad ... you need to stay away from it. It's not good for your career. The more you can distance yourself from your family, the further you'll go in this town."

I couldn't believe what I was hearing. At the core of it, if we weren't talking about a potentially dead woman, I might have laughed.

"Got it," I said. "You brought me in here for career advice. Duly noted, Jack. When you come to your senses and drop these charges, you know how to get a hold of me."

I took the report, the file with the security footage photos, and tucked them into my leather bag. Jack stayed frozen with his hands folded on the desk as I turned on my heel and walked out.

I kept my back straight as I made my way past the reception area. I ignored the polite smiles from two other assistant prosecutors as I hit the stairwell and went down to the first floor. By the time I charged past the security desk off the main lobby, I could feel steam coming out of my ears.

I got to my car, threw the bag on the passenger seat and slammed into reverse. I skirted the speed limit as I made my way out of downtown Delphi and took the main drag all the way to Matty's apartment.

I didn't even bother knocking on the front door. I slammed it shut behind me. My father and Matty were sitting at the kitchen table splitting a foot-long sub from the deli down the street. Thankfully they had soft drinks in front of them or I'm pretty sure I would have brained my father with my bag.

As it was, I took the security footage photos out and threw them at him.

"When were you going to tell me?" I yelled.

"Cass," Matty rose. "What the hell ..."

"Matty," I said. "I need you to leave. This is between Dad and me. And it's privileged anyway. Go outside. If you're sober, take a drive. Just be ... elsewhere."

Matty knew me well enough not to argue. He wrapped up the remains of his sandwich and threw it in the fridge. He shot a look at our dad then made his way out the front of the house. My father just kept right on eating his, unconcerned.

I sat down in the chair Matty had vacated. "You were with her," I said. "Sheila Brewer. Those photos were taken two days before the incident in your hotel room. You told the cops and me you hadn't seen her in weeks."

He raised a brow, tilted the grainy House of Waffles photo, then took another bite of his sandwich.

"So?" he said. "We had waffles. That's not a crime."

"It is if it proves you lied to the cops. And you did, Dad. They're not letting these obstruction charges go. I know your priors. Best-case scenario, Sheila Brewer turns up alive somewhere. I think they're still going to jam you up for lying. If she's never found ..."

He stabbed a finger into the center of the picture. "I did nothing wrong. Who cares about the dates? Two weeks, four weeks, so I forgot how long it had been. Big deal."

"Do you even care?" I asked. "This woman. Her family is worried sick. There's blood all over a hotel room registered in your name."

"Which I wasn't at," he said. "If you can't prove that,

you're not worth the money I wasted sending you to law school."

I saw red. Then purple. I sputtered. "You never spent a dime on me, Dad."

He raised a brow. "You lived under my roof, didn't you? Were you making the house payments?"

I shook my head in disbelief. He was delusional. He was out of his damn mind. Then I saw that maddening smirk settle in. This is what Joe Leary Sr. did best. He brought out the worst in people. He had me sputtering and acting from anger, not logic. No. Not this time.

"This is going to get way worse before it gets better, Dad," I said. "And I'm doing more harm to you than good. Never mind what you're doing to me. The Woodbridge County prosecutor's office doesn't really like me much right now. They're sporting a black eye that I gave them. Never mind the fact I've got a conflict of interest. There's a few scenarios where I might actually get called as a witness. I came here to tell you these charges aren't likely to go away. You need to get a different lawyer."

"You mean a better one?" he smiled.

"I'm not taking your bait. Not today. I mean a different one. Give me a day or two and I'll come up with some names."

My father shook his head. "Don't bother. I'm not spending a damn dime on this."

I shook my head. "You need to take it seriously. The hole you're in you dug for yourself by talking to the cops without me there. If you don't have someone counseling you through this, you're going to wind up convicted of another felony. You'll do time, Dad. And that's the best-case scenario. Do you get what I'm telling you?"

"You think you're smarter than me."

I flapped my hand then smacked it to the table. "Give me a break."

"You're not," he said. "But we're family, Cassiopeia. We take care of our own."

"This *is* me taking care of you," I said. "The best thing for you is to have competent representation by someone who isn't as close to you as I am."

He leaned far forward. "Either you take care of this, or I'll do it myself."

"You're impossible," I said, rising. I gathered the paperwork and shoved it back into my bag. My father just picked up his sandwich and started eating again as if we'd been discussing nothing more serious than the weather.

Matty was waiting for me next to my car when I walked out.

"Cass," he said. His eyes were filled with concern ... near panic, actually.

"Matty," I said. "I'm doing the best I can."

He gripped my arm. "He's doing good," Matty said. "He's been working in Jackson until he got laid off. But he's been helping me. We finally got the engine on my truck running right."

"Matty," I said. I was going to say a dozen other things. Don't trust Dad. This was his pattern. He would seem good for a while. You'd think maybe this time things would stay calm, normal. Then he'd slip. He'd blow up. It would be chaos all over again and the cops and social services would show up at the front door.

I smiled. "Matty, just be careful, okay? Take care of you, not him."

"He's worried," Matty said. "It's keeping him up at night. He doesn't want you to know. He's ashamed. He really did come to town with good intentions. All this stuff with this woman. I don't know what's going on, but I know it's not him. He didn't have anything to do with whatever happened to her."

I wondered how much my brother really knew. How many lies had my father spun to keep Matty's sympathies on his side? I was in this strange limbo where I couldn't really tell Matty anything. Like it or not, I'd acted as my dad's lawyer already. I couldn't discuss the case with him.

"I think he's different this time," Matty said.

"Matty, he's already set off a bomb in your life. Where's Tina?"

I knew the answer. She'd called Vangie late last week. She just didn't want to be around Matty if Joe Sr. had his hooks into him. She had seen this cycle play out one too many times. So had we all.

But at the moment, all I could do was pull my brother into a hug and pray.

Chapter 8

"Show me what you've got," I said. Grateful for the diversion of another case, Tori sat across from me at the conference room table. She had her laptop pulled up to a genealogy website.

"I was able to find yearbooks for twenty high schools with gymnastics teams in the counties you asked me about for '84 and '85. I've written down the names of the girls on those teams and did some digging. There were five private gyms in that area. I've got some calls out trying to see what information I can get about star athletes who might have been coached in that time frame. And I pulled up local newspapers. Those were actually the most helpful as they all make scholarship announcements usually right around May or June for the incoming college freshman classes."

It was still going to be a wild goose chase tracking down potential candidates for Alicia Romaine's birth mother, but Tori's work just made things a little less wild.

"Wow," I said. "You've been busy."

Tori gave me a weak smile. "I like it," she said. "It was the perfect busy work I needed to keep my mind off the holidays."

I felt like an ass. With Christmas a few days away, this would be a hard one for her. It had only been a couple of months since her father passed.

"Do you have plans?" I asked.

Tori raised one shoulder but didn't answer. She was still living with Miranda but had her name on a waiting list for a nicer apartment complex on the outskirts of town.

"Well, I have no idea what kind of shit show Clan Leary has in store, but you know you're welcome to join it. Christmas Eve. My sister's place on the lake."

"Thanks," Tori said. "I might just take you up on that offer."

"It was more of a direct order than an offer," I said. "I insist. I just wish I could host it myself."

"Do you have an ETA on when your new construction will start?" she asked.

"As soon as the ground thaws in March, probably. Then I'm looking at three to four months before I'm move-in ready." It might be longer than that. I'd shown my contractor the plans to Great-Grandpa Leary's Someday House. We were ironing out whether we could make all or part of it work.

"Ugh," Tori said. "So you're living on top of your sister for the next six months or so?"

I raised a brow. "Unless you want me taking your second bedroom when you get your new place."

I was teasing. Tori stuttered. I laughed.

"I mean, you could," she said. "I'll have plenty of room."

She really was one of the sweetest kids I knew. "So how many names are we looking at?" I asked, pointing to her list.

Tori looked down at her laptop. She hit the print command then walked into my office to grab the paper as soon as my printer spit it out.

"Initially," she said. "Sixty-three. But I was only able to

58

get reliable contact information on half that. For the other half, I'm thinking I'll actually call the schools or even go to them to see if somebody remembers something. It's doubly hard because many of them have married and changed their names. And I figure we ask the women we do get a hold of whether they've kept in touch with those who are MIA from the internet and social media."

"That many?" I said. "Well, it's a solid start. Very solid. Good work, Tori. And we can try and figure out if any of them had a lot of sisters."

"So," Tori said. "How do we do this?"

She handed me one page of her list. She'd typed out names, addresses, and phone numbers for the high school gymnasts who matched our filters.

I ran my finger along the line and pulled out my cell phone. "It's not glamorous," I said. "But it'll get the job done."

I punched in the first phone number. I got an answer on the third ring and looked back at the name.

"Hello?" she said.

"Hi, there," I started, trying my best not to sound like a telemarketer. "My name is Cass Leary and I'm an attorney in Delphi. I know this is going to sound strange, but are you the Jennifer Wayland who went to ... uh ... Lincoln High, Class of '84?"

"Er ..." she said. "Yes."

"Ms. Wayland, it's kind of a long story, but my client was given up for adoption thirty years ago and your name came up during our research. Is there any chance you or one of your teammates on the gymnastics team gave up a baby girl at that time?"

I made a face at Tori as I waited for Jennifer Wayland to process what I'd just said.

There was a pause, then startled laughter on the other end. "What did you say your name was again?"

"Cass Leary," I answered. "I'm an attorney working in Delphi."

"Well, Ms. Leary, I'm afraid I have no idea what you're talking about. I didn't start having babies until after college and I never gave any of those away."

"I knew this was a long shot," I said.

"You think one of my teammates had some secret baby?" she asked. "Wow."

"I don't think that," I said. "I'm just working on the field of possibilities. So I take that to mean you're not aware of any of those girls being pregnant just before college?"

"No," she said. "And we were a pretty tight-knit group."

"I appreciate that. And I really appreciate your time. I won't waste any more of it."

Tori's eyes widened. She tapped her pencil on four names she had circled next to Jennifer Wayland's. These were women she wasn't able to find online.

"Oh," I said. "Ms. Wayland, one more thing. Is there any chance you have updated contact information for Sue Pohler, Maggie Wendig, Kelly Bishop, or ... uh ... Terry Burt?"

There was a pause on the other end. "Maggie and I are still close. I don't feel comfortable giving out her number, but I'd be glad to pass yours along. This is one of the wilder phone calls I've ever gotten."

"I'm sure," I said. "And yes, that would be helpful if you'd pass my information along."

I gave Jennifer Wayland my cell phone number and thanked her one more time for her help. Exhaling, I set the phone down.

"Wow," Tori said. "We've got to do that sixty-two more times?"

I raised a brow. "Well, we can send emails where we find them. But I feel like getting these women on the phone is worthwhile. I'm cocky enough to think I might be able to hear a lie ... or the truth ... in their voices."

"You think Jennifer Wayland was lying?" she asked.

"I do not. And I also think it would have been the biggest stroke of luck in the world to have hit the target on the first phone call. But I suppose stranger things have happened."

"I guess I have the rest of my afternoon planned." She reached across the table, intending to take the list back from me.

"It's okay," I said. "Let me do this half. Just like you, I don't mind the distraction."

Tori gave a knowing nod. I folded the piece of paper and slipped it into my purse.

"I'm heading over to the Romaines' coffee shop. You want anything? Or want to join me?"

"You go ahead," Tori answered. "I'm going to crack through a few of these numbers. I'll let you know if anything pans out. Say hi to Alicia for me. She seems like a really nice lady. I hope we can help her."

"Me too."

I said goodbye, grabbed my coat on the way through my office, then headed down the block to Sweet Delights.

Last week's snow had already melted, but there was a bite to the air that tickled my lungs. I stood at the intersection, waiting for the walk sign to turn. From my left, a group of men headed down the other way.

I raised a hand. It was Detective Wray and two command officers, no doubt out to grab a bite just like I was.

They halted upon seeing me. A look passed among them. Eric said something I couldn't hear to his companions. One gave him a terse nod and they headed in the other direction.

Eric crossed the street and stood beside me. "I was hoping I'd run into you," he said, just as the light changed again.

I headed toward the shop. Eric kept up.

"Buy you a coffee?" he asked.

I smiled up at him. "How about we go dutch?"

He tilted his head to the side. He had the warmest smile. It lit up his pale-blue eyes beneath dark brows. Today he wore a long, black wool coat with the collar askew. I resisted the urge to reach up and straighten it.

We walked into the Romaines' shop together and took a booth near the door. I didn't see Terrence or Alicia right away. A waitress came and took our orders.

"So," I said. "Was this just a coincidence or were you coming to talk to me?"

Eric dropped his head. "Maybe both. I just didn't like how we left things last time I saw you. I know you're hopping mad at me for my part in the investigation into your dad."

"And I know you're hopping mad at me for defending him," I said.

The waitress brought our coffee. Eric curved both hands around his cup, warming them.

"Are you still doing that?" he asked.

"Are you making small talk or are you interviewing me?"

His face fell, recognizing the impasse.

"Right," he said. "So the subject of your dad is off-limits."

"I think it has to be. His prelim is next week. You might be one of Jack LaForge's main witnesses."

Eric nodded. "I just ... I need you to know how much I hate this. I don't like being at cross purposes with you."

"Eric, you're a police detective. I'm a defense lawyer. Delphi is as big as a postage stamp. This isn't the first or last time this is going to happen."

He tightened his lips into a bloodless line. "What?" I asked. "You want me to quit my job so we can stay friends?"

"Friends," he said. "Are we?"

It was a legitimate question. There really wasn't the right word for what we were. I knew things about Eric no one else did. He knew them about me. He'd saved my life once. I returned the favor. I couldn't deny I got that little flutter in my heart when I saw him. But neither of us had time for it. Then there was the not-so-small detail that Eric was still very much married.

Granted, Mrs. Wray was more or less a vegetable at Maple Valley Rehabilitation Center and in the years before that, word was she'd cheated on him backward and forward. Only, Eric still wore his wedding band and that wasn't something I was in the habit of letting slide.

Friends though. No. That was exactly it.

"I won't apologize for what I do," I said.

"I'm not asking you to. No more than I would for what I do. I just ... for once I'd like to be able to stop worrying about you."

I smiled. "That's your deal, Detective Wray. Not mine. I don't need you to take care of me."

"Except when you do," he laughed. I let it go.

"How's it going at Vangie's?" he asked, navigating to somewhat safer ground.

"Crowded," I said. "Chaotic. And I'm worried about my brother."

"Matty," he said, setting his mug down. "I gotta be honest, I am too, Cass. So far, I haven't seen him show up at Mickey's, but I gotta feeling it's only a matter of time."

My heart felt heavy. I was torn with the old instinct to protect my family from outsiders. At the same time, Eric had helped me look out for Matty more than once.

"I'm afraid of that too."

"Your dad hasn't been the greatest influence on him," he said.

My back stiffened. Eric saw it and his face changed.

"Listen," he said. "I'm not judging. We've all got our baggage. I know you know mine's worse than most. What I'm trying to say ... I'll keep an eye out. If I hear or see anything where Matty's concerned, I'll try to give you a heads-up. But if he gets in the way of what's going on with your father ..."

I put a hand up. "Don't. I can't sit here and tell you I'm just doing my job without expecting you to do yours just as well. We're on the same page as far as that goes."

I had more to say. I didn't get the chance. Eric's radio squawked. He turned the volume down, but the call code was enough to make his brow furrow. He gave me an apologetic look and I smiled.

"I've got this," I said, reaching into my purse to pull out a twenty. "I know. You've gotta go."

Eric reached across the table and gave my hand a squeeze. He nodded to Terrence Romaine as he came out from the kitchen. Then he rose to his full, considerable height and made his way out into the cold.

"Anything?" Terrence said to me, hopeful. He wiped his hands on his apron as I slid out of the booth, grateful once again for the distraction. I just wished I had more fruitful news to share.

Chapter 9

Four days before Christmas, I appeared in court with my father for his preliminary examination on the obstruction charges. I'd found an empty jury room in the Woodbridge County Courthouse and ushered him inside. So far, he'd followed my directions.

Matty loaned him a suit. Though it was too big through the shoulders, he looked nice in it. He looked so much like my older brother Joe, sometimes it was hard not to let my guard down. Dad had the same deep-set brown eyes, strong jaw, and lopsided grin as Joe Jr.

"Your main job today is to sit quietly beside me and look humble. Can you do that? No outbursts. No cocky swagger. You're not smarter than everyone else in that room."

He smirked. "You sure about that?"

"Dad, I explained all this and it's not like this is your first time at this particular rodeo." My father had a couple of D.U.I.s under his belt. Years ago, they took away his license. He eventually got it back but he also sported a string of drunk and disorderlies from back in his younger days. Luckily, his record for the last ten years was clean. As much as I worried about his influence over Matty, my dad at least appeared to be legitimately sober.

"Judge Tucker is newish," I said. "He doesn't know you so consider that a good thing. His only job today is to determine whether there's enough probable cause to bind you over to circuit court for trial. It's a ridiculously low standard. Jack LaForge is a good prosecutor. He can do these hearings in his sleep."

"What about you?" he asked.

"You won't like it, but my best strategy today is to stay quiet. I'm not putting any witnesses on. I'll challenge Jack's when it's appropriate."

My father sneered. "What the hell kind of weak ass shit is that?"

"It's smart ass shit," I said. "I don't need to give the prosecution any advance warning of trial strategies I might use down the road. In all likelihood, you'll get bound over. So be prepared for it and keep your mouth shut."

"You need to let me get up there and tell my side."

"No way. Probably not ever. Certainly not today."

He leaned forward and gave me a mean look. That used to work on me when I was little. Even now, I felt a familiar cold churning in my gut. But I stared right back at him.

"Stay quiet or I'm walking away from this right now," I said. "The only reason I'm here at all is for Matty. Don't delude yourself about that. Just as soon as we can find you one, you're hiring a different lawyer for trial if it comes to that. I have no doubt any good lawyer will advise you to plead out. The trouble is, they're currently not offering one."

"This is all lies," he said.

"There's a missing woman out there," I said. "You're not helping yourself by being so flippant about Sheila Brewer."

He waved me off.

66

There was a soft knock on the door. Judge Tucker's clerk poked her head inside. "You're up next," she said.

"Thanks," I said. I gave my father one last hard glare before gathering my things and following the clerk out the door.

I said a silent prayer. Please let my father keep his cool today. Please let me keep mine. While there wasn't much I could do to make this problem go away today, there was plenty he could do to make it worse.

Matty sat in the corridor. He rose as we walked out.

"Dammit," I muttered.

"We'll be right in, Syl," I said to the clerk.

She threw a look to my brother and father, then disappeared into the judge's chambers.

"I told you not to come," I said to Matty.

"I didn't feel like sitting around waiting for a text," Matty said. "We're on shutdown this week. Where else am I gonna go?"

I bit my lip past the urge to tell him to go to an A.A. meeting. My father's drama was nothing but a big, shiny trigger for him.

"We're family," my dad said. "We show up for each other."

It was a thinly veiled dig at me and I couldn't believe it. I was doing everything I could to clean up his mess but it would never be enough.

"Come on," I said. "Matty, will you just wait out here?"

I didn't say the other half of my speech. I was going to have enough trouble keeping my dad's temper under control. I couldn't add the wild card of Matty's to the mix.

My father held the door for me in a bizarre act of chivalry. Matty didn't look happy, but he parked his butt back on the bench in the hallway. I adjusted the strap on my leather bag and we walked inside.

I didn't have to tell my dad where the defense table was. He'd sat at it often enough. Judge Tucker's courtroom was oddly empty. He heard his landlord-tenant docket right after his criminal one. I wondered if the landlords of Delphi were in rare, holiday spirit.

I arranged my notes on the table. Jack LaForge still hadn't entered. I found that odd as well. Punctuality was a hallmark for him. In fact, he usually showed up at least ten minutes early for everything. I didn't see so much as a paralegal roaming around from the prosecutor's office.

Judge Tucker's bailiff came in from the door beside the bench. I looked behind me. Still no Jack. What the hell?

"All rise," the bailiff spoke loud and strong. I nudged my father and he rose to his feet, grunting through the kinks in his spine.

I straightened my suit jacket as Tucker took the bench. He cast his first glance at the prosecution table and scowled.

"Did I get my dates wrong?" Tucker said, his tone dripping with sarcasm.

"Not as far as I know, your Honor," I answered. "If the prosecution can't be bothered to show up, I'd like to move for immediate dismissal."

The judge cleared his throat. He leaned over and whispered something to his bailiff.

"Let's give Jack a couple of minutes grace," he said.

"This is bullshit," my father muttered but loud enough for the judge to hear.

I pretty much shot lasers out of my eyes as I looked at my father. I had the beginnings of a tingle along my spine. Something wasn't right. Irritated though I was, the judge was right. It wasn't at all like Jack LaForge not to at least have a junior staff member or paralegal checking in with the court if he was running late.

"We'll do this again in ten minutes," Judge Tucker said. He cast an irritated glare to his bailiff. "Next time make sure all parties are here before you knock on my door."

"Uh ... sorry, Your Honor, Mr. LaForge was just here."

"Sit tight," I said to my father. I saw no point in letting him back into the hallway to cause more trouble. In the meantime, I wanted to figure out for myself what the hell was going on.

"If Jack's not here in ten," the judge said, "I'll consider that motion to dismiss. Looks like your counterpart may have gotten his wires crossed."

I rose when the judge did. He disappeared through his private chamber door.

"I mean it," I said to my dad. "Stay put and zip it. I'll be right back."

The bailiff was fuming as he exited the courtroom through the gallery behind me. As he opened the door to the back of the courtroom, I saw a crowd gathered. A commotion. My heart sank. Every spidey sense I had told me I was about to have a very bad day.

I admonished my father one more time to sit still as I followed the bailiff out. As the door closed behind me, I came face to face with two uniformed Delphi P.D. officers. Jack LaForge stood right behind them.

"What's going on?" I asked. From the corner of my eye, I saw two detectives standing with their backs to me. One was Eric Wray. He turned at the sound of my voice, his face colorless, his expression grim.

"Your father inside?" Jack asked me.

"Of course, shouldn't you be?"

He nodded to the officers. Wray and his partner, Megan Lewis, started walking toward me.

"New charges," Jack said. He put a hand on one of the officers. He was holding a piece of paper. At Jack's direction, he handed it to me.

"Cass!" Matty charged down the hall toward us. I barely had time to read the warrant Jack handed me before my brother got to my side.

My eyes darted over the small print. With each word, the blood drained from my head.

"Cass," Jack said, explaining the obvious. "We've got a warrant for your father's arrest. These officers are here to take him into custody."

"The hell you are!" Matty shouted.

"Don't!" I snapped at him. "I mean it, Matty. I don't need you making a bad situation ten times worse."

As if on cue, my father walked out of the courtroom.

"Mr. Leary?" one of the officers said. "We have a warrant for your arrest for the murder of Sheila Brewer. Will you please turn and put your hands behind your back."

"Cass," Matty said. "You better stop this."

Eric had gotten to me by now. The uniformed officer was in the process of reading my father his rights.

"I didn't do this," he shouted. His bravado slipped as the cuffs went on. "I'm being railroaded."

"Not another word," I said to him.

"Cass!" Matty lost it. He charged the officer cuffing my dad.

Eric was quicker than I was. He stepped in between us, getting my brother by the arms. He pushed him back and pinned him against the wall, face first.

"You need to calm down," he said.

"Fuck you," Matty said to Wray.

"Matty!" I yelled. I didn't know which fire to put out first. I chose my brother's.

"They're doing this because of who he is," Matty said. "Dad, I told you not to come back here. I told you this would happen."

"Please," I said. "I can handle him. Let him go."

"I don't think so," Eric said as Matty proved his point by trying to shove off the wall. My brother was snorting like a bull about to charge.

As I got closer, my insides hollowed out. Matty reeked of alcohol. His eyes were glassy and red. I'd been so focused on keeping my father under control, I'd missed the signs with Matty.

"Eric," I said. "Please. I'll get my brother home."

"You gonna behave?" Eric said to Matty.

Matty gritted his teeth. As Eric eased up on him, he staggered sideways. He jerked his arm away as Eric let him go.

"Go home, son," Dad said. He was cuffed now.

"I'll meet you down there," I called. "At some point," I said under my breath. My main concern was Matty.

"Will you sit down and just wait for me for two minutes?" I said to him. "You're not helping Dad and you're definitely not helping yourself like this."

Matty gave me a nod and plopped back down on the bench where I'd first found him.

I walked down the hall with Eric until we were out of Matty's earshot.

I still held a copy of my father's arrest warrant in my hand.

"She's dead," Eric said. "Forensics came back on your dad's hotel room. The blood in his bathroom was of sufficient quantity to be not survivable. And it's a positive match to Sheila Brewer's."

Matty didn't do as he was told. He'd been quiet enough I didn't hear him, but he came up on us just as Eric uttered the words.

The world spun as Matty curled a fist and drew back his arm. Eric was quick. He ducked as Matty threw a sluggish punch. His hand made contact with the wall beside Eric's head and my gut twisted as I heard the tiny bones crack.

Chapter 10

I OWED ERIC WRAY. He could and should have arrested my brother for attempted assault on a police officer. Instead, he called down for one of the sheriff's deputies on staff at the courthouse. He made arrangements for the deputy to take my brother home.

I called my brother Joe and gave him the highlights. He would babysit Matty until we could figure out what to do about him.

"This is crap, Cass," Matty said. The fight had gone out of him. He just looked sad. I smoothed the hair out his eyes. I felt twin urges to hug him and kill him. Mostly kill him.

"Matty, you're not helping. Not Dad and definitely not yourself. Go home. Sleep this off. Then get yourself to a meeting."

"You have to do something about Dad," he said. "He can't go to prison, Cass. He won't survive it. And he didn't do this. He didn't kill that woman. They're framing him."

"You let me worry about that for now," I said. There was so much more I wanted to add. Why did he care so much?

Couldn't he see how toxic our father was to Matty's own well-being?

Those were questions for another time. Matty was in no condition to hear reason. At least he was more or less placid for now. The deputy Eric called was actually someone Matty went to high school with. They'd been buddies once upon a time. I saw no judgment in the man's eyes and smiled with gratitude. Matty went with him, his head hanging low.

As soon as he got on the elevator, I buried my face in my hands but stopped just short of screaming into them. I picked my leather bag up off the floor and heaved the strap over my shoulder. Eric came to me.

"I know," I said.

"Do you?"

"I've got to get down to the jail," I said. "I know I don't have to tell you nobody ..."

He put a hand up to stop me. "Nobody's going to question Joe Sr. outside your presence."

"You should recuse yourself from this, Eric. Hand off this investigation to George Knapp or someone else. You keep telling me I'm too close to this. Well, so are you."

The muscles in his jaw jumped. "Cass, this is Delphi. If I recused myself from every case involving people I know personally, I'd be out of a job."

It was more than that and we both knew it. But I was just too damn tired of it all to argue. I left things like that and headed for the stairwell. I was grateful Eric didn't try coming after me. That said, I knew I'd see him soon enough at the station.

The Delphi P.D. Public Safety Building was only half a mile from the courthouse. If the snow hadn't kicked up again, I might have just walked it. I could have used the air. I pulled into the visitor's lot, grabbed a notepad and steeled myself for what confronted me behind those steel doors.

My father had already been processed by the time I got in. Somebody fast-tracked him. It was probably a call from Eric. A patrolwoman showed me to interrogation room three. My father was waiting for me. He was cuffed, but not chained.

He barely looked up at me as I took my seat across from him and snapped the end of my pen. I had a small file with the new charging documents, and the preliminary police report.

"How can they charge me for murder if they don't have a body?" my father asked. I found that odd. I expected another declaration of innocence or an accusation about how the cops were out to get him.

"Blood," I said. I opened my file and turned the third page of the police report so he could read it.

"No body, no murder," he insisted.

I gritted my teeth. "Dad, let me explain this to you like you're five. They found a massive amount of Sheila Brewer's blood in your hotel room. Here's the lab report. Read the summation. What they collected amounts to over eighty percent of a human being's blood volume. Whatever injury caused it would be unsurvivable. They don't need a body."

He cocked his head and his eyes darted back and forth as he read the report. That smug expression never left his face. Finally, he shoved the papers back at me.

"Doesn't matter. I didn't kill her. I wasn't in that room that night. I've said it a million times and I've got a witness to back me up. If Sheila's dead, somebody else did it."

"Dad, you're lying."

He slammed a palm to the table. The sound of it echoed like a gunshot. "You will show me respect!"

"No," I said. "You'll show it to me. And you'll show it to

those cops out there. And for the love of Christ, you'd better start showing it to Sheila Brewer. You know, that's the thing that's pissed me off the most out of all of this. You've never once acted like you cared what happened to this woman. Whatever other nonsense you're peddling, you were seeing her. You dated her. And you definitely don't seem to care that she's dead except for how it's impacting you. So, tell me why that is. Tell me about her."

He let out a great big breath and leaned back in his chair. "She was nice. Pretty. Not too bright."

I rolled my eyes. He was doing it to goad me, even now. I knew no matter what else was going on, one of the worst parts about this for my dad was the knowledge that he needed me. That I was the expert here.

"When did you start seeing her? How did you reconnect?"

"I've known Sheila since we were kids," my dad said. "We got to talking again. She emailed me or I emailed her. I don't even remember. I'd been living in Jackson for the last year up until a few weeks ago. One day about a year ago, I bumped into her at a bar I like there. Total coincidence. I asked her to sit down with me. We got to talking. One thing led to another. We went out a few times. She was fun. For a while. Then she wasn't."

I tapped my pen against my legal pad. "What do you mean?"

My father's face went hard. He stared at me for a good ten seconds before he finally answered. "You sure you want me to get into this?"

I dropped my pen. "There's nothing about this I want. You're facing murder charges now, Dad. First degree. That means life in prison if you're convicted. You can't bullshit your way out of this. It's not thirty years ago. This isn't you getting out of hand at Mickey's. This is a dead woman. Her blood spilled all over your hotel room. And you've been lying to the cops all along."

"The hell I have," he yelled.

"Really? Don't pull your crap about how you just didn't care enough about Sheila Brewer to remember you went to the House of Waffles with her a few days before she went missing. Why did you lie about that? Tell me the truth."

He sneered but didn't answer.

"Fine," I said. "Let's see how close I get. You made her promises. Told her your kid was about to come into some money. Did Matty tell you about my house burning down? Or maybe you read it on the internet."

His face froze and I knew with sickening clarity that I was getting warm. He said nothing.

"Right," I went on. "Big man. Bigger talk. Maybe you bragged about how you were going to try to screw me over on my insurance claim somehow. You got bored with her and ditched her. But she wasn't going to give up so easily. Was that it?"

He clenched his fists. Sure.

"I didn't kill Sheila Brewer," he said, his tone measured. "I have an alibi. I forgot about the waffle place. I was trying to be discreet. I wanted to end things with her. She was too needy. That's all that happened."

"Did you ever take her to that hotel room?"

He shrugged. "Once or twice. But that time at the waffle house was the last time I saw her. I swear. Cass ..."

"I'm not going to be your lawyer," I said. "The most I'll do is find you a good criminal lawyer to take it from here. I'll handle your bail hearing if I can't find someone before that, but that's it. For now, you're not giving a statement to the police. I'll see you in the morning."

"Cassiopeia," he said, using the sharp tone he did when I was a kid. It still sent a little stab of dread through me and he knew it.

"Try to get some sleep," I said. "I'd put your chances of getting reasonable bail tomorrow at about seventy-thirty against. I told you, this isn't the Delphi of thirty years ago and you're not that charming."

"Where are you going?" he asked. For the first time since he came back in my life like a wrecking ball, my father sounded scared.

"We're done for now," I said. Rage simmered in my heart. "Thanks to you, I've got other fires to put out. Matty's in trouble, Dad."

"Not my fault that kid's always been weak," he said, all traces of fear gone. "He takes after his mother."

A monster reared its head inside of me. My heart turned black. I wanted to punch him. I wanted to gouge his eyes out.

I learned some things about my mother over the last few months. I never knew she had a problem with pills. I'd always believed my father was the addict. But she was dead now. She crashed her car after taking a curve too fast on a rain-slicked road. I'd always hated the fact that my father had got to be there when she died. I'd been at school.

I might have vaulted across that table. I might have given in to every dark impulse I had and live up to my last name. It didn't matter, there were two deputies standing right outside the door.

In the end, my father's satisfied smirk is what stopped me. He enjoyed provoking me. It fit into his narrative that I was no better than him. I stiffened my spine and turned my back.

My hands were shaking as I raised a fist and knocked on the door. My father's soft chuckle cut through me like razors as I waited for the deputies to let me out of the room.

Chapter 11

THE NEXT MORNING, Judge Tucker denied my father's bail. He stood red-faced beside me as the judge ticked off all the reasons I'd warned him about.

"Mr. Leary," he said. "You've got a colorful history with this town. While I can appreciate your claims that you've embraced sobriety, that doesn't erase the fact that you've challenged authority in virtually every brush with the law you've had. Obstruction of justice, resisting arrest, disorderly conduct. The list goes on. The heinous nature of this crime, your solid record of thumbing your nose at the legal system, the fact that you've been out of this jurisdiction for the past several years with minimal contact with your family, and your apparent utter lack of regard for the police has convinced me that the prosecution's arguments against bail are well taken."

He banged the gavel and my father drew a great breath, ready to launch into a tirade that would have only underscored every point Judge Tucker made.

"Save it," I whispered. "Or I'm walking right the hell out of here and you'll be on your own."

I have no idea why my words sank in with him at that

time. His shoulders dropped and he put his hands in front of himself, waiting for the deputies to transport him back to jail.

I made a strategic decision to waive the prelim. There was just no way the judge wouldn't find probable cause and bind my dad over for trial. I saw no point in tipping my hand at any defense strategies my father might use.

"Sit tight," I told him. "I'll be in touch as soon as I can with suggestions for your new lawyer."

"Don't need one," he said. "I want you."

I felt relief when the deputies finally came to march him out of the courtroom. Now I'd have a few minutes to think before dealing with the next family fire, my brother Matty.

When I walked into my office, Joe was waiting for me, his expression wary. Beside him stood Vangie. She'd clearly been crying.

Miranda gave me a sympathetic look. "You want me to move back your meeting with the Romaines?" she asked.

Alicia Romaine. I'd almost forgotten about her over the last forty-eight hours. Tori and I promised to update her on the investigation into her birth parents. Sadly, there wasn't much to tell. Between the two of us, we'd made over thirty fruitless cold calls to former high school gymnasts around the state.

"No," I said. "Don't put her off. Tell Tori to start without me and I'll be down as soon as I can."

I took Joe by the arm and put a hand on Vangie's back. I led them into my office where they took the two seats at my desk.

"He's going to trial," I said. "And he's going to sit in jail until then. This is a bigger mess than I can fix, guys."

"I'm worried about Matty," Vangie said. "He won't go to a meeting. He hasn't taken a drink since last night as far as I know, but he won't talk to me either."

"Where is he now?" I asked. I tried to keep the accusation out of my voice. If they were both here, who was watching him?

"He went to work," Joe said. "I dropped him off and watched him head into the shop."

"Good," I said. "That should keep him out of trouble for the next few hours at least. As far as the rest of this, here's what's going to happen. Dad needs a different lawyer. I'm working on finding one and I need both of you and Matty to back me up on that."

"Cass," Vangie said. "He's going to want you. I mean ... I want you. What you did for me when I was the one on the hot seat ... That's what Dad needs. I know what he is. Believe me. But he's not wrong about the deck being stacked against him here in Delphi."

I sat back hard. There were so many things I wanted to say. Foremost in my mind was the simple fact that our father might actually be guilty. It was a point I hadn't spoken out loud to anyone.

Joe's eyes narrowed. I could guess what he wanted to say. Damn his ability to practically read my mind. He stayed tight-lipped though. Our instinct to always protect our younger brother and sister from the harshest truths of our family was deeply ingrained.

"Look," I said. "You've both heard me say this a thousand times. There's a lot I can't discuss, even with you guys. He's our dad, but up until now, I've been acting as his attorney. And if you can't see why that's the exact reason he needs somebody else to represent him, I don't know what to tell you."

"Matty's going to stay over at my place tonight," Joe said. "I took his car keys last night and haven't given them back yet. He's kind of dependent on me."

I raised a brow. "You sure that's not just going to piss him off?"

"Probably," he said.

I let out a sigh. "Okay. If I can count on you to deal with Matty for now, that'll be a huge help. The good news is I don't think Eric's interested in jamming him up on any attempted assault charges. He easily could have. There were about four witnesses to Matty's outburst in the courthouse."

"Idiot," Joe muttered. I wasn't so sure Joe wouldn't try to tune Matty up himself to try and knock some sense into him.

My phone buzzed. It was Miranda. "I've got to get back to work," I said. "I'll check back in with the two of you later this evening. Dad's not happy, but he's fine where he is for now. Trust me."

Vangie and Joe slowly rose. As they shut the door behind them, I leaned far back in my chair and propped my feet up on the desk. All the reasons I'd left Delphi in the first place after law school came flooding back. I hated to admit the idea had appeal once again.

Chapter 12

TERRENCE AND ALICIA ROMAINE were just the balm I needed. The two of them sat holding hands at the conference room table. Jeanie and Tori were already waiting.

"Thank you," Alicia started, smiling up at me as I found an empty chair and sat down.

"I haven't done anything yet," I smiled.

Terrence and Alicia exchanged a nervous glance. She reached down and picked up a paper bag with straw handles up from the floor and slid it across the table to me.

"Just a little of our special brew," she said. "I thought maybe you might need it after the week you've had."

I looked inside. Alicia had carefully packaged four different flavors of coffee in cellophane gift bags with little red bows. The heavenly aroma enveloped me. I couldn't wait to snuggle up in bed on some cold winter day and drink it while watching my niece skate on the frozen lake. Right now, that seemed a million miles away.

"I think you might be a good witch, Alicia," I said. "And you really didn't need to go to all the trouble."

She shifted in her chair, trying to find a comfortable position under the weight of her growing belly.

"We've made a lot of calls," I said. "So far, it's gotten us nothing but a dead-end, I'm afraid. None of the former athletes we've spoken to knew anything about your mother. Now, it's possible we've actually talked to her and she's just not interested in coming forward."

Alicia blinked rapidly. "I knew that was a risk once we started all of this. I just ... I can't bear to think about giving up just yet. I feel like it's now or never."

"Hey," I said, smiling. "Nobody's talking about giving up. We just may need to get a little more creative, is all."

"I had an idea about that," Jeanie said. She had a small green box in front of her on the table. She slid it across to me. I read the label. It was a Tree of Life ancestry kit.

"Have you thought about this?" I asked, looking Alicia Romaine squarely in the eye. I flipped the box so she could read it too.

"I've seen commercials for those," she said.

"I did one myself about a year ago," Jeanie said. "Found out I'm more Eastern European than people who currently live there. Strong peasant stock and proud of it." She smiled and flexed her biceps.

Alicia took the box. It had a lid flap that opened to a picture of a green tree intertwined with the hallmark double helix of a DNA strand.

"Does it hurt?" she asked. "I'm not good with needles. Terrence has to hold my hand and sing to me when I go in for bloodwork for the baby."

"Nope," Jeanie said. She took the box back from Alicia and opened it. Inside, nestled in a neat little plastic liner, was a test tube, instruction booklet, and a return mailer.

"You just spit in this thing," Jeanie said. "You haven't

eaten or drunk anything in the last half hour, have you? Wouldn't want it to come back that you're related to a pork chop or anything."

Laughing, Alicia took the test tube.

"There's a restroom through that door," I said.

Alicia gave her husband a smile, then disappeared into the bathroom.

"Thank you," he said as soon as she'd shut the door. "She's been worried about you, Cass. I don't mean to get into your business, but everyone in town knows about your dad's drama."

"Story of my life, Terrence. And I appreciate the concern."

He looked uneasy, like he had something more to say. He cleared his throat and started again. "I don't mean to stick my nose where it doesn't belong. It's just ..."

My heart sank. I knew where this was headed by the look on his face.

"You saw something," I said.

Terrence shrugged. "Your dad came into the coffee shop with Sheila Brewer a while back. A few days after we opened, actually. I mean, at the time I didn't know he was your dad. But I knew Sheila. I mean, you live here long enough you know everybody. I don't mean to speak ill of the dead, but she wasn't my favorite customer. Never tipped the waitresses. Bossy."

"Terrence," I said. "What do you want me to know?"

Alicia came back out holding her test tube. She slipped it in the mailer Jeanie held out for her. Jeanie sealed it as Alicia sat back down next to her husband.

"Monique, one of my waitresses, came to me yesterday. I didn't see any of this myself. I wasn't in the restaurant at the time. But Monique said they were kind of hot and heavy in a back booth," Terrence said. "Then, I don't know. Monique said Sheila got mad. Called him, well, a name I'd rather not repeat. She stormed off and he went after her without paying his bill."

"Terrence, I appreciate you telling me."

He looked like he was going to be sick. "I really hate having to do it," he said. "I'm one to mind my own business. But I told Monique she's got to tell the cops what she saw."

I reached across the table and took his hand. "Terrence, it's okay. I appreciate you telling me. And you're right, Monique should tell the police what she knows."

Jeanie cleared her throat and, breaking the tension, held up the little mailer with Alicia's DNA sample. "Well, let's get this little puppy out into the world. It'll take a few weeks to hear anything. Don't get your hopes up."

Terrence and Alicia rose together. They were a team. A unit. A family. Part of me wanted to warn her. She'd hit the jackpot with both Terrence and the family who chose her. At the moment, I wanted nothing more than to escape the one I'd been born into.

Chapter 13

THREE LAWYERS IN, and no one would touch my father's case with a ten-foot pole. My best hope had been a former prosecutor friend of mine from Oakland County named Ronald Whitney. His wife was actually a police detective in Wayne County who I'd come up against in a recent murder trial. I respected him as tough, fair, and honest.

Whitney went so far as to meet with my dad. Their interview had lasted all of ten minutes before my father threw him out.

"Ron, I'm sorry," I said over the phone. I had a sick feeling rising in my core.

"Your dad is his own worst enemy," Ron said.

"I know," I answered. "I appreciate you even taking the time to talk to him."

"The thing is, there are real holes in the prosecution's case. I wouldn't have minded sinking my teeth into this one. I actually think it's a winner. Davy Monroe will make a good alibi witness and he hasn't budged from his story. But I'm sorry. Joe's impossible. He won't take responsibility for lying to the cops. He's still doing it. He flat out denied what your friend Terrence Romaine had to say. Terrence is unimpeachable. If I were Jack LaForge, I might put him on the stand as one of my first witnesses."

I rubbed my forehead. "Yeah. I was thinking the same thing."

"You want my advice?" he asked.

"Always."

"Cass, walk away from this. Let some public defender handle it."

"Thanks," I said, feeling my shields going up. I knew every ugly thing about my father and his temperament. And yet, when an outsider started to throw them at me ... even though I'd more or less asked for it ... I felt defensive. It was that old "he may be an asshole, but he's my asshole" mentality I'd been raised with.

"I'll tell you one thing, if I *had* decided to take this case ... By the way, don't let your old man tell you it was his decision not to hire me. I flat out don't need the headache. It's a good move not to waive speedy trial on this one. The blood's damaging. But with your dad's alibi witness, that's more than enough for reasonable doubt. To be honest, I'm really surprised they arrested him as quick as they did. Somebody's in a rush. So use it to your advantage. Why give them more time to get organized?"

"Yeah. That's what I'm thinking too," I said.

We said our goodbyes and I stared at the four walls of my office. They seemed to be closing in on me. Jeanie came to the doorway. She'd probably heard enough from my end of the conversation to know what was up. Besides that, it was a safe bet the Woodbridge County gossip mill had already made its way to her from the jailhouse.

"You hanging in there, kiddo?" she asked.

I gave her a weak thumbs up then filled her in on the gist of Ron Whitney's advice. She reacted with an impressed nod.

"Too bad old Joe scared him off," she said.

"Him and two others."

"So make him get a public defender," Jeanie said. "Ron's given you a few bits of solid advice. Take them, honey."

"I know," I said. "But something else Ron said sticks in my craw. Truthfully, it's been there for a while anyway. Davy Monroe. He's been solid with the cops, but he's avoiding my calls, and I was hoping to have someone else in place for Dad before I had to press the issue, but ..."

Jeanie's eyes sparked with understanding. I hadn't wanted to drag her into this any further, but Davy Monroe and she went way back. Like a lot of old-timers in this town, Davy had carried a torch for Jeanie way back when. I knew his affections went largely rebuffed the way she told it. By all accounts Davy had had a happy marriage until his wife passed away a few years ago, but maybe Jeanie could work her magic.

"You want me to get Davy in here for you," she said.

"I do. I can subpoena him, but I'd really like to have a conversation without it. I'm not even sure Davy knows you're working with me now."

Jeanie shook her head. "That little weasel. You know the minute I call him, it's just going to encourage him. I can look forward to about a dozen calls from him just wanting to 'shoot the shit' for the next year or so."

"Jeanie, I'll owe you," I said.

"Big time," she answered. "I'm thinking Joey and Matty can put on my new roof come spring. And my Mercedes isn't running as smoothly as I'd like. They'll gouge me if I take it into the shop."

I gave her a salute. "Consider it done," I said.

"And my living room could use a coat of paint. My bedroom too, for that matter."

She was rambling. Her voice trailed off as she wandered back down the hallway. I knew I could expect a list of chores for Matty and Joe by this evening.

The thing was, Jeanie knew she didn't have to call in a favor to get any one of those done. My brothers loved her as much as I did.

True to her word, Jeanie came back about twenty minutes later. She slapped a sticky note in front of me.

"Davy Monroe. Mickey's. Seven o'clock. You're buying."

Smiling, I gave her a thumbs up then called my sister and told her not to expect me for dinner.

Chapter 14

OF ALL PLACES TO meet with Davy Monroe, Mickey's bar seemed like a terrible idea. Nothing happened in that bar that didn't become grist for the Delphi rumor mill within about ten seconds.

Davy was waiting for us when we arrived and had a half-empty beer mug in front of him. Mickey Jr. held the door open for me. As I passed him, he whispered in my ear, "That's all he's had from me, I swear. Can't say for sure what he came in with, but he's steady. Let me know if you need anything."

"Thanks, Mickey," I said.

"Jeanie!" Davy Monroe's face lit up. He was a short man with pale skin, his cheeks permanently reddened. He was hanging on to a wisp of blond hair right at the front that he curled with pomade.

Jeanie was a good sport. She gave Davy a brief, platonic hug, but pushed him back into his seat with a firm hand. Davy sat down like an obedient cocker spaniel. With his big brown eyes, I realized he favored the breed in more ways than one.

I reached across the table to shake Davy's hand. "Good to see you, Cass," he said.

"Thanks for meeting with us," I said. It was always better for me to interview witnesses face to face. There was more to it for a jury besides their story. I needed to see for myself how they held up to questioning; did they have any bothersome tics or habits that might annoy a jury and make them a less-than-compelling witness?

"You know what we're here for, Davy," Jeanie said. "I need you to tell Cass what happened the night of December 1st."

Davy stiffened. "I gave my statement to the cops. I know you can pull strings and get it."

"I've read your statement, yes," I said. "But I want to hear what happened in your words."

"How's Joe doing?" Davy asked. He took a sip of his beer.

"He's holding up," I said.

"I told him he never shoulda come back here. Still a lot of old-timers who have it in for him. You know Georgie Knapp still thinks he stole money from him?"

George Knapp was currently the longest-serving detective on the Delphi P.D. I had no idea my father had entanglements with him. I filed that away. It probably meant nothing, but one never knew.

"No," I said. "I didn't know that. Why?"

"Georgie used to sometimes get in on our weekly poker game. That was, I don't know, more than twenty years ago. He was just a street cop then. Accused your dad of cheating. That always pissed me off. Joe's a lot of things. But he doesn't cheat at cards."

"So how'd you hook back up with Joe?" Jeanie asked. "How long had it been since you'd seen him?"

"Can't say that we ever lost touch completely. I'd say about a year ago he asked me what I thought of Sheila Brewer. Was she worth the trouble and all of that. I said she was a nice gal. That she'd probably be good for him. I took it as good news they hit it off."

"Can you tell me what happened the weekend after Thanksgiving?" Jeanie asked.

I held my breath for a moment, waiting to see if Davy would change any detail of the story he'd been telling the cops. Davy smiled and answered.

"We made plans. Me and Joe. I asked him what he had goin' on that Sunday night. He said nothing. I said a group of us were maybe getting together to play some pool here. We got kind of a league. So he came."

"How'd you get here? Who drove?" I asked.

"Joe parked at my place and we walked. It's only a few blocks."

"Were you drinking?" Jeanie asked.

Davy looked down. "Aw, come on, Jeanie. That's why we walked. We were just having a little fun. It was me, Joe, Hank Rayburn. Al Connely too. Though those guys all left early. By ten, I think. Scotty was working at the bar. You can verify."

The cops already had. That part of Davy's story was true. There was also security footage of Davy leaving with my dad at closing time. From two a.m. to eight a.m., when my father showed up to meet Matty, was the critical window.

"I knew Joe was staying at the Harmon Arms. That seemed kinda sad to me with the holiday and all his kids still living here. He didn't seem like he wanted to go back there and we were having such a good time reminiscing, I told him to come on and crash on my couch. He did that from time to time. He said the motel air conditioning was messing with his asthma. So we hung out."

"Do you remember what time you went to sleep?" Jeanie asked.

Davy smiled. "Oh, we didn't. We talked all damn night.

Watched some old movies on cable. There was an Eastwood marathon."

"You sure Joe never left the whole night?" Jeanie asked.

"Nope."

"And you didn't fall asleep?" I asked. "Or doze off or pass out?"

Davy's eyes narrowed. "No, ma'am. Your pops was with me the whole night. I'll swear that on my Kim's grave."

Kim Monroe had been dead for at least a decade. She'd been a kindergarten teacher; Matty had her. I remembered her as a sweet lady with big green eyes and a mass of red curls. What she'd seen in Davy I'd never know.

Jeanie and I passed a look. A tiny bit of the dread I'd been carrying eased. Davy had stood up to police questioning. He'd been willing to testify at the preliminary exam we waived. Now he'd kept his story straight with me down to the last detail.

He was imperfect, but every witness was. As Jeanie let him shoot the breeze with her for another twenty minutes or so, I felt confident for the first time that my father's mess might not be as hot as I originally feared.

Chapter 15

Two DAYS into the new year, and my father scared off another lawyer. This one was an old friend of Jeanie's named Scarlett Lawrence. Jeanie had talked her out of retirement just to take the meeting with my father. It lasted all of five minutes from what Jeanie said. She was fuming. I sat behind my desk as she paced in front of it.

"Cut him loose, Cass," she said.

"He's facing the rest of his life in prison," I said.

"So, maybe he deserves it."

"Do you really think he killed Sheila Brewer?" I asked. "I mean, in your heart of hearts. Do you think Davy Monroe was lying?"

"Davy's a drunk. A smarmy little cockroach," she said.

"That's not what I asked you. And we both know any help I give my father isn't really for him. I'm trying to keep Matty from going all the way off the deep end."

"Yeah?" she said, turning on me. "How's that going?"

I winced when she said it. She didn't back down.

"He's going to his meetings. He goes to work every day. One day at a time and all that."

"Matty's a grown man," she said. "He's twenty-seven years old and it's not your responsibility to keep him straight. Certainly not at the cost of your own sanity."

The conference room door adjoining my office stood wide open. From where I sat, I could see the whiteboard we'd prepared with my father's case notes on it. Jeanie and I always worked with pro and con columns. On the con side were my father's lies and misdirection to the police, the blood evidence found in his hotel room along with Sheila's personal belongings. On the pro side was his alibi and the absence of key pieces of physical evidence. No scratch marks or any signs he'd been in a fight. No murder weapon. No body. In the bottom corner of the board, Tori had taken a red marker and written the looming trial date in huge letters.

April 1st. We were at the point of no return. "I don't know who else to recommend for him," Jeanie said, coming to the same conclusion I had. My father had burned through every good attorney I could think of and a handful of not-so-great ones.

"So, it's me or someone else from the court-appointed list."

Jeanie shrugged. "So be it, Cass. You're so worried about Matty's well-being. Well, I'm worried about yours. You let that man run you ragged. I didn't want to say anything, but you look like hell."

"Thanks." I gave her a wry smile.

"No, I mean it. You're losing weight. Miranda says you just pick at the lunches she has delivered every day. By the bags under your eyes, I'd say you're not sleeping."

"Jeanie, you're not my mom," I snapped and instantly regretted it.

"Nobody in your life is looking out for you but me right now, Cass. You know how much I love your brothers and sister. But every single one of them is adding to the weight on your shoulders. You're trying to pull them all to shore and they're dragging you under the waves. It scares me. And I know it's why you left Delphi in the first place. That's how you operate. You go and go and go until you're backed into a corner and then you make big, wild decisions that put you in worse shape than when you started."

I folded my arms on my desk then rested my forehead in the crook. The beat of Jeanie's voice pounded away at my skull. While I understood the truth to her words, I flat out didn't want to hear them.

My voice was muffled against my arm when I spoke. "I'm all there is," I said. "If I don't keep pulling them to shore, they'll all sink, Jeanie. It's happened before."

She took the seat across from me. Reaching across the desk, she pulled my arms straight and made me look up at her. Her eyes were filled with concern.

"Sometimes, you gotta just let 'em, honey. It's not always your job to fix everyone. Please, for your sake. Hell, for mine. Walk away from this one for a while. Let Nancy Oleson assign him a public defender."

"What makes you think he'll accept that?" I asked.

"What makes you think I care?"

There was a soft tap on the door frame. Tori had a weak smile on her face as she stood there holding an envelope in her hands.

"Sorry to interrupt," she said, waving the envelope. "I've got something you might want to see."

Jeanie and I shared a look. I could pretty much guess what just went down. Miranda didn't like it when Jeanie and I fought. No doubt she'd just sent poor Tori up here to throw a flag on the play in the form of whatever was in that envelope.

"Come on in," I said, trying to find a smile for her. "What's up?"

Tori's shoulders dropped with relief when Jeanie didn't bite her head off. She came fully into the room and took the seat next to Jeanie opposite me.

"Results came back on Alicia Romaine's DNA test. She wanted everything to go through us. You ready to take a look?"

Chapter 16

Tori lobbed the envelope on my desk. I picked it up and opened it. There wasn't much to see from it other than a giant pie chart representing the various nationalities and ethnic groups Alicia's sample revealed.

"Seventy percent western European," I said. "She's got some Scandinavian and a bit here from the Iberian Peninsula."

"May I?" Tori asked. She pointed to my closed laptop. I slid it over to her. Tori fired it up and put in the office password.

"The interesting thing," she started, "will be to see if there's anyone else among the registered users who pulls up as a familial match. That was the whole point of doing this."

I waited as Tori pulled up the Tree of Life website and punched in a twelve-digit code printed on Alicia's test results. A cartoon tree popped up and as a status bar loaded, the branches of the tree spread out in all directions. Tori's generic avatar sat at the root of it.

We waited.

After about a minute, the tree finished populating. I

leaned in trying to make sense of what I was seeing. I ran my finger over the screen. The center and immediate branches of the tree remained blank with giant, grayed-out question marks over them. But further out, names and pictures began to pop up.

"Well, I'll be damned," Jeanie said. "What the hell does that all mean?"

"No parent matches," I said. "No immediate family member matches. But there are some clusters here. Cousins, it looks like."

"Does it say whether it's a maternal or paternal match?" Tori asked.

I pulled the laptop closer to me and clicked on one of the little avatars.

"Maternal," I said. A little pink bar appeared under the user's name. I clicked a few others.

"It looks like nothing closer than second or third cousins."

"Shoot," Jeanie said. "So all we did was find another haystack with a needle inside of it."

"Maybe," I said, my wheels already turning. I clicked a button on the screen with a graphical view option. The tree went away and a flow chart popped up instead. It wasn't definitive, but this way, I could see the lines to Alicia more clearly.

"What is it?" Tori asked. I stared at the screen for a full minute before answering.

"Maybe nothing," I said. "Probably more dead ends. But I keep seeing a name repeated fairly frequently. Evans. Tori, what else is on your schedule today?"

"Whatever you say is on it, boss. I was just proofreading the brief for the Daniels's summary disposition motion. It's not due for a few days yet. Then I was going to do some deposition sumaries on Martin and Bialecki."

"Those can wait for now," I said. "Do you think you can do some digging for contact information on some of these names? Cross-reference it with what we know about Alicia's mother's estimated date of birth. Start zeroing in on where these distant relatives were concentrated. If you find a cluster living in Michigan, I'd start there. I think we're going to have to start a whole new round of cold calls."

"You bet," she said. "I know this probably makes me a weirdo, but I really like doing this. It feels like detective work. Like solving a logic puzzle."

"Oh," I said. "And definitely cross-check what you find with the list we already have with the high school athletes. I know we've worked our way through most of those, but if we find an overlap, it'll be worth another call. I'm not convinced everyone we talked to was entirely forthcoming. And don't forget to look for clusters of families with lots of girls."

"That's a great idea," Tori said. "I'll get right on this. I'll have the first list by the end of the day. Do you want me to start making calls?"

"Hold off," I said. "At least show me the lists first. Let me think my way through how to approach these people. For some reason, I think we might get better attitudes with this round. Everybody in this database is there because they took that same DNA test. They *wanted* to know more about their family tree."

"Right," Jeanie said. "But none of them are Alicia's mother or father. I can't shake the fact that whoever they are, they don't seem to want to be found."

"Maybe not," I admitted. "Only you're assuming they're still alive. Alicia's mother would be in her fifties now. Certainly young enough to have living parents. I mean, if her mother's dead, don't you think *her* mother would jump at the chance to have a connection to a granddaughter?"

Jeanie pursed her lips. "I think it's naive to assume we can put ourselves in any of these people's shoes, Cass. People give children up for adoption for all kinds of reasons. In my experience, no matter what the reason, it's never easy. It isn't always a joyous reunion like you see on those sappy love story channels."

I smiled. "You spend a lot of time watching sappy love story channels?"

The minute I asked the question, Jeanie's face flushed.

"I like my stories," she said. "Don't judge me."

I put my hands up in surrender. Tori's expression was as dumbfounded as mine. Gruff, tough, Jeanie Mills still had some layers to her I hadn't seen. It made me smile. Things were easy between us again and I was glad of it.

"Okay," I said. "So we've all got stuff to do today. Let's touch base at the end of the day."

Jeanie and Tori rose. "Give me a piece of that list when you make it," Jeanie said to Tori. "I could use the distraction too."

With that they left my office. I sat staring at the gaps in Alicia Romaine's family tree. Once again, I was struck with the contrast of her story to my own. She wanted to find her family. Today, I just felt like I'd been buried by the weight of mine.

Chapter 17

Two WEEKS LATER, I got a call from prosecutor Jack LaForge. His tone went from the hard-ass cockiness I was used to to something more subdued.

"I've got a deal for you on your father's case," he said.

Tori sat in the corner of my office writing up the last of her notes on the Romaine birth parent search from what we'd learned online. During lunch, I planned to make my way through a half dozen or so names. The handful I'd already tried on the Evans side turned up nothing.

"I'm listening," I said.

"You have to realize how bad it is for him," he said. "You know I'm going to be able to introduce his statements to the police. The jury's going to know Joe Sr. is a liar. There's the physical evidence in his hotel room. The blood. Sheila's wallet."

I bit my lip. If Jack thought he could call me up and have me start arguing legal strategy with him or tip my hand to my dad's defense, he was nuts.

"Are you still authorized to speak on your father's behalf?" he asked.

"For the moment," I said.

"But you can't possibly be thinking you're going to try this case, right?"

"Jack, which is it? You're calling to offer a plea or you want to discuss the trial?"

Jack cleared his throat. "Cass, this is a professional courtesy on my part. Get out of this while you still can."

"What's your offer, Jack?" I asked.

"You know I'm going to rip Davy Monroe apart. I mean ... you *know* that, right?"

I had a keen sense someone else was listening in.

"Do you have me on speaker?" I asked.

Jack paused. "No. It's just us, Cassiopeia."

"You must be worried about the motion to suppress," I said. I'd filed one just last week. Regardless of who tried this case, I felt my father had at least a fifty-fifty shot at getting the hotel room evidence thrown out on a search and seizure violation. If I could win that, the prosecution's case would evaporate and I could be done with this. If they regrouped and refiled, I made it a vow it would be someone else's problem.

"Voluntary manslaughter," he said. "And you need to know this wasn't my call. If it were strictly up to me, I wouldn't be talking to you at all. I like my chances on this one. It's going to be fun to try."

I cringed. No matter what else was happening, a woman was dead and missing. I would describe no part of this as fun.

Manslaughter. It meant my father could be out of prison in a few years. Jack was right about one critical fact. Though I felt confident in Davy Monroe's story, you just never know how a witness will perform under pressure.

"I'm curious," I said. "Why the change of heart? If this is coming from your boss, I'd like to know why."

Jack stayed silent.

"Jack?"

He let out a breath. "Take it to your father and get back to me. There's a ticking clock on this one. I need to know by Monday morning at most."

"I'll communicate it to him," I said. "Is there anything else we need to discuss?"

"No," Jack answered.

Tori had moved from the corner table and took a seat on the other side of my desk. She had a curious expression on her face as she tried to read mine and parcel out my end of the conversation. I had a pen poised on a pad of paper but had yet to write anything down.

I hung up without saying goodbye. I quickly filled Tori in on the plea deal.

"It's something to think about," she said, her tone tentative.

"Maybe," I said. "But it's got me wondering, why now? Maybe Jack's boss is more worried about our chances at the suppression hearing than I would have guessed."

"Could be," she said.

"Can you make arrangements at the county jail so I can visit my dad first thing in the morning?"

"No problem," she said, rising. She had a slip of paper in her hand and gave it to me. I looked at it. It was another round of names she'd generated from the genealogy website. There were ten of them. All people who lived within a hundred-mile radius of the hospital where Alicia Romaine was born.

"Thanks," I said. "This will be a welcome distraction. How many calls are we up to now?"

"Between the two of us, including the ones we made when we were just tracking down gymnasts, we've made over fifty calls. There's about another hundred that I'd consider warm leads in terms of the geography and the DNA and just intuition on my part. Evans is just a ridiculously popular name. There's a ton more that I'd consider total shots in the dark."

I nodded and set the paper on my desk beside my landline. "Good work," I said.

"Do you think so? Because I've gotta admit. I'm feeling less confident that we'll ever be able to help her."

I tilted my head. Tori had taken the Romaine case personally. She was still grieving the loss of her dad. I knew in some small way, helping Alicia made her feel like she was giving back.

"You've got a good heart, Tori," I said. "And as far as Alicia goes, we *are* helping her. Even if none of these names pans out. She'll at least know she tried every possible thing. And I think she understands there's no small amount of fate at play. If she's meant to connect with her birth parents, she will."

Tori nodded. "You're right. Then, you always are."

I smiled and rolled my eyes. "If you could get a tee-shirt printed with that on it and then make my family members wear it, I'll buy you a car."

Tori laughed. She picked up her things and left my office for lunch.

I listened as the back door opened and shut. Jeanie was off for the day. Miranda had walked down to Sweet Delights as had become her habit over the past few months. That just left me alone with my thoughts in the office for the first time in forever.

I looked out the window. I had a view of the courthouse and jail beyond. My father was in there somewhere. I wondered if he felt the walls closing in the way I did. This was real. He'd had more brushes with the law over the years than I could remember or count. And yet, I couldn't believe he was guilty this time. He'd threatened my mother. They'd thrown things, broken lamps, dishes, once a chair. He'd smacked my older brother and I hated him for it. But to stab a woman to death. I just couldn't see it. I hoped that didn't make me blind.

Drawing my eyes away from the window, I picked up the paper Tori had left, grateful for something else to do.

The Evans name kept coming up. If we could just find a way to match it with the non-identifying information we had in Alicia's file.

Marilyn Evans was one of the names that might be a first or second cousin match for Alicia's mother. The woman would be in her nineties if she were still alive. But she had the strongest familial connection to the other names on my list so I made the call and crossed my fingers.

The phone rang five times and I nearly hung up. Then a male voice answered with a sing-song "Hallo, dare!" that made me smile. The memory jolted me. My grandfather used to answer the phone in a similar manner.

"Good afternoon," I said, then launched into my pitch.

I got silence on the other end for a moment. "Well," he said. "I'm not Marilyn. Suppose you've figured that out though, Missy. You can call me Newt."

"Hey, Newt," I said, writing the name on my pad of paper.

"Miss Marilyn, well, she passed. It's been oh, five or six years now. Great lady. She was my wife's mother. My wife was Patricia, her oldest daughter. Is she on your list?"

"Patricia," I repeated. "Patricia Evans?"

"That's right," he said. "She kept her name."

"May I speak to her then?" I asked. I realized I was on shaky ground. It was a long shot that Patricia Evans was actually Alicia's mother, but if she was and I'd just revealed it to her husband, this could be a disaster.

"Well," he said. "Patricia passed about ten years ago now. Brain cancer. Poor thing. Miss Marilyn and I were the ones there for her in the end. I thought it was gonna kill Miss Marilyn. She was stronger than I was. Damn near killed me."

"I'm sorry," I said. "Truly. I hope my call hasn't brought you any distress. It's not at all my intention."

"Where'd you say you were calling from, honey?" he asked.

"Delphi," I said. "I'm an attorney in Delphi and it's my client who is looking for her birth mother."

He grew silent for a moment. "That's gotta be rough. Patricia and I never got to have a kid of our own. She had endometriosis. Horrible pain. Used to lay her up for days until they finally took all that stuff out of her. Broke my heart. You know, we thought about adopting. Isn't that funny? And you're saying maybe a cousin of Patricia's had a baby she gave up? How old is she?"

I hesitated. Then finally, "My client is in her thirties."

"Wow," he said. "I sure wish I'd have known. Patricia and I would have taken that baby as our own. We were never rich, but she'd have been our princess, I'll tell you that. Is she okay though? Your client?"

Newt's voice took on a wistful tone that tugged at my heart a little. He was just a sweet old man who lived alone. The women who had taken care of him were all gone now. "Is she a lawyer like you?" he asked.

"Um. No. But yes. To answer your question, my client is doing just fine. She's happily married. She has children of her own. She was raised by loving parents."

Newt let out a sigh. "That's good to hear. Makes me happy to think it. You hear so many sad stories these days about kids in the system. Bullies. School shootings. I'm glad for her. And I'm sorry I don't have more I can tell you."

"It's okay," I said. "I really do appreciate your time."

"You know," he said. "Maybe I can do something for you after all."

"Oh?"

The doors downstairs started opening and closing as Miranda and Tori came back from lunch. Miranda made her way upstairs. She stopped at my door when she saw me on the phone. She had a stack of pink messages in her hand and my stomach dropped. I knew I was in for a busy afternoon.

"Miss Marilyn, well, she was the matriarch of this family, you better believe it. If she'd known one of her nieces or their daughters or any blood of hers was in that kind of trouble, why she'd have swooped right in and handled it. Even if she ended up raising that child herself. I'm sure of it. Family was everything to her. It's why I'm still here living in her house. Once I married my Patricia, that was it. I was part of the tribe. And, man, she had occasion to fix quite a bit over the years. If anyone had a problem, they'd come to Miss Marilyn. I swear if any of 'em had robbed a bank she'd blame the bank for having all that money in it, I'll tell you what."

I laughed to myself. It was something I said about my own Grandma Leary before. I found myself wishing hard that I could have met Miss Marilyn Evans. And it gave me strange comfort to know Alicia was related to her somehow, even if distantly.

"How do you think you can help?" I asked, trying to steer Newt back to the matter at hand.

"Well," he said. "We still get together now and again. The sisters are all gone. Patricia had eight of them. But the nieces and nephews. They still check in on me from time to time and they're welcome here at Miss Marilyn's whenever they want.

That's why she left the place to me. She didn't want to pick favorites and she knew I wouldn't either. A neutral party, if you will."

"Sure," I said. My pulse quickened. Marilyn Evans had eight daughters? This could be the break we were looking for if the information Alicia's birth mother wrote to the adoption agency was accurate. Perhaps one of Patricia Evans's sisters was that woman.

Miranda came in and set the messages down. The top one came from my dad and it was marked urgent. I pressed my fingers to my forehead.

"The nieces and nephews are all scattered to the four winds now. It'll take me some time to get a hold of them. I'm willing to try."

"I'd surely appreciate it," I said, hopeful.

Newt rambled on for a few more moments while I smiled and nodded. Then we said our goodbyes with his promise to see what he could find out. It was worth a shot at least.

Dread filled my heart again as I picked up my pink message and called the county jail.

Chapter 18

"No."

My father's answer was dark and definitive.

"You haven't even heard me explain it," I said. I sat across from him at the beat-up metal table in the lawyer's room at the county jail.

"Whatever deal they offered," he said, "is gonna require me to admit that I did something I didn't do. Manslaughter. Is that it?"

I felt my nostrils flare. "Dad ..."

"Right," he answered. "Tell Jack LaForge to go fuck himself. I didn't kill Sheila Brewer. I hadn't seen her for days. I told you a thousand times. We didn't argue. We didn't have some falling out. I hooked up with her when it was convenient. She understood that. It was our arrangement. She wasn't looking for more than that and neither was I."

"Dad, that's all well and good," I said. "But you could go down for this."

"Not if you do your job," he said.

"I've sent you five different lawyers. All highly competent. All perfectly capable of putting on a rigorous defense for you. You've run them all off. Your trial is ten weeks away."

"There isn't gonna be a trial," he said. "You're gonna go in there and get that hotel room search thrown out. End of story. Then all they got is their interpretation of what I said to the cops. There's no body. They can't even prove a murder took place."

"Fifty-fifty," I said. "Those are your odds on the motion to suppress. You lose that, you're going to trial and LaForge proves you're a liar and Sheila's blood was all over your hotel room."

He banged on the door. "Fix it, Cassiopeia. You're in this family and it's your job. Cheer up, I'm giving you a compliment."

"Great," I said. "Forgive me if I don't take it as such."

I rose to meet him as he pounded on the door again.

"This isn't a traffic ticket," I said. "It's a first-degree murder charge. You think I have some magic wand I can wave. Some string I can pull. You're nuts if you think I have that kind of pull in this town. We have the same last name, remember?"

He made a shooing gesture with his hands and something inside of me snapped. What the hell was I even doing here? I didn't need this. Didn't deserve it.

"I'm done," I said. "There's no talking sense into you and I'm not going to let you drag me down with you. Tomorrow or the next day, you'll hear from the court. Ask for a public defender to be assigned. I quit, Dad."

I don't know what changed. It wasn't like I hadn't said the same thing to him a dozen times. This time, for whatever reason, he must have believed me. He sank back into his chair and I swear within the span of two seconds, I saw him age twenty years.

"Cass," he said, reaching for my hands. "I need you. I know how good you are. And I know that's what I need. Honey, you don't really believe I killed that woman."

There was a quiet desperation in his voice. Something flickered behind his eyes and for the first time, I realized how truly afraid he was. No, he was terrified.

"No," I said, deflating. "I don't think you killed her. But I need to understand why you lied."

"She wanted me to," he said. "Sheila didn't want anyone knowing we were seeing each other. She caught flak for it from her family. She was trying to figure out a way to break it to them. I didn't know she was dead when I talked to the cops. I thought Sheila was just trying to get the hell away from her nosey-ass cousins for a while. She always told me she wanted to. Had fantasies about just hopping a plane and flying off somewhere. She didn't take me breaking up with her well. The last thing I said to her, I told her she should do it. I told her I'd give her money for the ticket."

"Did you?" I asked.

He shook his head. "Nah. And she probably wouldn't have taken it."

It was the longest stretch of honesty he'd given me. Unless he was playing me all over again. But it was the first time I'd seen any show of emotion from him over what might have happened to Sheila Brewer. It was a start.

The deputy came to the door. My father's face changed again, becoming hard. He fixed his smirk in place and held his hands out for the cuffs. This time, when the deputies led him out, I jumped when the heavy metal door clanged shut.

I got to my car and let out a sigh. The day seemed brighter. Early February and we were getting off lucky this winter. It was in the high thirties. Warm enough for native Michiganders to forgo wearing coats even.

I sent Miranda a text letting her know I planned to take the rest of the afternoon off. I wanted nothing more than to curl up on the couch and watch trash television with Marbury snuggled up in the crook of my arm and Madison at my feet. I had two hours before Jessa got off school and Vangie made it home from her day-shift-bartending gig. It was perfect. Heaven.

I should have known even thinking it would jinx my day to hell.

My phone rang as I pulled out of the jail parking structure. It was Tina, Matty's wife. My stomach dropped. She rarely called me.

"Can you get over here?" she said, her voice breaking.

"Where's here?" I asked.

"My place," she said. "I need you to come pick up your brother or I swear I'm calling the cops. I've already called Joe to bring his truck. I'm throwing the rest of his stuff out on the lawn."

I could hear Matty yelling in the background. He sounded enough like my father to send a cold chill through me.

He wasn't though. I told myself that over and over again as I raced out of the parking garage and headed to the north side of town.

Chapter 19

JOEY HADN'T ARRIVED YET. True to her word, Tina had the first few boxes lined up on the driveway. She stood there, red-faced from crying. I didn't hear Matty shouting anymore. I hoped he hadn't gotten behind the wheel and driven off.

"Tina?" I parked my car at an angle and got out. She set the box down and came to me.

My arms went up instinctively and she went into them. She sniffled against my shoulder. "What?" I said. "Tell me what's going on."

She pulled back. "You know. How many more times do I have to go through this with him? He promises he'll change. He got fired this morning. The machine shop threw him out. It's not a layoff this time, Cass. Not some diversion program where he can come back or for a probationary period. It's a flat-out firing for just cause. He's been lying to me for weeks. He's already been through a hearing with the union and everything. He's out, Cass."

My heart shattered. It meant Matty had been lying to all of us. He'd shown up to work drunk.

"Where is he?" I asked.

"He took off," she said.

"In his car?!"

"No," she said. "I have his keys. He started walking toward Scarlett Street. He's probably only made it five or six blocks by now."

I hugged her again. "Hang in there. We'll get him back."

"No," she said. "Cass, you don't get it. I don't want him back. I can't do this anymore."

"How long of a head start did he have?" I asked, looking down the street.

"He left about ten minutes ago," she sniffled. "And Cass, I mean it. Please don't bring him back here. He's got an apartment. Make him use it."

"Tina," I said, my voice dropping low. "Did he ... has he ..."

Her expression turned horrified. "No. Oh. Cass, he's never hurt me. He's not like that. He goes quiet with me."

I believed as much, but I had to ask. If my brother had ever so much as raised a hand to Tina, even piss drunk, Joe would kill him and I wouldn't stand in his way.

"I don't want anything bad to happen to him," she said, fresh tears falling. "But I can't fix him. And I can't keep letting him break my heart. I let him in just a little and I get flattened. Every time."

"It's okay," I said. "You know I'm on your side too. I love you both. And as messed up as Matty is, he loves you with all of his heart."

She nodded. "Sometimes it's just not enough."

With that, she withdrew. Wiping her face, she walked away from me and back into the house. I got in my car and drove no more than fifteen miles down the street in the direction Tina pointed. I made it five blocks before I found my brother sitting on a bench just inside Shamrock Park.

I pulled into the gravel parking lot by the baseball diamonds and headed toward him. The way Matty was sitting, I thought he might have passed out. His chin was on his chest. He wasn't moving. I steeled myself for whatever might come and took a seat beside him.

"I messed it all up," he said after a great breath. When he looked up, my heart broke for him. Matty's face was swollen from crying.

"Yep," I said. "You sure did."

"She changed the locks this time. It's for good. I know the difference."

I nodded. "Probably."

Matty gave a choked sound. He reeked of whiskey. But I knew the stages of drunk Matty. He got sad like this as he was sobering up.

"You need help," I said.

"It doesn't work."

"It does if you work it," I said.

"Don't give me the lines. I can't stand it."

I turned to him. "Yes, you can. You have no choice. None of us do. I love you, Matty. Tina loves you so much it's breaking her. You're worth loving. But me saying it doesn't help. You have to believe it."

He shook his head. "There's no help. There's no winning. If Dad can't do it, neither can I."

I snapped. I grabbed my brother by the shoulders and shook him. "You're not Dad! Matty, when are you going to get that through your thick skull? His sobriety doesn't have anything to do with yours."

"You can't say that," he said. "This thing doesn't live inside of you."

"You're right," I said. "I don't have your disease. But I get to live outside of it and watch it eat away at you. And you are *not* the same person he is. You have a good heart. You have everything in the world to live for."

"She's done with me," Matty said.

"Maybe," I said. "But I'm not done with you."

"God," he said. "Aren't you sick of it? Haven't you had enough of trying to take care of me?"

"Well," I smiled. "That's two questions. Yes to the first. No to the second."

Matty went quiet. He stopped crying and his face went white. "I'm done, Cass. I know you've tried to help. And I could quit for a little while. Maybe a few years even. But it's going to come back. It always does. Dad's been lying to you too. He's been drinking since he came to town. A lot."

I felt a little lightheaded. I thought I had a moment of honesty with my father at the jail.

"Fine," I said, breathing again. "But what the hell does any of that got to do with you?"

Another tear fell from his eye. "It's my path. We're the same. If Dad ends up here, I'll be next."

"No," I shouted. "It's not the same. Not even close. You still have a chance. You have a million of them. You just have to take one."

"He has to make it too," Matty said. "If Dad can't get out from under this, I can't either."

I wanted to throttle him. "Stop it!"

"You have to fix this, Cass. Because I *know* he didn't kill Sheila Brewer. But if he goes down for it ... Cass, he's scared. Terrified."

I knew he was right. I'd seen it for myself.

"He's covering," Matty said. "You may not want to believe this but I know him better than you do. I understand him. I'm serious. He's ... I think he's close to being suicidal. And he's scared you're going to abandon him."

"Matty," I said. "Our father is not a good man."

"He's me!" he said.

It was like arguing with a stone wall. My poor brother really believed he and my father were so much alike. I didn't know how to get through to him.

"Matty," I said. "He drags you down. He manipulates you. Every time he comes to town, you let him sabotage your sobriety and he enjoys it. It makes him feel better about himself. That man is toxic, Matty. And I need to be done with him. So do you."

Matty took my hands in his. "You can't give up on him. Please. Stick by him. Do it for me."

I hated myself for what I was about to say. What I was about to do. It seemed I would never get out from under any of it.

"Matty," I said. "Okay. I'll do it for you. I'll stay by his side and get him through this damn trial. I can't promise you he'll be acquitted. You need to prepare yourself for the very real possibility that he'll be found guilty. But only on one condition."

Matty jerked back. He knew me well enough to know what he'd just walked in to. I couldn't help that I hated them both a little for it. "Cass ..."

"No," I said. "I'll help Dad, but you're going to rehab or the deal's off. A real program. Ninety days. Then sober living. The whole nine yards. And you commit to it for real, Matty. Or Dad's on his own too. I love you, but I won't help you destroy yourself anymore. I mean it. I can pull some strings and get you into Maple Valley. I think I can get you admitted tonight. Now."

He blinked hard, considering whether to call my bluff.

"Your choice," I said. "I'm offering you a gift, Matty. Take it. Or I walk out of this park and I won't look back."

For the first time in his life, Matty understood I wasn't joking. The gesture was subtle. If I'd so much as blinked I would have missed it. My brother's face fell in defeat or surrender, but he gave me a nod and I took him by the hand.

Chapter 20

Two mornings later, I made good on my promise to Matty. At four o'clock that afternoon, he swore he would live up to his. "All rise," Judge Felix Castor's bailiff called out.

Tori stood beside me with her laptop open. She was ready with half a dozen tabs open to various points of law in case the judge took us too far into the weeds.

"You're up, Counselor," Castor said. The odds were stacked against me, considering how the judge peered at me over the top of his reading glasses.

"Your Honor," I started. "I know you're familiar with our brief in support so I won't rehash it."

"Please don't," he said. "Just remind me, what's the time frame here on the welfare check versus what the maid had to say?" Judge Castor would have preferred deciding all motions just on written briefs. Half the time, I think he humored the lawyers in Woodbridge County to lull them into thinking they stood a chance.

"At least six hours, Your Honor," I answered. "The maid at the Harmon Arms gave an equivocal report of what she described as shouts at one point, an argument, and then later, after the police arrived but several hours after the so-called incident, screams. She went on with her shift without reporting what she heard. It was only when the manager came in the next morning she reported it. That report didn't even alarm management enough to key into room seven. Therefore, there is no justifiable reason the police had to circumvent the Fourth Amendment on a so-called welfare check. They had no right to be in that room without a warrant so anything they found incident to that search is the fruit of a poisonous tree."

"Mr. LaForge," the judge asked just as Jack started to wind up. "Was Mr. Leary already a person of interest at the time the cops showed up at that hotel room?"

"He was, Your Honor," Jack said. "But they didn't know he was staying at the Harmon Arms. And they didn't know he was in room seven. They performed a lawful welfare check based on credible information from a reliable witness. There is no Fourth Amendment violation."

Judge Castor pursed his lips. He pushed his glasses up his nose.

"Your Honor," I started. He cut me off with a wave of his hand.

"I get it, Ms. Leary," he said. "Abundantly."

He closed the file on his desk. "All right. I've heard all I need to. You'll get a written order by the end of the week. That is all."

He banged the gavel and dismissed us. Jack stood slack-jawed. I had to admit, I was a bit shocked too. Castor usually ruled from the bench on stuff like this. I couldn't tell if that was a good or bad sign.

Castor left for his chambers. Jack walked over to me. "So you're still in this?" he asked, incredulous. "Did you lose a bet or something?"

I clamped my mouth shut. There was no reason to tell

Jack how close he was to the truth. I checked my phone. I still had a few more hours before I met Joe, Vangie, and Matty over at Maple Valley. I'd begged Tina to come too, but understood why she wouldn't. She was too in love with my brother. She could only stick to her bottom line if she did it from a distance today. For the moment, Matty was staying at Vangie's house. She took the day off work to make sure he didn't disappear or go on a bender for old times' sake.

"Good seeing you as always, Jack," I said.

"My offer still stands," he said. "What did your father ... er ... client have to say? It's only good up until the time Castor rules."

"After Castor rules, I expect you'll dismiss the charges against my dad," I said.

He was rattled. I could tell by the red spots in Jack's cheeks. Every question Judge Castor asked was pro-defense. Even I was a little surprised by that. For the first time in a while, I felt a little cocky. But I had enough trial experience to know it was very bad juju to act out on that. Instead, I shook Jack's hand and got out of that courtroom as fast as I could.

I just made it to my car when my phone rang. I braced myself as I looked at my caller ID. It was my new buddy, Newt. He'd called me two other times on the Alicia Romaine matter with new family details about Miss Marilyn Evans's nieces. He was still working on getting current phone numbers.

He was a sweet enough old guy. Well-meaning. He was lonely though and I got the impression he thought of me as his new pet project.

"Good afternoon, Newt," I said, trying to make my voice more cheery than weary.

"Hallo, dare," he said in his trademark way. "Hope you're not working too hard, Miss Cass," he said.

"Or hardly working," I said, finishing his corny joke for him. "What's up?"

"Not much," he answered. "I talked to Eileen Evans. She's Miss Marilyn's younger sister. Did you know she had one?"

I did. Tori had done a pretty good job piecing together a list of Evans women who might have been closer relations to Alicia. We were closing in but still had a long way to go.

"Well," he continued. "Eileen's in a nursing home out in Florida. She was always the family historian. She and my Patricia were close once upon a time. Eileen was her godmother and all that. Anyway, I think Eileen might be someone for you to talk to. I've got a phone number for you. You ready?"

I hoped Eileen's mind was still sharp. She had a handful of granddaughters who made Tori's cut for potential candidates as Alicia's mother. I didn't yet know if she'd had all girls like Miss Marilyn did. Only none of them had ever lived in Michigan and as far as we could tell, never competed in gymnastics. I was starting to think that part of the story was a lie or a fantasy. Maybe Alicia's mother had only dreamed of being a gymnast or wrote it down as a way to throw a red herring should her long-lost daughter ever come looking.

"Thanks, Newt," I said, writing down the number as he rattled it off. "I'll put my girl on it. I really do appreciate it."

"You okay, honey?" he asked. "You don't sound so good. Did you have a rough day?"

I smiled. He did this grandfatherly routine with me a lot. Though it was definitely overfamiliar, once again he reminded me a lot of my real Grandpa Leary.

"I'm good, Newt. Honest. Just busy today."

"Oh, I'm sorry. And here I am calling to ramble on. Last thing you need is some doddering old fool slowing you down."

I instantly felt like an asshole.

"I really don't mind," I said. "We're gonna crack this case. And you'll be part of the reason why."

I could practically see him smiling through the phone. I didn't even know what he looked like. I imagined him with a bald, shiny head, wrinkly elbows that poked out from a short-sleeved golf shirt. He probably wore Old Spice and maybe even smoked a pipe. Sometimes, I could hear him puffing away between sentences.

"Well, that'll be something," he said. "You let me know if you have any trouble getting ahold of old Eileen. She's a tough old bird. A little hard of hearing, but her mind's good. Just like Miss Marilyn's was up until the end. Strong mental genes, those ladies have. Wish I could be so lucky. I swear I walk into a room and forget why about twenty times a day."

"You're doing all right, Newt," I said. "Don't let the ladies tell you any different."

He laughed at that. I said my goodbyes as I pulled out of the courthouse parking lot. It was just past noon. I had a couple of hours to kill before our appointment at Maple Valley for Matty. So instead of spending my energy on my dad again, I went back to the lake.

My lot was empty. The last of my old house had been cleared away. With any luck, we would break ground on the new place by the end of the month. It would be bigger than before. I'd purchased the adjacent lot. The new house would sit higher on the hill, centered on a small peninsula.

I hadn't told my brothers and sister everything I planned. I'd have the main house with a master suite and home office like I'd always dreamed. I could look out at the lake from huge, wall-to-ceiling windows. I designed a massive kitchen that would become the heart of the house. But the biggest surprise was an apartment I planned over the new four-car garage. Once it was built, I could provide the sanctuary each of them needed from time to time without having them on top of me. With the exception of that surprise, the house was damn close to Great-Grandpa Leary's Someday House.

Heaven. I would carve out my slice.

Right now though, I just wanted a few solitary minutes where I could pretend to be an only child.

Chapter 21

I FOUND my brothers and sister waiting for me, piled into Joe's truck in the parking lot of Maple Valley nursing home. Matty sat in the passenger seat staring straight ahead.

"I'm proud of you, baby brother," I said as I leaned in his window.

He was stoic, setting his jaw in a hard line. Joe was no better. He gripped the steering wheel. Vangie had to remind him to pull the keys out of the ignition.

Then Matty got out. I looped my arm around his, ready to march up to the double doors with him.

"We have your back," I said. "You know that. I'll look in on Tina. I'll do what I can to take care of Dad. I hope we'll get some good news on that front soon."

"It doesn't matter," Joe said, sternly. "It can't. Matty, if you …"

"Stop!" Vangie said. "We're here. Matty's here. No more lectures. He knows how hard this is going to be. He's ready."

I rubbed Matty's back. He looked so young to me just then. No different than the baby boy who'd grown so used to taking care of. But that was the trouble. He had to take care of himself. He had to want this, or it was just a waste of time.

A nurse met us at the door. He was broad, burly, and strong. I supposed he was used to admitting patients far less docile than Matty currently was.

"You can come with me, Mr. Leary," he said. "My name is Cole. We'll get you set up at intake."

"Come on," Vangie said. "We're right here with you."

"Not after this point," Cole said.

Vangie started to cry. I could see Matty tense up. I took her by the shoulder and pulled her away from him. Not here. Not now. Matty just had to walk through those doors and stay there. Nurse Cole was right. We weren't helping by bringing any drama.

I hugged my brother. He didn't respond.

"I love you," I said.

Joe stood like a stone mountain to my right. He was angry at Matty and couldn't yet get past it. Vangie was just a nervous wreck. I didn't think any of this energy was good for him. It was a mistake all of us coming.

But the most important thing happened. Matty nodded and walked with Cole through the front doors. He never looked back.

Vangie fell apart beside me. "He's got to get better," she said. "He's just got to."

"He will," I said, hoping like hell it was true. There were only so many chances Matty had left. I wasn't sure at all whether he'd have a job waiting for him at the end of this process. But he wasn't the only one who had to take this one step at a time.

"Come on," Joe said. "Let's go back to Vangie's."

The moment he said it, a wave of dread came over me. I

needed a break from all of them. My father. My brothers. Vangie. Only, with my living arrangements, my means of escape were few.

Then the doors of the facility opened and I recognized a familiar swagger. I couldn't help that it made me smile.

"You guys go on ahead," I said.

"Cass," Joe said. "You can't go in there with him. You heard the nurse."

"I know," I said. "But I've got some other business of my own to handle."

Joe looked toward the doors. He saw Detective Eric Wray's approach and frowned.

Eric's step faltered as he saw the three of us standing there. He shot me a sly grin though. I wondered if he'd passed Matty on the way out. He knew enough about my family drama to guess what was going on.

"Got a minute?" he said, as if he could read my mind.

"Yeah," I said. "Joe, I'll be fine. Just take Vangie home. I'll talk to you tomorrow."

Joe scowled at Eric, but didn't argue. He put a hand on Vangie's back. Then he ushered her to his truck and opened the door for her. When he got behind the wheel, he managed to make even his truck sound angry, peeling out and jerking the wheel.

"Had enough Learys for one day?" he said.

"Something like that," I answered. "How's Wendy?"

Eric winced a bit. I hadn't meant my question as sarcasm. Eric was at Maple Valley for usually only one reason. His wife was a permanent resident. Though their marriage had been on the rocks before that, he still visited her every week, paying penance for something I knew wasn't his fault.

"You know what," I said. "Never mind. I'll make a deal

with you. I won't ask you about your problems if you don't ask me about mine. Let's just ... can you take me out for a drink?"

Eric smiled. "Yeah, Leary, that I can do."

With that, he took my arm and led me away from my problems, at least temporarily. Though I knew in my heart they would find me soon enough.

Chapter 22

Wray and I ended up at Mickey's. I knew the irony of "celebrating" my brother's voluntary admission to rehab with a vodka gimlet, but I sorely needed it.

"Cheers," Eric said as soon as the waitress handed him his beer. He chose to forgo the frosted mug she gave him and drank straight from the bottle. We clinked glasses.

"It'll be good for him," Eric said, skipping the preamble. I was grateful that I didn't have to explain it all. He knew my family. He didn't judge. Well, at least he didn't judge my brothers. My father was another matter and one we couldn't discuss.

"He's tired," I said. "We all are."

"You know," he said. "I really want to ask you how your dad's doing. Not because I care so much about him. But I know it affects you."

Eric and my entry into the bar together hadn't gone unnoticed. Two junior prosecutors sat on the other side of the room. I saw Justine Appleman at the bar ordering a pitcher. She was one of the deputy court clerks and she was married to a probation officer. Beyond that, the place was full of off-duty cops from both the sheriff's office and the Delphi P.D. This was Delphi; the eyes and wagging tongues were everywhere.

"I appreciate that," I said. "I really do. And you know, there's nothing I'd like to do more than unload my troubles on you about it."

I said it as almost a throw-away, obligatory comment. But the minute the words spilled out of my mouth, I realized how true they were. Eric had been a solid sounding board for me over the last two years. He had turned out to be a true friend. A rarity. And it flat out sucked that I had to stay on guard around him now.

"Well, I've had a hell of a year so far," I said, clinking glasses with him again.

"How'd your motion hearing go?" he asked.

I raised a brow. "I expect you already know the answer to that. You want to try and pretend you didn't have ears in the courtroom today?"

He smiled. Busted. "Well, it surprises me Castor didn't rule from the bench."

"Me too," I admitted.

"That's a good sign for you, I suppose."

"Eric," I said. "I think we know each other well enough to cut the crap. You think my dad murdered Sheila Brewer and you're not going to stop trying to prove it no matter what Felix Castor does with my motion to suppress."

He shifted uncomfortably in his seat. "It's nothing personal, Cass. It matters to me that you know that."

I finished the last of my drink. Our waitress was good. Her name was Crystal and I went to high school with her mom.

"You ready for another?"

I considered my options. I was probably better off just sticking with water.

Eric said, "Don't take this the wrong way, but you look like you need it."

I gave him a wry smile. "Fine," I said. "One more. Tell Scotty to ease up on the lime this time."

"Got it." Crystal gave me a salute and collected Eric's empty beer bottle. He stuck with water this round.

"Any ETA on your house?" he asked, moving to more neutral territory.

"Should break ground on the foundation in three or four weeks. They're telling me three months to completion after that but I'm bracing for closer to six."

"Pity," he said. "It'd be nice if you could have your first summer in it. You know I saw the design over at the planning commission."

"You spying on me?"

"Nah," he said. "I was over there working another case. They were spread out on a desk."

"Right," I said. "It's big news. There hasn't been any new construction on Finn Lake in decades. I'm getting all kinds of advice."

"I'll bet you are."

He grew quiet for a moment. We were quickly running out of things to say that didn't involve my father's case. It really was the giant elephant in the room.

"I hate this," he said. "I've been trying to figure out a way to tell you that."

I nodded. "I think you just did."

"Maybe. It just would make my life a hell of a lot easier if you'd just take a job in the prosecutor's office or stick with civil law."

"Your life?" I said, my voice going up.

"You know what I mean," he said.

"Actually, I don't."

Crystal came back with our drinks. I took a sip. Scotty had made this one even stronger. This would be my limit if I intended to drive myself home.

"Okay," I said. "Uncle. I like it better when you're on my side too."

Eric's face changed. For a moment, he looked wounded by my words. Then he got serious. He fixed his on me with such intensity, I felt my pulse quicken.

"Cass," he said. "I will always be on your side."

"No matter what?" I teased. It probably wasn't fair of me. The vodka was starting to do its work.

"No," he said. "But it turns out you're one of my favorite people and I'm getting damn tired of worrying about you."

"So don't," I said.

The silence settled between us again. This was Eric Wray and me. The dance we did. I cared about him. More than I wanted to admit to myself most of the time. But nothing was ever simple, least of all now. And there was still the matter of that gold band he wore on his left ring finger.

My phone buzzed. I looked at it as a welcome respite. It was Joe. His text read: "We're all at Vangie's. Emma's here too. When are you coming back?"

I swiped the screen and put my phone back in my bag.

"Everything all right?" Eric asked.

I closed my eyes and let out a breath. I couldn't think. Claustrophobia set in at the prospect of heading back to my sister's house. Three to six months. The time it would take to have my own house back currently seemed like an eternity.

"Cass?" Eric asked.

My eyes snapped open. "It's nothing. It's just ... I miss Chicago."

It was the first time I'd admitted that to myself, much less out loud. I instantly felt guilty. Eric blanched.

"Don't," he said. "Chicago wasn't right for you."

I took another sip of my drink. That was it. My head was legitimately swimming now. "I know this is going to sound strange, but my life was a hell of a lot easier back there."

He laughed at that. "Only you would say something like that. You honestly found working for the mob and skirting the law on the daily easier?"

"Hey," I said. "Who said I skirted the law?"

Eric shook his head and laughed. "Right."

"I didn't," I said. It was true enough. It was also true I looked the other way more than I should have until I couldn't anymore. It had nearly gotten me killed. I finished my drink and it was my turn to laugh.

"Okay," I said. "Uncle. Again."

I tried to play it off with a laugh and a joke. But Eric stayed serious. I felt the hairs rise on the back of my neck as he stared at me. My chest felt heavy. Heat flooded through me.

"Cass," he said. He struggled to find the words he wanted to say. I froze like a deer in headlights, afraid he'd say something I couldn't playoff. Finally, after a long moment, he settled on something simple. "I'm pretty damn glad you're not in Chicago anymore."

I smiled. "I think I am too."

Things grew easier between us then. I waved off another vodka gimlet. Though it was tempting, I would have been legitimately drunk after it and couldn't trust what I'd say.

We gossiped a little more. We split a plate of cheesy fries that I instantly regretted. Once again, I saw that flash of gold on his ring finger and it gave me pause. It occurred to me it wasn't usual to see Eric at Maple Valley when I did. He usually visited his wife on Friday afternoons.

"Wendy," I said, feeling a different wave of guilt. I'd been so wrapped up in my own crap, I hadn't meant to ignore his. "Is everything all right?"

Eric stopped mid-chew. He cleared his throat and wiped his mouth on a napkin. My eyes zeroed in on his full lips. I shook my head. Damn. The vodka was strong.

"I've got some decisions to make," he said. "She's not getting any better. In fact, she's starting to decline. There have been some complications."

"I'm sorry," I said.

He wiped his hands on the napkin and crumpled it, tossing it to the corner of the table. "I knew we were headed this way. It's been over two years since her accident. I held out hope for a while, but ... I don't know ... she's just gone, Cass."

"Eric," I said. "You've done so much for her. More than most would have."

"Yeah," he said, though his tone turned a little bitter. Rumor had it, Wendy Wray had a string of lovers in the years leading up to her accident. Jeanie told me she'd even begun divorce proceedings and tried to clean out Eric's pension. But they'd had a fight. She got drunk. She got behind the wheel. She hadn't been wearing a seatbelt and wound up thrown from the car into a ditch.

"What do the doctors say?" I asked.

"They want to move her," he said. "I've been fighting with the insurance. Then there's her parents. They're coming to town this summer. They're in denial."

"She had advanced directives?" I asked. "I'm sorry. I don't mean to pry."

"It's okay," he said. "Yeah. It's complicated."

"It shouldn't be," I said. "I mean, if she named you her patient advocate ..."

Eric took a long drink of water. There was something

about his expression that kept me from going on. He seemed agitated.

"It's okay," he said. "It'll all work out the way it's supposed to."

He was deflecting. I opened my mouth to call him on it but realized that would make me a hypocrite. I clammed up to him about my own family issues. I couldn't expect him to do anything less.

After Eric gestured, Crystal brought the check. I reached for my wallet. Eric put a hand over mine.

"Let me," he said.

The vodka made me bold. "Are we on a date, Wray?"

His eyes flashed darkly. "Not tonight, Leary. I'll tell you when."

I got that familiar flare of heat. Eric handed Crystal his credit card but I put a ten-dollar bill for her tip.

"Come on," he said. "Let's get out of here. I'll drive you back to Vangie's. You can come get your car later. You've had too much to drink."

I dropped my head. Just the idea of dealing with my sister and brother tonight made my head spin more than the vodka.

"So, not Vangie's then," he said. "Fair enough. Why don't you come back to my place?"

It was a loaded question, or could have been.

"The guest room, Leary," he said. "The guest room."

He held his arm out for me like a true gentleman. Laughing, I looped my arm through his. We drew some open-mouthed stares as we left the bar together. Delphi being what it was, I knew my brother would catch wind of it all by morning.

I hesitated for half a second as we walked outside. Then I decided I didn't care. The hell with it all. For tonight, I would find some peace.

Chapter 23

I woke to quiet. Unbelievably, the only sound I heard was the heavy thunk of wet snow sliding off the pitched roof.

I sat bolt upright, disoriented for half a second. This wasn't the foldaway bed I slept on in the middle of Vangie's living room. This was a real, queen-sized bed with bleach-cleaned sheets and delicate-patterned wallpaper on the walls.

Eric.

My heart caught. I slid a hand down my face then touched the pillow next to me, holding my breath for a moment. But I was alone. Nothing happened. It took a breath, willing my pulse to slow. The hazy memories of last night filtered back into my brain. I'd gotten slightly drunk and incredibly exhausted.

Eric drove me to his place. He had turned down the bed in the guestroom on his second floor and showed me where he kept the spare everythings in the adjoining bath. He'd been a perfect gentleman and I'd just had my best night's sleep in weeks. The smell of fresh coffee wafted up and my stomach growled.

I padded to the bathroom. The shower beckoned. Oh, just

the thought of taking one without running out of hot water or waiting for Vangie, Jessa, or Matty seemed like heaven. The hell with it. I was already here. I turned on the jets. Steam poured out in less than a minute and I marveled at that too. Vangie's house was older. She'd gotten it after a foreclosure and it had months' worth of repairs still ahead. My house had its list of quirks too before it burned down. Soon though, everything would be rebuilt and brand new. For now, I indulged myself with hot, city water.

When I finished, I dressed and went downstairs. I found Eric sitting at the breakfast bar eating a toasted bagel and reading the newspaper.

"They still make those?" I asked.

"I'm old-fashioned," he said. "And I like reading the comics."

Pursing my lips, I nodded. I pointed to the coffee machine.

"Help yourself," he said.

I poured a cup and went to the bar, leaning across on my elbows. "Thanks," I said. "It was nice to escape for a little while."

He nodded. "Glad to oblige. You know you're welcome anytime."

"Right," I said. "You sure you're ready for all the gossip? Wouldn't be surprised if everyone in the department thinks you knocked me up last night."

Eric grinned. His face flushed just a little. I meant it as a joke but the second I said it, my own heart fluttered. As good as it felt to hide out, this could get complicated ... fast.

"Relax," he said. "I've survived worse from the Delphi gossip mill and so have you."

I took a sip of my coffee. "I hope you're right. But you're the lead investigator on a murder case involving my dad. You don't think the police chief will have something to say about that?"

He folded his paper and put it aside. "I'll use one of your lines, Leary. I can damn well take care of myself."

I sighed as I pulled up a barstool. Nothing could ever just be simple about my life.

"Sleep good?" Eric asked.

"Yes, actually. I needed it. Thanks."

He slid my phone across the bar. I'd left it on his counter along with my purse.

"This thing's been blowing up all morning and part of last night."

"Ah, the real world," I said. I checked the lock screen. Most recently, Joe called. I opened the lock screen and my heart started beating again as I read Joe's texts. It wasn't about Matty. It was just a big brotherly check-in. I flipped the phone over and laid it face down on the bar.

"I really do appreciate your ear and your guest room, Eric."

The coffee felt good going down. I wanted more of it, but knew the longer I stayed, the more gossip we'd stir. I wished I could ignore it. Eric was right about one thing. The sooner this case concluded, the better for both of us.

"I'll drive you by Mickey's on my way in. You can pick up your car before you go home," he said.

"Thanks. I'll probably go straight to my office. I keep a change of clothes there. Let's just say I end up sleeping there as much as I do at Vangie's lately. It's quieter."

Eric shook his head. "I don't know how you do it sometimes."

Laughing, I slid off the stool. "Me either."

I grabbed my jacket off one of his dining room chairs. My

shoes were still in the foyer. I slipped those on then went back to retrieve my phone off the kitchen counter.

No sooner had I reached for it than it rang. Not two seconds later, Eric's rang as well. Our eyes met.

My caller ID showed Miranda's name. Eric's phone was next to mine. I saw Jack LaForge's name pop up. Eric took his phone and I steeled myself to answer mine.

"Hey, Miranda," I said.

Eric walked back into the foyer and answered his phone.

"Good morning," Miranda said. There was concern in her voice, but I didn't sense any judgment. I had no doubt she already knew exactly where I was.

"What's up?"

She took a breath. "Judge Castor made his decision, honey. Tori just came back with it."

I heard Eric say, "Oh?"

"Lay it on me," I said, turning my back to Eric.

"He denied your motion to suppress," she said. "I'm sorry. He's going to let in all the evidence from your dad's hotel room."

Eric was just hanging up with Jack LaForge. His expression turned to stone and I knew he'd just gotten the exact same report.

Game on, I thought. It made my being here all the more complicated for both of us.

"Thanks, Miranda," I said. "I'll be in within the hour."

I was about to hang up with her when she stopped me. "Cass, wait. There's something else. There's a woman here to see you."

"Miranda, I can't take any new clients right now. Can you see if it's something Jeanie can help her with? It looks like I've got a murder trial to prepare for in less than four weeks.

"Honey," Miranda said. "It's not about that. This is about

Alicia Romaine. She says it's urgent and I can't get her to leave."

"Trouble?" Eric mouthed the word.

"I'll get there as soon as I can," I said to Miranda then clicked off.

"Probably," I told Eric. "It's my middle name."

Chapter 24

"TOUGH BREAK ABOUT YOUR MOTION," Jeanie said. "But you knew it was 50/50 at best going in."

"Probably worse," I said. "Though, I gotta be honest. With the questions Castor asked I thought we might have had it."

Jeanie blew out a breath that lifted the hair on her forehead. "Welp, I guess it's down to Davy Monroe. He seemed pretty solid every time we and the cops have talked to him. As long as he doesn't crack, I just don't see how you don't have reasonable doubt."

I heaved my heavy leather bag on the chair next to Miranda. "I've got some discovery materials I took home. Can you have Tori help them find their way home up in the conference room?"

"No problem," Miranda said. "I put your, uh, visitor in your office."

I looked toward the stairs, then back at Miranda. "Any idea who or what she wants?"

Miranda shrugged. "She just said it's of a sensitive nature and she only wanted to talk to you. I think she's a lawyer. She's got that look."

The corners of my mouth lifted. "What look?"

She rolled her eyes. "You're all arrogant."

"I beg your pardon," I said, teasing. I knew exactly what Miranda meant. I could smell another lawyer a mile away. Truth be told, I didn't like most of them. But what the hell would another lawyer want to talk to me about on Alicia Romaine?

"How long's she been here?"

"An hour," Miranda answered. "Since eight. She apologized for coming in unannounced but that it couldn't wait and that she was one hundred percent sure you'd want to hear what she had to say."

"Hmm." I didn't like that. If she really was a lawyer, I would have liked the professional courtesy of a phone call. I wasn't a fan of walking into meetings without knowing the context.

"You want me to take this one with you?" Jeanie asked.

I shook my head. "No. I got it. I'll send out a flare if I get into any trouble. And I'll make it short and sweet. Miranda, can you call over to the jail? I need to find some time to meet with my father and tell him the news."

"Oh boy," Miranda said. "I don't envy you that one."

"You're committed to this then?" Jeanie asked. "You know how I feel about you representing that old bastard."

"I do," I said. "You and everyone else in town except for my family. But I made a deal with Matty. So far, he's living up to his end."

At least I hoped to hell he was. I half expected a call from Joe telling me Matty had checked himself out of rehab. I looked at the stairs. Well, it was going to be a one-fire at-a-time kind of day.

When I opened the door to my office, I found her staring at my framed law degree, hands on her hips. She had her back to me. Sleek, dark hair and an expensive gray wool suit, the skirt a little shorter and heels a little higher than I would have dared to wear, even in my Chicago days.

When she turned, I saw she was older than my first impression, short skirt notwithstanding. Probably pretty close to my age, actually. Pretty. Stunning, actually, with high-arched brows, full lips, and a square jaw that would make her striking no matter how old she got. With all of that, her most prominent feature was a shock of white hair on the right side of her part.

"Ms. Leary?" she said, her voice cold and serious. "You're Cassiopeia Leary?"

She came forward and extended her hand to mine. Giving her a sideways glance, I shook her hand. Firm. Strong.

"Forgive me for barging in like this. I don't think I made friends with your support staff."

"I'm sorry," I said. "Who are you?"

"Mara," she said. "Mara Brent. I'm an assistant prosecuting attorney from Maumee County. We're down in northwest Ohio."

"I know where Maumee County is," I said. It was one county over from Lucas, near Toledo, just over the Michigan border.

"May we sit?" she asked. I noticed she'd already set a brown-and-gold checkered briefcase against the side of my desk. Expensive, vintage Vuitton. How the hell did a Maumee County prosecutor afford that? I smirked, thinking of my beat-up messenger bag downstairs. The thing used to get me a few raised eyebrows when I lugged it around in Chicago. Everyone tried to get me to upgrade. I wouldn't hear of it. That bag was my good luck charm. A gift from Jeanie. It had belonged to her father.

"I have a few minutes," I said, gesturing to the chairs in

front of my desk. I could have shown her to the less formal seating I had in the corner of the room. For now, I wasn't ready to get that familiar with her until I knew what the actual hell this was all about.

Mara Brent, assistant prosecuting attorney from Maumee County, sat down keeping her back rod straight and crossing her legs.

"I've done a little research on you," she said.

I raised a brow and crossed my arms. Every alarm bell I had inside of me clanged. Who the hell sent her here? Maumee County. I'd never actually practiced in that court. My last foray into Ohio came courtesy of my sister Vangie. I'd dealt with the Toledo police when Jessa went missing last year.

"Word is," she said, "you left a hell of a gig with the Thorne Law Group."

There was no mistaking her dark tone. The Thorne Group's clientele was an open secret. Highly connected. Highly dangerous. But Liam Thorne and I had recently come to a meeting of the minds. I'd made a deal with him that I knew would ensure my safety and freedom. What could a small-town prosecutor from two states over have to do with the Thorne Group?

"You're good," she said. "What you did on the Drazdowski and Ted Richards murder trials was pretty miraculous. I wouldn't mind sparring with you one day."

"Ms. Brent, is it? I get the distinct impression you're trying to do it now. It's way past time that you stated your business. I have quite a bit of my own to get to."

Her eyes flicked downward. She had thick, dark lashes and I wondered if they were fake. I could never manage to get those things on right.

"I'm here about Alicia Romaine," she said.

I stayed quiet. I kept my gaze locked with hers. Mara Brent took a breath then reached down for her briefcase. She pulled out a folded piece of paper and placed it in her lap.

"You recently submitted her DNA to a national registry," she said.

Still, I said nothing. How in the seven hells did she know that?

"Ms. Leary, I believe your client's DNA is connected to a cold case of mine in Maumee County."

I blinked hard, taken aback. My guard went way up. Was I wrong about Alicia? She was one of the sweetest people I'd ever met. What possible connection could she have to some Ohio cold case?

"I'm listening," I said. At this point, I couldn't even confirm that Alicia was my client. Mara Brent should have known that.

"I'm sure you're aware," she went on, "that law enforcement agencies routinely submit cold case DNA into several national databases when it becomes available."

"Of course," I said. My neck felt hot.

Ms. Brent took the paper from her lap and unfolded it. It was a photocopy of a newspaper clipping from the *Toledo Blade*. I glanced at the date before the headline. It was thirty years old.

"Missing Waynetown Woman Found Beaten, Left for Dead."

"Okay?" I said.

"Denise Silvers," she said. "She was a twenty-year-old waitress at the time. She never came home from a shift one night and her boyfriend reported her missing. They found her on the banks of the Maumee River a few days later. Raped. Tortured. We think someone dumped her there. She stayed in a coma for weeks. She's in a wheelchair now. Paralyzed from the neck down. We never found the perpetrator. I've been tracking this case ever since I started at the prosecutor's office. Eight years. Denise and her family have kind of adopted me. Anyway, we have DNA on the guy. About a year ago, I started doing some digging on my own time. I don't know. This is one of those cases that has just stuck with me. Do you ever have those?"

I kept my face even. Did I ever have those cases? Aubrey Ames and Tori's own father came to mind. Yes. I knew what she meant. That cold snake of dread coiled itself around my spine.

"There were others," she said. "Another waitress in Gary, Indiana. A nurse in Kalamazoo. I could lay it all out for you. We've found traces of matching DNA in all of these cases. I can't discuss the particulars. Even telling you this much is skirting a line. But Ms. Leary, your client's DNA is connected to what was found in Denise Silvers's rape kit."

"I don't understand," I said. "You said Mrs. Silvers's attack was thirty years ago. Alicia Romaine would have been a baby if she was even born at all."

Mara Brent pulled another piece of paper out of her Louis Vuitton. She handed it to me. It looked like a print-out from the Tree of Life website where we'd registered Alicia's DNA. This was slightly different though. Alicia's name showed up. Above it was a line leading to a blue square. Inside of that was a generic male avatar. Beneath that, it read: "Paternal Match, ninety-nine percent probability."

It took me a second to register what I was seeing. Paternal match.

"Ms. Leary," she said. "Cass. I believe your client's father is my serial rapist and a murderer."

My head spun. Everything else Mara Brent had said

repeated in my mind almost on a loop. Other murders in Indiana, Michigan. Rape. Murder. Torture. Thirty years.

"I'm sorry," I said. "This man. You're saying you think you're dealing with a serial rapist? A murderer?"

"Yes," she said. "That's exactly what I'm saying. The database, Tree of Life. They cooperate with law enforcement. You would have seen that in the fine print on their terms of service."

"I'm aware," I said.

"Tree of Life is one of the few companies who agree to keep the crime-solving part of this confidential. We submitted my guy's DNA under their privacy clause. So far I'm the only one who has seen that match. Now you. I sent it into them five or six years ago, almost on a whim. I only check it every few months now. Anyway, last week I got a notification relating to Alicia Romaine. Your name was listed as a contact. So, here I am."

I was floored. We had zoned in on cousin matches for Alicia's mother. Nothing at all came up for her father.

"I need to speak with your client. And I need to see what you have on her. I'm aware she was adopted."

"Ms. Brent," I said. "You're going to have to give me a minute."

She produced a third piece of paper from her briefcase. This one was a subpoena for my file on Alicia.

"This won't hold up," I said. "Those files are protected by attorney-client privilege."

"Talk to her," she said. "I'm trying to catch a killer, Ms. Leary."

My head pounded. A killer. A rapist. And if Mara Brent were right, Alicia Romaine was his daughter.

Chapter 25

DENISE SILVERS'S FACE, smiling, frozen in time, stared up at me from Mara Brent's newspaper clipping. The details of her abduction and rape chilled me to the bone. She'd been beaten, hogtied with duct tape. Left for dead. She'd received a blow to the back of her head that should have killed her but instead, left her as a paraplegic.

My eyes scanned over the Tree of Life printout Mara had given me. Alicia's smiling face leading to the paternal line made a stark contrast to Denise Silvers's.

I rubbed my eyes. It couldn't be true. How the hell was I going to tell that sweet girl that her father might be a cold-blooded, Ted Bundy-level monster?

After Mara Brent left, I'd filled Jeanie, Tori, and Miranda in on what she had to say. Knowing me as they did, my team left me alone for a few minutes to collect myself to figure out just what the hell I would do next. Now Jeanie stood in the doorway holding two steaming Styrofoam cups of coffee.

"Did you have yours yet?" she asked.

"Not enough," I said. The pounding of my head under-scored my statement. I reached for one of the mugs.

"Oh, those are both for you," she said.

Smiling, I lifted the mug to Jeanie before bringing it to my lips. She plopped down in the same chair Mara Brent had vacated.

"So what's she expect you to do?" Jeanie asked.

"She expects me to share all of the research we've done for Alicia."

"She thinks if we find her mom, that'll help lead her to this psychopath of a father?" Jeanie asked. She picked up the DNA report and the newspaper clipping.

"Jeanie," I said. "I think we have to entertain the genuine possibility that Alicia's birth mother was one of this bastard's victims."

Jeanie's eyes went wide. "I hadn't even thought that far ahead."

"Well," I said. "It would answer some questions. I mean, think about it. Young girl gets raped. I would understand why she'd want to give that baby up for adoption."

No sooner had the words spilled out of my mouth than a cold chill went up my back. The exact same thing had happened to my sister Vangie. My own niece had been the product of rape. Vangie had given her up both because she was too young to care for her, and the horrible, violent circumstances surrounding her conception.

"Ugh," I said, burying my face in my hands. Jeanie knew my mind and how close to home this had all just hit.

"She deserves to know," Jeanie said.

"I know. And we talked about this very thing. I mean, not this exact thing. But Alicia's a shrewd woman. I know she's at least entertained the possibility that something like this might have happened."

"No," Jeanie said. "Not something like this. You said this

Brent woman claims this psycho's DNA is linked to dozens of other rapes?"

"Yes," I said.

"And where are we on the DNA clues we do have?"

"We've got the list narrowed down to about twenty-five women. The info your buddy Newt provided has been pretty helpful," Tori said. She put the list she'd made of the most likely candidates for Alicia's birth mother on top of the other papers Mara Brent left for me.

Half of the women were nieces of Marilyn Evans. Newt had helped me track down current addresses and a couple of the phone numbers. I had messages into two of them. A third Tori had spoken to just yesterday and she got a phone slammed in her ear for her trouble. The last two were on my list to call. Now I wasn't sure if I had the stomach for it before talking to Terrence and Alicia again.

"Well," I said. "As much as I hate this, why don't you call the Romaines and arrange for them to come in as soon as possible. Alicia needs to decide what to do."

"She's not legally bound to help," Jeanie said.

I raised a brow. "I mean, I suppose not technically. No matter what else happens, I made it clear to Mara Brent that I want Alicia's privacy protected. This psychopath doesn't need to know he's got a daughter out there looking for him."

"Honey," Jeanie said. "He might not even still be alive. Did this Mara tell you whether they think he's still out there actively raping and murdering?"

"We didn't get that far in the conversation. I hadn't even thought of that. This Denise Silvers's attack happened thirty years ago. Alicia is thirty years old. I mean, how old could this guy be by now?"

"I think I'm going to be sick," Tori said, echoing my own sentiment.

"Let's just take this all one step at a time," I said. "I need to think my way through how best to protect Alicia. That's got to start with telling her the truth. Tori, get them in here. Today, if possible."

Tori shook her head. "Cass, they're gone. With only a few weeks left before her baby is due, Terrence and Alicia decided to go away for the weekend."

I nodded. "Well, maybe that's for the best. It'll give me some time to figure out just exactly how to break this to her. I know I want you all here when I do. She needs to feel supported and Alicia's grown close to everyone in this office."

"What are you going to do in the meantime?" Jeanie asked.

I rose and grabbed my coat off the rack. "I have the small matter of my father to deal with. He needs to know Castor torpedoed our motion."

Tori's expression turned even grimmer.

"What?" I said, my throat running dry.

"The written opinion just came through," she said. "He attached a new scheduling order to it. Now that discovery's done and your motion's been disposed of, he wants to stick to the hard trial date. April 1st. Do you want me to file a motion for a continuance?"

April Fool's Day. The irony wasn't lost on me. I slipped my arms into my coat sleeves. I was off to tell my father he had just a few more weeks until he went on trial for first-degree murder. And the jury would now hear every gory detail about what the cops found in that hotel room.

Chapter 26

My father sat in the common area of the visitors' room on a couch, lounging with his arm draped over the back as if we were just meeting in my living room. The fear came back. It started as a twitch in his right hand. "You know I wasn't there. The cops know I wasn't there. And Davy Monroe will tell them I wasn't there. All you gotta do is put Davy on the stand, then me on the stand, and this will be over. Quit worrying so much."

I took a breath. "I haven't decided whether I'm putting you on the stand or not."

"That's my choice, not yours," he said.

I was tired. Exhausted, really. I didn't feel like hopping on the mental merry-go-round my father liked to spin.

"I want you to think some more about the manslaughter deal LaForge's office put on the table. As far as I know, it's still live. Jack would have called me immediately to gloat and pull it after Judge Castor's decision came down. He's done neither."

He leaned forward and locked eyes with me. "Do you think you can win?"

All of my law school ethics lessons ran through my head. Guarantee no outcomes. Never give odds on a verdict. But my father, damn him to hell, knew me.

A slow smile lifted the corner of his mouth. "You've got fire in your belly. You're a Leary. Doesn't matter that you've got some fancy degree. You still like a fight. And you just can't wait to get in there and hand Jack LaForge's ass to him again."

I went still and silent, not wanting to give my father even the slightest piece of me. He was right though. There were so many holes in the prosecution's case against my father I could almost have fun exploiting them. Only I hated that his approval apparently still mattered to me.

"That's my girl," he said. "You tell Jack LaForge to stick his plea deal up his ass. I got me the best lawyer in town and she's going to show him up again."

I shook my head. "You talk about this like it's a playoff game you just bet on."

He smiled. "Maybe it is, sugar. Maybe it is."

"Are you sure?" I said. "Juries are still unpredictable. If they convict ..."

"They won't," he said. "And I'm sure. Now get the hell out of here. They're showing *True Grit* in the rec room. I'm taking a front-row seat."

"Fine," I said. "I'll call you in a couple of days. We have some things to go over after I finish my witness prep."

My father waved me off. Lord. He actually seemed happy in here. In his glory. Only Joe Leary Sr. could still feel like the cock of the walk from behind bars.

I hoped he was right, but meant what I said. Juries could fixate on anything and he'd been away from Delphi far too long for any of them to potentially know who he was, or care. That could be good or bad.

I left the building through the lawyer's entrance. My

phone buzzed in my bag as I fished for my keys. Newt's name popped up on my caller ID. Alicia Romaine's family tree popped right back into my brain.

"Hey, Newt!" I said as I slipped behind the wheel.

"Hallo, dare!" he sang out.

"Whatcha got for me?" I asked.

"Oh, I gotta hot message for you," he said. "I found some more numbers on a couple of Patricia's nieces you were looking to find."

I grabbed my notepad out of my bag and scribbled down notes as Newt spoke as fast as I could.

"Wonderful," I said. "That's good, Newt. That's really helpful. Did you actually talk to any of these girls?"

"Well, I thought about it," he said. "But I figured it'd be better if you or your people did that. I think it'd be strange them hearing from Uncle Newt after all this time. Most of these girls haven't seen me in years."

Newt rambled on for a full minute. When he finished, I thanked him again. I wondered why he thought it would be less strange for these women to get called by a random lawyer out of nowhere like me. But I'd take whatever help I could. It wasn't my news to tell yet, but I couldn't help but worry how Newt might take it when he found out one of these nieces might very well have been the victim of a brutal rape. Part of me still held out hope that wasn't true.

Chapter 27

Ten days later, Alicia and Terrence Romaine came back from vacation. Her belly hung so low I marveled at how she could stand for very long, let alone walk. But she was somehow graceful with it, as only a mother could be. From time to time, I caught her gently rubbing the curve of her stomach to soothe the child within. It seemed to work. She grew calmer, more settled as she found a more comfortable position on Jeanie's office couch.

"We've had some news," I said. I worried how to tell her what I knew. I'd thought about trying to talk to Terrence ahead of time so he could prepare her for what was to come. But Alicia had never given me permission to do that. This was her business, her news, and there was little I could do to brace her for it.

Alicia's eyes filled with the same hope and fear I would have had in her situation. I cleared my throat and took out the file. I kept the newspaper clippings inside but held the Tree of Life printout.

"We have a possible lead on your birth father," I said.

Alicia's face fell a bit. For the last couple of months, we'd focused on her birth mother. That was all we had from the DNA results until now.

"You found him?" she asked.

"No," I said. I'd rehearsed this conversation a hundred times, or tried to. But how the hell do you tell someone their father was probably a psychopath? Once again, my thoughts turned to my niece Jessa. It was a conversation Vangie would one day have with her. But she would have the benefit of years of therapy leading up to it. Still, I felt once again entirely too close to this case.

Jeanie watched me closely. Her color had gone ashen. There was no help for it. I had to deliver the hammer blow.

"Alicia," I said. "What I'm going to tell you is going to be hard to hear."

"Is he dead? My birth father?" she asked. She tightened her grip on Terrence's knee. He leaned in and kissed the top of her head.

"I don't know," I said. "Here's what I do know. It appears you share some commonalities with a DNA profile that's been submitted to a crime registry. The man belonging to that profile is suspected of committing some fairly serious crimes over the last few decades."

Alicia blinked rapidly but beyond that, she went still as a statue.

"I don't understand," she finally said. I carefully explained my meeting with Mara Brent. "A rapist," she said. "We think my birth dad was a rapist."

I could only nod and give her a moment to absorb my words. Alicia stayed remarkably calm. Of course we'd discussed this very possibility. I knew she probably went over it in her head a thousand times. But here it was in black and white and columns of numbers on a piece of paper. I handed the printout to her.

She and Terrence read it. He looked up first.

"You said decades. This guy's DNA was found at more than one crime scene?" he asked.

"That's what I was told," I said.

I took the newspaper article on Denise Silvers out of my file and handed it to her. Alicia took it with trembling fingers. She drew her hand to her mouth as her eyes darted over the words. Terrence read along with her.

After a few moments, Alicia put the paper on the coffee table between us. She folded her hands in her lap. Tears came to her eyes, but never fell. She simply nodded and drew in a breath. Then she locked eyes with me.

"There were others," she said.

"Suspected," I said.

"Other rapes?" she asked.

"Yes," I answered. "And at least one victim didn't survive. I'm not privy to all the details, only what this prosecutor shared with me. These are still unsolved cases. Open investigations. She may not be at liberty to tell us everything."

Alicia pressed a hand to her forehead.

"Baby," Terrence said. "You okay?"

"Can I get you some water?" I asked.

Alicia shook her head. "I'm fine. I'm not going to break, you guys. I'm ... I don't know what I am."

"Cass," Terrence said. "Do you think Alicia's mom was one of this guy's victims?"

"I honestly have no idea," I said. "We've made some headway with the Evans family. That was the branch of the family we found on our own through the T.O.L. database. One of the family members in particular has been very forthcoming and has helped us narrow down the pool of candidates for your birth mom. It's still a long shot, but I feel confident we might just find her."

"I can't even," Alicia said. "Then what? Cass, if this woman was raped by this guy, what makes you think she wants to be found? I know I wouldn't. I think I'd want to put all of that behind me. And what would I be? I'd be a living reminder of what was probably the worst day of her life."

"Baby," Terrence said. "You'd also be her daughter. She'd want to know. I mean, I think she would. No matter what the circumstances were, she had you. It was her choice to try and make sure you had a better life than what she might have been able to give you. It might bring her comfort to know she succeeded."

His words were calm, soothing. I'd liked him the day I met him, but my respect for Terrence Romaine went up considerably at that moment. I hoped I could be just as comforting to Jessa if the time ever came.

"Terrence is right," I said. "You married a smart man, Alicia." I smiled at them. They seemed to have the kind of marriage I'd never seen before. Terrence looked out for her well-being. It was little things. A touch. A shoulder for her. He protected her when she needed it.

"This prosecutor," Alicia said. "What else did she say?"

Her voice was stronger now. Maybe the impact of what I'd told her would hit her harder later, but for now, Alicia was solid as a rock.

"She wanted to know if you'd be willing to help her," I said.

Alicia's brow raised. "How could I help her? I never met my birth father."

"She wants us to compare notes," I said. "If your birth father is guilty of these crimes, your very existence builds a timeline of sorts. What little we've been able to piece together about the circumstances surrounding your birth may be helpful. Or it may not."

164

"Or if you actually find Alicia's mom through one of these leads, she might know something too?" Terrence asked.

"That's the idea," I said. "For now, I've told her nothing. I couldn't even if I wanted to. This is your call, Alicia. She'll try to subpoena my file, but I believe that's privileged unless you're willing to sign a waiver."

Terrence and Alicia looked at one another. He squeezed her hand. "What do you think I should do?" she asked him.

"Baby," he said. "I can't tell you that."

Alicia turned to me; her eyes went stone cold. "How many victims?" she asked.

"We don't know," Jeanie answered. "And this man, even with the DNA connection. He hasn't been convicted of anything. This is all just suspicion."

Her lip quivered, but Alicia Romaine stayed strong. "Okay," she said, taking a breath that reminded me a little of what they probably taught her in Lamaze class.

"Okay," she said again. "Let's do this. If this guy ... this bastard ... if there's something in my veins that can help bring justice to these women ... tell that prosecutor I'll do whatever I can to help."

The fierce look in Alicia Romaine's eyes gave me chills. I had no idea where this path might lead, but I knew in my heart she was strong enough to face it.

"You bet," I said. "And I'll be with you every step of the way."

Chapter 28

"IT'S AS good a deal as your father will get, Cass," Jack LaForge said. We stood outside courtroom number two. In ten minutes, the court would let the fifty-odd members of the jury pool in for the start of voir dire.

"Second-degree murder," I repeated Jack's offer. Manslaughter was off the table now that he'd defeated my motion to suppress the hotel room evidence. I was shocked we were even having this conversation in light of that. It meant someone in the prosecutor's office was nervous. They should be.

"Why now?" I asked. Jack was smart. Plus, he seemed uneasy, not really meeting my eyes.

"Sheila Brewer's family wants her back," he said.

I shook my head. "I don't get it. Why now?"

"Does it matter?" he asked.

I also already knew what my dad would say. No deal. It would be my advice to him as well. He didn't kill this woman. I had the strong sense that Jack LaForge and the prosecutor's office felt very much on their heels leading into this.

"I'll meet you in there," I said.

Jack grumbled. "You're making a mistake," he said. "You both are. You really willing to kill your career for that man?"

I wouldn't stand here and let him bait me. The door opened to the stairwell. The sheriffs led my father in. He was wearing a suit I brought for him. The deputy removed his cuffs just outside the door.

"Private conversation or can anyone join?" he said, smiling at Jack. I grabbed my father's elbow and ushered him into the courtroom with the deputies right behind.

We sat at the defense table and I gave him the highlights of my conversation and the plea deal he'd just been offered.

Dad laughed. "They're scared," he said. "They should be."

"Well, I'm glad you're in a good mood, at least," I said through gritted teeth. If he didn't wipe that smirk off his face before the jury pool came in, we could be sunk before this thing started.

Jack walked in and caught my eye. I clenched my jaw and shook my head no. No deal. Game on.

To his credit, my father sat quietly and mostly docile as we waded through voir dire. It went smoothly. Within an hour, we had a panel of twelve jurors and four alternates. They ranged in age from twenty-five to sixty-three. Six men, six women. I had my eye on a female chemistry teacher from Delphi High School. With the highest education of the bunch, I'd bet my dinner they'd make her foreman. She was also newer to the district and admitted to hearing about me from the Larry Drazdowski trial. They all had. I hoped that made them see me as a winner.

Judge Castor ran an efficient courtroom. He wanted to get through opening statements and maybe even Jack's first witness before lunch.

Jack rose, cleared his throat, and addressed the jury.

"Ladies and gentlemen," he said. "I wish you could have met Sheila Brewer. By all accounts, she was a kind soul. A hard worker. She wasn't rich. She wasn't famous. She liked daytime soap operas and lived a quiet life. She worked at the library part time and never gossiped. She never had an unkind word to say about anyone.

"She gave what little she could to her favorite charities. She volunteered at the veterans' center because her dad died in the early days of the Vietnam War. She made weekly trips to the Delphi Animal Shelter to drop off kitten food and towels and anything else she thought dogs and cats might need. She couldn't even have one of her own because of a debilitating dander allergy.

"She'd known the defendant, Joseph Leary, for quite a while. She found him charming. He probably said all the right things. She trusted him. But ladies and gentlemen, the evidence will show that trust got her killed. We don't know exactly what happened in Sheila Brewer's last moments. But we know it was violent, bloody, and she screamed for her life. All the trust she put in the defendant, he used against her. Maybe he didn't think Sheila Brewer's life mattered. She had no real close friends. She kept to herself. Maybe he thought she was expendable. But we know better. After you hear the testimony and see the evidence in this case, I trust that you'll come to the same conclusion I did. Sheila Brewer *did* matter. She had worth. She had years ahead of her to chase her dreams and bring good into the world. She didn't deserve what happened to her. And she's relying on you now to see through the lies. You'll hear so many. Sheila Brewer never had a true champion when she was alive. I hope that you can be that for her in death. Thank you."

My father sat stock still, his eyes cast down. He looked truly sad. If it was a show, it was timed well. Jack shook his head and stared at my dad as he left the lectern and took his seat at the prosecution table. I had to admit, as openings went, Jack's was sparse. It didn't feel like his heart was in it and that gave me pause. No matter what else was going on, this was a damn murder trial.

My father reached under the table and squeezed my hand as Judge Castor motioned for me to take my turn at the lectern.

"Good morning," I said to the jury. "Thank you for your time. This is a sacrifice we ask of you. Your duty here is great. The prosecution's burden here is great. It's the highest required in a court of law. Mr. LaForge said so many things I agree with today. Sheila Brewer was a good person. And she didn't deserve what happened to her. But before this trial ends and we leave it to you to weigh the evidence, I'm confident you'll find the state hasn't met its burden of proof.

"You don't have to like my father. Sometimes I don't. But he's no killer. At the end of the day, I'm confident you'll have more than just a reasonable doubt about Joe Leary's guilt. I believe you'll realize there is no doubt he wasn't involved with whatever happened to Sheila Brewer. So for now, I ask that you keep an open mind. It's tempting to want to find a bad guy ... any bad guy ... to pay for what may or may not have happened to Ms. Brewer. But you can't do that. You must hold Mr. LaForge to his proofs. When you do, you're going to see the gaping holes in the prosecution's case. You may not even believe a crime occurred here at all, let alone who committed it.

"The doubts surrounding this case and my client's involvement aren't just reasonable, they are overwhelming. And although we have grave concerns about what happened to Sheila Brewer, I trust you'll come to the conclusion the state has not done its job. I'm as angry as anyone for Sheila. She deserves better. But what you're about to hear from the prosecution should shock you. Not about the brutality of what might have happened, though that's disturbing enough. But you may be shocked by the lack of evidence on every single element the state is required to prove. And I think it'll make you just as angry as it did me. For Sheila. For the defendant. And for justice itself. Thank you."

"Mr. LaForge," Judge Castor said. "Are you ready to call your first witness?"

"We are, Your Honor," he said. "The state calls Claudia Christie to the stand."

"I liked that," my dad whispered to me.

I put a finger to my lips as the bailiff directed the Harmon Arms housekeeper to the stand. She was a small, slight woman with dark hair pulled into a bun and wisps of gray at her temples. She raised her right hand and was sworn in. She sat with her hands folded and had to be instructed twice to speak into the microphone.

"Miss Christie," Jack started. "Can you tell the jury where you work?"

"I'm the third shift housekeeper at the Harmon Arms. I've worked there for the past two years."

"Thank you. What are your duties at the Harmon? Specifically."

She cleared her throat. "Specifically. I clean the rooms. Change the bedding. Vacuum. Wipe down and disinfect the guest bathrooms. Replace the towels. You know. Everything that's required to make the room clean."

"Were you working the night of December 1st?"

"Yes, sir," she said. "I was. It was me and Rose Taylor. I had rooms one through fourteen, Rose did the other half. The Harmon isn't very big."

"Do you have occasion to actually clean rooms in the middle of the night?"

"Um, we do when there is later checkout. But that night we were working in the laundry. Washing the bedding and towels so day shift had everything fresh to start with."

"Okay," Jack said. "I understand. Can you tell me if anything out of the ordinary happened on that Sunday night going into Monday morning?"

Claudia's eyes darted to me. I tried to form a non-threatening smile. "Um, well. I heard some shouting."

"Do you know where it originated from?" Jack asked.

"Not at first. I heard like a scream. I stopped what I was doing. I'd been loading the dryer. Rose had already left for the night. I was a little mad about that. It was my turn to leave early. Anyway. I heard what I thought was a woman's voice coming from the west side of the hotel. I finished loading the dryer and I walked outside."

"What time was this?" he asked.

"It was between three fifteen and three twenty a.m."

"How can you be so precise?"

"Because, like I said, Rose just left. I was with her when she clocked out at exactly three a.m. The break room where the time clock is is right next to the laundry room. I went in there and checked the dryer load. It was still a little damp so I set it on a twelve-minute cycle. I head the scream exactly after the cycle buzzer went off."

"Then what happened?"

"I waited for maybe ten or twenty seconds. Then I heard another scream. A woman's voice. She was saying no. She was saying don't. She was crying."

"What did you do?"

Claudia adjusted the microphone. "I walked a little closer to the sound. It was coming from room seven."

"How can you be sure?" Jack asked.

"Well, rooms six, eight, and nine were empty that night. It was a Sunday right after a holiday. Lot of people already checked out. On that wing, only rooms one through four were occupied. And also seven. One through four were on the other side of the bend. The hotel is shaped like a U, you see."

"How long did this screaming go on?" he asked.

"I don't know. Maybe thirty seconds."

"What did you do?"

"Look," she said. "I try to keep to my own business. The Harmon, it's not ... people come there a lot so they don't have to be at their houses. You know?"

"No," Jack said. "I'm not sure I do."

"I've heard stuff like that. Not quite like that. I just didn't want to get involved."

"So what did you do?"

"I listened for maybe a minute, but I didn't hear anything else so I went back to the laundry. But it was bothering me all night. That woman. She sounded ... scared."

"Objection," I said. "This calls for speculation."

"Sustained, Mr. LaForge," Castor said. "Let's stick with facts instead of conjecture."

"What did you do then, Miss Christie?"

"I get off at eight," she said. "That's when the manager gets in. As soon as I clocked out, I went and told him what I heard. I thought I didn't do the right thing. I should have checked on that woman."

She started to cry. Jack directed her to a pitcher of water.

"I went to my manager at eight that morning and told him what I'd heard. He was pretty mad at me for not saying something the night before. He called the cops."

"Thank you, Miss Christie," Jack said. "I have nothing further at this time."

It was short, sweet, to the point. Jack was trying to establish a timeline. With Davy Monroe's upcoming testimony, that actually helped me more than hurt me.

"Your witness, Miss Leary," the judge said.

"Thank you. And thank you for being here this morning, Miss Christie. I just have a couple of quick questions."

"Okay."

"You said you heard a woman's voice screaming," I said. "You're absolutely sure of that?"

"Yes," she said. "It was a woman's voice screaming no and stop. And ... um ... it wasn't from pleasure."

I smiled. I could have objected and asked that last bit be stricken as calling for more speculation. But that wasn't the main purpose I had for my questions. I was hoping to show the jury why it didn't even matter.

"So, Miss Christie, you only heard one voice then, correct?"

"Uh ... right. Just one voice."

"A woman's voice," I said.

"Yes. One woman. Screaming."

"Got it. For all you know, she was the only person in that room then, right?"

"Uh ... well ... she was probably screaming at someone."

"But you don't know that at all, do you?"

"No. I don't."

"You never heard a male voice."

"No."

"You didn't hear glass breaking?"

"No. Just the screams."

"And you didn't see fit to tell anyone until your manager showed up five hours later."

"No, I ... I try to mind my own business," she said.

"Before you heard the screaming, when was the last time you were in room seven?"

"I worked a double that weekend. Nobody wanted to come in because it was the weekend after Thanksgiving. But it was good money. I'd been there since four the afternoon before," she said. It wasn't an answer.

"So you were at the hotel from four p.m. through eight o'clock in the morning the next day?"

"That's right."

"In that time, isn't it true you never once saw that man, the defendant, coming or going from room seven?"

"What? Uh ... no. I didn't see him," she said.

"I have your statement to the police in front of me. Do you remember them asking you whether you saw any cars parked outside room seven that evening or at any time during your shift?"

"No, I don't remember."

"You don't remember them asking or you don't remember a car?" I asked.

"I don't remember a car. I know they asked me that."

"But you told them there was no car, isn't that right?"

"Um, yes. I told them I never saw a car."

"Thank you," I said. "So to be clear, you never saw a car parked outside room seven for nearly twelve hours prior to when you say you heard this screaming. And you never saw the defendant coming or going from that room in that time frame either."

"Right. I never saw him."

"But you know who he is, right?"

"I know he's Mr. Leary. I know that was his room. Room seven. I saw him a day or two before that. But no, I never saw him that shift when I heard the screaming. No."

"Thank you," I said. "That's all I have."

Jack rose, adjusted his tie, then sat back down. "No redirect from us, Your Honor," Jack said. Even Castor raised a brow at that.

"Okay then," he said. "We'll break for lunch."

My father stood beside me as the judge rose and exited through the door behind the bench. Jack's paralegal whispered something in his ear. He shot me a look, then hustled out of the courtroom.

"What's up his ass?" my father said.

"Shut up," I said through gritted teeth. Though the exact same question had just popped into my head.

Chapter 29

Jack LaForge had a lousy afternoon. Until he didn't. His next three witnesses after lunch were friends and coworkers of Sheila Brewer. They painted the picture Jack foreshadowed in his opening statements. Sheila was a nice, albeit lonely lady who kept to herself but was looking for love.

Candace Dobson worked with Sheila on Tuesdays at the library.

"Did Sheila ever talk about the defendant, Joseph Leary?" Jack asked.

"A couple of times," Candace said. She was a fifty-something former beauty queen with plump, rosy cheeks and blonde hair piled high on her head.

"What did she have to say about him?" Jack asked.

Objection," I said. "Counsel's asking for hearsay."

"Sustained," Judge Castor ruled.

"Did Sheila seem happy?" Jack tried again.

"Objection," I said. "Calls for hearsay."

"Sustained."

This was about the fifth time I'd had this little dance with Jack. It was starting to rattle him. These were uncharacteristic

177

mistakes he was making. This was a first-degree murder trial. If it were anything less, I might have taken it easier on the guy. Well, probably not. But it was in me to think so.

"When was the last time you saw Sheila," Jack asked.

Candace considered the question. "Oh, I mean, I was on vacation Thanksgiving week. I went down to visit my daughter in North Carolina. I just had a new grandbaby. Sheila and I didn't work full time and so we were ships passing in the night a lot. I'd say it was about two weeks before they said she went missing since I'd seen her."

Jack went to the lectern and thumbed through his notes. He threw a scowl at his paralegal.

"Mr. LaForge?" Castor said, growing increasingly irritated with him.

"I ... I've got nothing further for this witness," Jack said.

"Ms. Leary?"

I got to my feet. "I have just a couple," I said. "Ms. Dobson, do you know whether Ms. Brewer was close with her family?"

"Uh ... what do you mean, close?"

"Well, she had no immediate family, but there were cousins, right?"

Candace Dobson rolled her eyes and I tried to hide a smile. "Oh jeez, yeah, those cousins. Always in Sheila's business. Calling all the time while she was at work. A bunch of busybodies. Sheila used to say she wished she could just hop a plane and disappear for a while."

"Objection!" Jack popped up. "Hearsay."

It was already too late. The jury had heard what I wanted. I decided to quit while I was ahead.

"Thank you," I said. "I have nothing further."

The jury sat a little straighter in their seats. Good. They seemed to pick up on the futility of Jack even calling Candace

Dobson. She'd only established one vague fact. Sheila Brewer had been seeing my father, though that wasn't even in dispute. But she'd just planted the seed I wanted. Sheila Brewer might just have been looking to escape from her life.

Jack had similar trouble with the rest of his witnesses. He kept trying to elicit testimony about what Sheila Brewer might have said about my dad. My objections and Castor's rulings went against Jack every single time until we'd hit the four o'clock hour.

"Um, in light of the time," Jack said. "I propose we recess for the day. My crime scene expert is subpoenaed for first thing in the morning."

Castor nodded. "We can dismiss the jury and deal with any housekeeping matters."

The bailiff ushered the jurors out. It was then that Jack LaForge's day got better. I did what he knew I would. I renewed my objection to Jack's crime scene expert testimony.

"Your Honor," I started. "We've now heard from the hotel housekeeper. She stated under oath that she didn't even bother telling her manager about whatever she heard until five hours after the fact. There was no justification for this so-called health check. Again, I put to you that the warrantless search of room number seven contravened my client's constitutional rights. Any evidence collected incident to that search is inadmissible under the Fourth Amendment."

Castor let out a sigh. "Counsel?" he said to Jack.

"We renew our arguments from Ms. Leary's pre-trial motion to suppress which the court rightly granted. Exigent circumstances were more than met. Plus, we haven't even heard from the detectives who conducted that search yet. In addition to being unsupported, Ms. Leary's renewed motion isn't ripe."

"Agreed," Castor said. "On both counts. Your motion is denied, Ms. Leary. I'll wait until the detectives testify."

He hesitated as if he were going to say more. I had a good idea what it might be. If the police testified they were running a routine welfare check and the evidence they collected was in plain sight upon entry, the jury was going to get to hear about it. And then, all of Jack LaForge's floundering today would be forgiven and forgotten. Castor banged his gavel and we were adjourned for the day.

The deputies stepped forward to take my father back to jail. "Same warning," I said to him. "Head down. Mouth shut. Some good things happened today. But also plenty of not so good. Tomorrow is going to be rough. Get a good night's sleep if you can. I need you cool and calm tomorrow. We clear?"

"Crystal clear," Dad smiled. "I'm proud of you."

His words took me aback. I don't think I'd ever heard him utter them to me or any of my brothers or sister. I could only manage the word "fine" in response.

Smiling, my father held out his wrists so the deputy could cuff him and lead him out the back of the courtroom.

I gathered my things. I'd been solo this afternoon. I sent Tori to make more calls on the Romaine case. So far, we'd had little success reaching the Evans cousins Newt recommended. I adjusted the strap to my bag and turned, ready to leave what I thought was an empty courtroom. Only there was one spectator left.

Mara Brent sat along the back wall. She rose to her feet as I opened the wooden gate separating the lawyers' area from the spectator gallery.

"Interesting case," she said, smiling. "So that was your father?"

It wasn't so much judgment I sensed in her tone. If

anything, it was genuine curiosity. "Yeah," I said. "Long story."

This got light laughter from her. "You know, I kinda think I'd like to hear it sometime. It's got to be a damn sight more interesting than mine."

I snorted. "I don't know if interesting is the word."

Mara held the door open and we walked out into the hallway together.

"So," I said. "You gonna tell me you just happened to be in the neighborhood?"

She laughed. "Well, sort of. I'll admit. I was kind of checking up on you."

"On me?" I stopped walking.

"Point of fact, I really was just in the neighborhood. I've got a murder trial of my own next week and one of my star witnesses lives about ten miles west on M-50. I decided to stop off on my way back. I heard about your trial. Wasn't planning to stay as long as I did. But this was ... intriguing."

I looked back at the courtroom. "You think so?"

"Yeah," she said. "I can't figure out what the hell Jack LaForge is doing."

Her words stunned me a little. "Hmmm. And here I was thinking all prosecutors stick together."

"Just calling it like I see it. He's right about that hotel room search though. You know that."

I shrugged. "I don't think so."

"How tight is your dad's alibi?" she asked.

I pursed my lips. I think she was actually trying to be of help. I wasn't sure how I felt about that. My silence was an answer.

"I get it," she said. "I wouldn't talk to me either in your shoes. Just ... well ... good luck with this one. I hope it turns out how you want. For you and for your family."

"Thanks," I said. We stopped at the elevator. "I'm looking forward to our meeting with the Romaines. You should know Alicia is very interested in trying to help you with your case."

Mara's face brightened. I knew that look. We try not to, but it's hard not to let certain clients or cases get under your skin. I surmised Denise Silvers, her cold case assault victim, had done that for her. I felt warring emotions about it. Whatever happened to Denise had to have been horrific. I wanted to string the bastard up myself. But I worried for Alicia. This case would end up in a dark place, no matter what.

"Mara?" a familiar male voice came from further down the hall.

Eric came toward us in his firm, sure stride. Mara's smile was bright and instant. Something black flickered inside of me as Eric got close and stuck a hand out to shake Mara's. Their greeting was warm, familiar, and for a second I wanted to scratch Mara Brent's eyes out. I shook my head to clear it.

"The hell you doing in my neck of the woods?" he asked.

Mara eyed me then turned back to Eric. "Just some follow-up on a witness who lives out here."

"You know Mara?" Eric asked me.

"We've just met," I said. Things grew quickly awkward between us. I don't know if Eric sensed some shift in my demeanor with my momentary flare of unwarranted jealousy. Or maybe it was the weight of the knowledge that I might have to cross-examine him tomorrow or the next day. We kept our distance from each other over the past few weeks since I crashed in his guest room. We made a sort of unspoken pact to keep to our neutral corners until this trial ended.

"Well, she's one of the best there is," Eric said. He turned to Mara. "And so is Cass, actually."

"So I've heard," Mara said. "Who knows, maybe someday we'll get to lock horns."

"I'd look forward to that," I said, trying to keep the humor in my tone. I meant it, really.

"Well," Eric said. "It was good seeing you, Brent. If I had a second, I'd try to snag you both for a cup of coffee. I've got to catch Castor before he leaves for the day. Babysitting a warrant on another case."

"Good luck on that," Mara said. "Your boy Jack put him in a bad mood." She shot me a look of solidarity. I appreciated it.

"Great," Eric said. "I'll, uh … I guess I'll see you tomorrow, Cass."

Things got awkward again. Mara sensed it and cast her eyes downward.

Eric gave me a tight-lipped grin, then disappeared down the hall as Mara and I stepped on the elevator together.

"Good guy," Mara said. "Great cop."

"That he is," I agreed.

"He taking the stand tomorrow?" she asked.

"Could be. Though his partner's the one who did the hotel room search."

"Bad break for Jack then," Mara said. "Eric's an iceman on cross. I've seen him in action a few times. He was on a gang task force a few years back and had occasion to testify down in Maumee County for me once or twice."

"I'll keep that in mind," I said, dreading the prospect of going toe to toe with Eric. Not that I couldn't handle him on cross. I could be every bit as ice-cold as he was. I just didn't want it to get personal.

"I want to thank you," Mara said, shrewdly changing the subject. "Any help that you can give me on the Silvers case will go a long way. And I can't imagine how rough it must be on your client to hear all of this. I mean it's got to be every adoptee's worst nightmare."

"Yes," I said, feeling weirdly defensive about my own sister.

"Well," she said. "I look forward to meeting the Romaines. They sound like special people."

The doors opened and Mara and I said our goodbyes. I liked her. She had a direct, no-nonsense demeanor that I could appreciate. Plus, she clearly cared deeply about the victims she advocated for. I respected that. I just hoped that when the time came, my research on Alicia's case might help bring peace to Denise Silvers. I knew it wouldn't for Alicia.

Chapter 30

I COULDN'T power down that evening. I was ready for whatever Jack had to throw at me. I knew that. But seeing Mara Brent stirred me up. I wanted to bring both her and Alicia something concrete when we met in two weeks.

It was just past nine o'clock at night as I sat on my foldout bed at Vangie's with Tori's notes spread out in front of me. I had a million other things on my plate. While intriguing, Alicia's case wasn't an emergency. And yet, as I sat alone in the house, I decided to give Newt a call.

"Hallo, dare!" he answered as usual.

"Hey, Newt," I said. "It's Cass Leary. Do you have a second?"

"For you, pretty lady, I've got all night. Surprised you're not out on the town with some handsome stud on your arm."

I smiled. His jokes were corny. Next-level dad humor. "I'm working."

"Can I help?" he asked.

"That's why I'm calling. We're running into some trouble contacting the cousins you shared with us. Getting a lot of disconnected numbers. Unanswered messages. I'm wondering if you might be able to help us crack through that."

I heard him whistle on the other end of the phone. "Well, you know I love a good mystery. Most exciting thing to happen to me in ages. But I don't know what more I can tell you. These were Patricia and Miss Marilyn's people. I didn't even know all of them personally. Oh boy, did they like their family reunions though."

"One name on your list, Cindy Holcomb," I said looking at Tori's notes. "She's got a record. It just got me thinking ..."

"Cindy?" he said. "Patricia didn't get along with her all that much. Well, she didn't get along with Cindy's mom, her sister Louise. Miss Marilyn thought she was a bad influence. But my Patricia had a soft heart. Sucker for lost causes and all that. You know the type?"

I smiled. "Yes. I do. There are some who say I'm that type."

"Well, I just bet you are," he said. "Pretty girl like you. How come you're not married by now? Did some man break your heart?"

It was an odd, overfamiliar thing for him to say. But also in keeping with his hokey personality.

"Cindy Holcomb," I said, steering the conversation back to the matter at hand. "Is there anyone else in Patricia's family who might still be in contact with her?"

Newt breathed into the phone. "Well, I'll have to think about it. You know, I'm getting worried about you, Cass."

"Why's that?"

"You're burning the candle at both ends, probably. And I'm thinking, maybe this mama ... maybe she don't wanna be found."

I took a beat. "Maybe not," I said. "But we've come this

far. I'd just like to at least talk to these cousins so I know for sure."

"I understand," he said. He grew silent for a moment. "Can I ask you something?"

"Of course."

"Do you think maybe this girl's father was a bad man?"

The question floored me. I'd been very careful not to let on the deeper urgency this case had taken. I couldn't. Not without betraying Alicia's confidence.

"I don't know anything about him," I said. It wasn't exactly a lie.

"Well, I just wonder. What kind of man would leave a girl like that knocked up and not care for her?"

"Maybe he never knew," I said.

"Maybe," Newt said. "But it's a sad, sad story. Your client is lucky to have you on her side. You keep fighting for her. You're a winner. I can tell."

"Thanks, Newt," I said. "I've kept you long enough."

"Never a bother," he said. "Anytime."

"Well, if you can think of any other family member that might be able to put me in touch with Cindy Holcomb, I'd appreciate it. I'll call you in a week or so."

"I'll be looking forward to it."

We said our goodbyes. As much as I wanted to help both Alicia Romaine and Denise Silvers, tonight, it felt like justice might slip away.

Chapter 31

I RAN into Eric in the exact spot the next morning, right outside of Judge Castor's courtroom. He was in a suit. I expected Jack LaForge would call him to the stand today.

The deputies picked just then to lead my father down the hall. He and Eric were nearly the same height. My father puffed out his chest and looked Eric up and down. I wanted to murder him. Forcing a smile, I turned to him.

"Just wait for me inside," I said. I stared so hard at him, I expected laser beams to shoot out of my eyes. If he could make it through today's testimony without losing his cool, I might start seeing some light at the end of this particular tunnel.

"You up first?" I asked.

Eric cast a nervous glance down the hall. "I'm testifying in another case downstairs."

"Detective?" Jack came up behind us. He wore a similar expression to my father's as he stared at Eric. What did he think? That I was capable of attempting witness tampering right outside the courtroom?

"Good to see you, Jack," Eric said, his tone harsh. He clearly didn't like the vibe Jack threw off either. Jack cleared his throat and made a hasty exit through the courtroom door.

Megan Lewis stepped off the elevator. She looked sharp in a tailored blue suit, her hair pulled back in a neat bun. So, Jack planned to call her first today. I had no idea how that would go for me. I'd never seen how Megan performed in a witness chair.

"Good luck today," Eric said. "I mean that."

"Thanks. Same to you. For whatever case you're testifying in."

Eric gave me a cocky grin and all at once, things got easier between us. He spared me the comment I knew he wanted to make. He wouldn't need luck.

"You know my reputation," he said. "I usually make quick work of defense lawyers."

That got a genuine laugh out of me. "You've never squared off with me before, Eric. Am I to assume we won't get the chance this time either?"

He cast a glance over his shoulder at Megan. She actually looked a little nervous. Eric saw it too and his smile tightened.

"Maybe I'll see you at the end of the day," he said. Then he was gone.

I smiled politely at Megan and made my way into the courtroom. I took my seat beside my father and pinched his arm under the table.

"Keep your mouth shut and your expression neutral today. No matter what you hear."

"Cool as a cucumber," he said. "I trust my baby knows what she's doing."

"All rise!" The bailiff had already brought the jury in. Castor always started his day at nine on the dot. His court reporter once told me he actually stood behind his chamber door with his eye on the second hand of his watch.

He took the bench. "We ready to proceed, Mr. LaForge?"

"The state calls Officer Rob Daniels to the stand."

Rob Daniels was a rookie cop. To me, he looked to be about twelve years old. He wore an ill-fitting suit and had his hair shaved to a buzz cut. He took the stand.

Jack asked his establishing questions. Rob was in field operations, a street cop. He had been dispatched to the Harmon Arms on the morning of December 1st incident to a 911 call placed by hotel management after Claudia Christie reported what she'd heard.

"So what did you do next, Officer?" Jack asked.

"I went to the room. The door was closed and locked. The occupants didn't respond to my knocking or shouting. I identified myself as a police officer."

"Then what happened?" Jack asked.

"At that point, I asked the maid to tell me again what it was she'd heard. She described screaming. She felt confident that she'd heard a woman call for help."

"Objection," I said. "This calls for hearsay."

"Your Honor," Jack said. "The statement isn't being offered for the truth of the matter asserted. It informs the officer's next actions."

"Overruled," Castor said. "Continue."

"Officer Daniels," Jack said. "What happened next?"

"I asked the manager if he had a key to the room. When he answered in the affirmative, I directed him to open the door."

"What did you find?" Jack asked.

I renewed my objection to the testimonial evidence on the grounds of unlawful search and seizure. At a sidebar, Judge

Castor denied me once more as I knew he would. But I preserved the issue for appeal if we ever made it that far.

"What did you find, Officer?" Jack asked.

"Well, the bed was still made. There was a woman's wallet lying face down on the floor in front of it. The bathroom light was on and I could see the mirror had been shattered."

"Had you entered the room at this point?" Jack asked.

"No, sir," Officer Daniels replied. "I was still standing on the sidewalk outside the room."

And this is where my objection always died. If the court found the welfare check was sufficient exigent circumstances to circumvent the warrant, anything Officer Daniels saw in plain sight was fair game. Once again, I found myself praying Davy Monroe kept himself together.

"What else did you see?" Jack asked.

"What appeared to be blood covered the broken mirror. It dripped down over the vanity and I could see a large amount of it splattered over the wall."

"What did you do next?" Jack asked.

"I told the maid and manager to stay back. Not to enter the room. I immediately radioed my Sergeant and asked him to call in a detective and the crime scene unit. I shouted into the room again, identifying myself. Then I carefully entered the room to determine if there was anyone still inside needing medical attention."

"Was there?" Jack asked.

"No, sir," he said. "I checked the closet, under the bed, and deeper into the bathroom, including the tub. The room was empty."

"Thank you," Jack said. "I have no other questions."

"Your witness, Ms. Leary," Castor said.

"Officer Daniels," I said. "To be clear, you're saying you

entered that hotel room before the crime scene unit or a lead detective arrived?"

"Yes, ma'am," he answered. "I had no choice. I had to make sure the victim didn't need medical attention."

"Did you ever attempt to contact the defendant to ask for permission?"

"No, ma'am," he said. "I didn't feel there was time to wait. I had to ascertain whether I had a victim needing medical attention inside."

"You never found a victim?" I asked.

"No, ma'am."

"And you walked through the crime scene, correct?"

"Yes, ma'am. As I explained, I had no choice."

"Thank you," I said. I ended my cross. Officer Rob Daniels was essentially a neutral witness since I couldn't get his search suppressed. He was a likable, young kid. I would score no points going too hard on this one. Daniels left the stand.

Jack said, "The state calls Detective Megan Lewis to the stand."

Megan was led in through the back. It struck me how tiny she really was. She was maybe five foot two though she wore high heels today. But she had fine bones and slight shoulders. Her path to detective hadn't been easy. It might be the twenty-first century, but Delphi was still a parochial town. She was only the second female detective in the police department's history and the only one currently serving. She took the stand, kept her back rod straight as the bailiff swore her in.

"Can you state your name for the record?"

"I'm Megan Lewis. I'm a detective with the Delphi Police Department in the crimes to persons unit," she answered loud and clear.

"How long have you held that position, Detective?"

Megan adjusted the microphone downward. "Three years. Before that I was in field operations. What you'd call a beat cop. I was hired in after college so it's been seven years since I joined the force in total."

Jack took her through her list of accolades. Megan had gone to school for accounting. She joined the force with the aspiration to move up the chain of command. Though Sheila Brewer was only the tenth homicide case she'd worked, she cut her teeth working on a sex crimes task force. In fact, that's what first led to her being plucked off the street. She didn't say it specifically, but I knew the Delphi Police Chief had faced mounting pressure to get more women in the detective bureau. From everything I'd so far seen, Megan Lewis was smart, sharp, and good at her job. Still, she had to put up with many lesser cops assuming she was a token hire. I also knew she'd likely face that presumption for her entire career. I was in the odd position of rooting for her at the same time I prepared to poke holes in her testimony.

"Ms. Lewis," Jack said, getting to the meat of Megan's role in this case. "Can you tell the jury how you came to be called to the Harmon Arms on the morning of December 1st?"

"We received a call about a guest in possible distress. A maid reported she'd heard screaming from room number seven earlier that morning. So, a 911 call was placed."

"What happened next?" he asked.

"That call was dispatched to a field operations unit. Officer Daniels responded and performed a welfare check. When no one answered the door, they went in with the manager. I was called in shortly after that."

"What happened next?"

"The information I received was that this was the scene of a possible homicide. I called for the crime scene unit to accompany me. We arrived together and began sealing off the scene. Once my warrant arrived, we searched the room."

"Your Honor," Jack said. "At this time, I'd like to mark exhibits eight through twenty-seven for identification."

Jack approached the bench. He had the crime scene photographs. After Megan authenticated them, Jack moved to have them admitted into evidence. Once again, I objected on my Fourth Amendment grounds. Once again I was denied.

Jack pulled the photos up on the overhead screen. They were gruesome. As Megan and Officer Daniels described, they showed blood dripping down the mirror, the vanity, and splattered all over the wall leading into the bathroom. A large, oval-shaped pool of it stained the carpet and ran into the grout of the nearby bathroom tile.

"Detective," Jack said. "Can you tell me what else you found in that room?"

"There was a woman's wallet on the floor by the bed. Inside, we found Sheila Brewer's driver's license, her ATM card, a key to room seven, and a few wallet-sized school photos that we later confirmed belong to her cousin's children."

Jack moved for admission of the wallet and its contents.

"Then what did you do?" Jack asked.

"I confirmed with hotel management who told me the room was registered to the defendant, Joseph Leary, Sr.," she said. "As I indicated, I secured an arrest warrant based on the evidence at the scene and Mr. Leary's prior statements to us. I worked with the officers on scene and Sergeant Willis to question the other hotel guests and canvass the area. While that was going on, Mr. Leary arrived on scene with his attorney. He was taken into custody. I oversaw evidence collection at the scene then joined my partner at the police station where Mr. Leary was being held."

"Detective," Jack said. "Can you tell us whether an arrest was made in this case?"

My father cast a hard glance my way. As much as I hated every second of it, I had no grounds to object here. The minute he'd opened his mouth to the cops, every damn thing he uttered was admissible.

"Mr. Leary was questioned by my partner. We had reason to believe he was in a dating relationship with the victim, Ms. Brewer. He informed us that he hadn't seen her in several weeks."

"That's hearsay," my father whispered to me. "Do something."

I'd already explained this to him ad infinitum. It wasn't hearsay if the statement actually came from him and was against his own interests. A lie always was. They would get it all in, including the security tapes showing my father with Sheila Brewer just days before her disappearance.

"Quiet," I mouthed to him.

"Were you able to verify those statements?" Jack asked.

Megan leaned forward. "We were able to verify that they were untrue."

"How?" Jack asked.

"We received information that put Mr. Leary in the victim's presence far closer to the night of December 1st."

At that point, Jack walked Megan through the canvassing that was done and her securing of the security footage from the waffle house. Later, when he had the manager on the stand, the jury would see my father chatting it up with Sheila Brewer three days before she went missing. He would be able to underscore my father's falsehoods to the cops as her blood in his hotel room was still wet.

When he finished, Jack scowled and looked at his notes.

"Your Honor, I have nothing further for the detective at this time, but would like to reserve the right to call her later."

"Your witness, Ms. Leary," Castor said.

"Detective Lewis," I said. "I just have a few items to go over. In your report, Officer Daniels filed a supplemental indicating that he arrived ... strike that ... that it was 0848 hours when he directed the hotel manager to open the door to room seven. Is that right?"

"If that's what's in the report, yes," she answered.

"And in that same report, you indicated that you arrived on scene at nine forty. Correct?"

"Yes," she said.

"And you arrived with the crime scene unit, correct?"

"Yes."

"Fifty-two minutes later, by my calculations," I said.

"Yes. We did not enter that room until the warrant was secured. You were there for that. I wrote one up on scene and had another officer take it to the courthouse."

I left it there. It was thin, but I could argue to the jury we were dealing with an unsecured crime scene for nearly an hour. I'll admit, it was a cheap tactic, but the goal was reasonable doubt.

"You canvassed the area," I said. "But at no point was the defendant ever seen coming or going from room seven that night or that morning, correct?"

"It's only correct that he wasn't seen," she said.

Indeed, Megan Lewis was sharp and smart.

"And it's also correct that as of this moment in time, you still have no idea where Sheila Brewer is, do you? No one claims to have seen her coming or going from the hotel. She isn't seen on any security footage coming or going."

She bit her lip. "No."

"No body?" I asked.

"No."

"No cell phone?"

"No."

"You found a wallet with Sheila Brewer's driver's license, an ATM card, and a few personal photos. What about car keys?" I asked.

"No. Ms. Brewer's car was found at her place of residence, parked in the garage. Her keys were on a hook near her back door. We only found one key to the hotel room."

"And you found no physical evidence that Mr. Leary had ever been in her car, isn't that true?"

"That's true," she said. "Yes."

"You searched Mr. Leary's car as well, didn't you?"

"Yes," she said.

"Did you find any blood in Mr. Leary's car?" I asked, knowing her answer full well.

"No."

"You didn't find Sheila Brewer's blood in his car?"

"No."

"You didn't even find any of Joe Leary's blood in the car, did you?"

"No."

"No hairs matching Sheila Brewer's?"

"Not in the car. No."

"And you didn't find any of Sheila Brewer's hair in room number seven, did you?"

"No. We didn't."

"Mr. Leary was examined while he was in custody. He didn't have a scratch on him, did he?"

"Um, not that I'm aware. He was uninjured."

"You only found blood in the bathroom and on the vanity and mirror, correct?"

"That's correct."

"Nothing on the carpet in the actual sleeping area near the bed?"

"None. No."

"No blood trail leading out of the hotel room? None on the door? None down the sidewalk?"

"No. We found no blood evidence in those three areas. It was confined to the bathroom and vanity area."

"Did you find any clothing fibers that belonged to Sheila Brewer in that hotel room?"

"No," she said.

"Uh huh," I said. I wore a puzzled look on my face.

"Did you see any other signs of a struggle in that hotel room?" I asked.

"You mean other than the shattered mirror and the copious amounts of blood everywhere?" she asked.

"The bed was still made, correct?" I asked, ignoring her sarcasm.

"It was."

"There were still fresh towels hanging on the racks, correct?" I asked, pointing to the neatly folded white terry-cloth towels in one of the crime scene photos still on screen.

"That's correct."

I would use this evidence to later bolster Davy Monroe's alibi testimony. My father just plain wasn't in that room that night, or the day before, no matter what else might have happened.

"Thank you, Detective," I said. "I have nothing further."

"Mr. LaForge?" the judge asked.

"Just one question on redirect. Ms ... er ... Detective Lewis. Did you have any concerns that your crime scene had been left unsecured before your arrival that morning?"

"None at all," she said. "Officer Daniels is a trained field operations officer. He followed proper protocol until we arrived."

"Thank you," Jack said. "I have nothing further for Detective Lewis."

She was dismissed.

I let out a breath. I got some jabs in. But those crime scene photos would leave the biggest impression on the jury and would be tough to overcome.

Chapter 32

JACK ENDED the day by calling crime scene unit detective Lloyd Cameron to the stand. Cameron had a humorless, down-turned mouth that gave him a turtle-like countenance. He moved just about as fast. But he immediately came off as a thorough, serious witness.

His was the driest of testimony. The science always was. He went through his methodical collection of evidence at the scene. He described the testing used to isolate the various DNA markers that positively identified the blood samples as belonging to Sheila Brewer. She'd actually had bloodwork done for a thyroid condition within the month prior to her disappearance. To his credit, Jack kept Cameron's testimony relatively short and sweet as these things went. Just before three o'clock, he turned the witness over to me.

"Detective," I said. "You have no idea how that blood got in the hotel room, have you?"

"What ... I mean ... presumably the victim bled there."

"But you can't actually establish the manner of death, can you?" I asked.

"I'm not sure what you mean." I knew damn well he did.

"There was no body, correct?"

"There wasn't, no."

"No murder weapon?" I asked.

"No."

"This could have been a gunshot wound?" I asked.

"It's possible, but with the splatter pattern we identified, the wound would have been far more consistent with a stabbing. The pool of blood found on the carpet is what we classify as low velocity. Generally, this occurs from blood dripping from a wound such as a stabbing wound. We also found a medium velocity pattern against the wall near the bathroom door. This was also more consistent with a stabbing wound, likely if an artery was severed. Perhaps the neck. Gunshot wounds generally generate high velocity splatter patterns. We found none of those. The largest concentration of blood was found soaked into the carpet. As I testified on direct, the victim likely slumped to the floor and exsanguinated."

"You think she died right there on the floor?" I asked.

"Most likely."

"You testified on direct that you recovered approximately four liters of Sheila Brewer's blood in that hotel room."

"Yes," he said. "The human body holds at most five to six liters. The amount recovered would have therefore been seventy-five to eighty percent of her blood volume. From what we know of Ms. Brewer's height and weight, four liters are far more likely to be in the eighty percent range for her total volume. That is not a survivable injury."

"So there's no chance, in your opinion, that Ms. Brewer could have walked out of that hotel room?"

"No chance," he said.

"And yet," I said. "No body was found. So in your opinion she had to have been dragged out, correct?"

"Dragged or carried."

"But you found no blood trail," I said.

"No," he said. "She could have been wrapped in a tarp or a sheet though."

"Your Honor," I said. "I'd ask that the witness's last statement be stricken as non-responsive."

"Sustained, the jury will disregard everything after 'no'."

"So, all you really know is that there was an amount of blood in that room that fits the math of what you consider fatal, is that right?"

"That's correct," he said.

"But you cannot establish the manner of death, whether it was from a gunshot or a knife, or any number of other implements, correct?"

"I don't know that with one hundred percent certainty, no," he said. "But as I testified, we did not find splatter patterns that would be consistent with a gunshot wound."

"And likewise, you have no idea whether the defendant, someone else, or Sheila Brewer herself inflicted these wounds, isn't that right?"

He set his jaw to the side. "No. But like I said, if they were self-inflicted, we would have found a body, because no one could walk out of that room leaving eighty percent of their blood behind."

He meant to be snide. It took everything in me to suppress my smile. Detective Cameron had just used the magic word I planned to drive home to the jury.

If. If was the stuff of reasonable doubt.

Chapter 33

ON THE THIRD morning of trial, Jack LaForge called Davy Monroe to the stand. There were rumblings in the courtroom behind me. Tori and Jeanie had just walked in. Jeanie gave me a silent nod. I'd asked her for one main favor this week. I wanted her to keep my brother and sister away from the courtroom. It was one of a hundred other reasons I was glad Matty was safely ensconced in rehab. I couldn't trust the rest of Clan Leary to keep their tempers. I had my hands more than full with Joe Sr.

"What the hell's he doing?" my father whispered to me. "I thought he was our witness."

"He is," I said. "It's just strategy. Jack's probably hoping to attack Davy's credibility on offense. I might have done the same thing."

Davy came up the aisle. He was wearing a cheap brown suit and a pink tie. He had his fine hair slicked back and his scuffed shoes squeaked on the floor. He blushed when he passed Jeanie. She shot him a resigned look that read, "you better not screw this up." I shared her sentiment.

Davy was sworn in and Jack wasted no time getting into it with him.

"Mr. Monroe," he said. "Can you tell me how you're acquainted with the defendant?"

The microphone squawked as Davy got too close to it. Every hearing person in the courtroom winced.

"Sorry," he said, leaning back. "Joseph and me have known each other since high school."

"You're friends?"

"Uh ... yeah. Buddies. Joe's always been a character. I mean, we don't always see each other. We can go years. But when he calls up, or I do ... it's like no time has passed. It's good to have friends like that."

"Indeed," Jack said. "Have you stayed in contact with the defendant over the past, say, five years?"

"Ah ... not all the time, no," he said. "Joe left town, oh, I don't know. Maybe seven, eight years ago. His kids were all grown and gone and didn't really need him anymore. His wife, Lynn. Man, she was a saint. I had a crush on her. I can admit that now."

"Mr. Monroe," Jack said. "Can you answer the question?"

"Oh. Sorry. Right. So Joe left Delphi maybe seven years ago. He had a girlfriend. Margie? Marty? Something like that. She inherited her mom's place in Coral Gables, Florida. So she invited Joe to move down there with her. It was a big place. Rundown. Joe's handy. So off he went. I'd get calls from him every few months. Just sort of a hey, how you doin' kind of thing. He'd come back into town or near town and when he did we'd meet up. Go have a beer or two."

"Mr. Monroe," Jack said. "Did you and Mr. Leary have occasion to reconnect in person recently?"

"Uh. Yeah. He, uh ... well, he'd been calling a lot. Actually, I started calling him a lot. I think I may have started it.

Back and forth over this past year. Joe was asking about his kids. He knew his two daughters came back to Delphi, that's Cass here and the younger one, Vangie. He kinda wanted me to check up on them for him."

"Did you?"

"Well, I mean, I didn't bother either of them none. Just had my eye on 'em when I'd see them about town. Told Joe if I did. It was all real casual. He was just a concerned father."

If I'd been eating, I would have choked.

"Okay, so Mr. Leary came back to Delphi at some point. Do you know how that came about?" Jack asked.

"Well, I know he started talking to Sheila Brewer. He told me. And she told me. First they were just on the phone talking. Getting reacquainted. Sheila was a few years younger than us growing up. Good girl. She even asked me what I thought of Joe. You know. Whether or not I thought it was a good idea getting into it with him?"

"Getting into what?" Jack asked.

"Oh, you know. Dating. She asked me if he was over his wife. Lynn."

"Objection," I said. "Can we stay out of hearsay territory, Your Honor?"

"Sustained."

"Mr. Monroe," Jack said. "To your knowledge, your first-hand knowledge, did the defendant and Sheila Brewer get more serious than phone conversations?"

"Oh yeah," Davy said. "They were hot and heavy. Joe came back to town for her. He told me that. She had boundaries though. He told me she wouldn't let him stay over to her place. Always a hotel. He liked the Harmon Arms. What a dumb name that is. Especially now, right? I told him he should be talking to his kids. He said he would. He just wanted to wait for the right time. Anyway ..."

"Mr. Monroe," Jack said. "At any point, did you ever become aware of trouble in the defendant and Sheila Brewer's relationship?"

"Objection," I said. "Counsel is leading the witness."

"Rephrase, Mr. LaForge."

Jack scowled. "Do you know whether the defendant and Ms. Brewer were still dating as of November 30th of last year?"

"Oh yeah," Davy said. "I asked Joe if he had plans for Thanksgiving. I mean, I don't do much. Usually have my nephews and nieces over. I've got the bigger house. They do all the cooking and whatnot. I knew Joe hadn't really reconnected with his kids yet. I asked him if he was going over to be with them for the holiday and he said he didn't know. Anyway, he told me he was planning to spend it with Sheila. They were gonna go out to eat, he said."

"Do you know if that happened?" Jack asked.

"You know, I never asked him. But the Sunday after, Joe and I went out for drinks. We met up at Mickey's bar."

"What time did you arrive at Mickey's bar?" Jack asked.

"I'd say it was between eight and nine. We shot some pool. Polished off a couple of pitchers."

"Did you talk about Sheila Brewer?" Jack asked.

"Yeah," he said. "Jack was feeling kinda down. He told me Sheila was going kind of cold. They weren't getting along."

My back stiffened. My father's fists curled as he rested them on the table. In all my conversations with Davy Monroe, he had never mentioned that. Neither had my father. He'd said the opposite, that he was the one who had cooled things off with her. Color came into his cheeks. I knew that look. I shot him a withering stare aimed at keeping him quiet no matter what else came out of Davy Monroe's mouth.

"How long did you stay at Mickey's, if you recall?" Jack asked.

"We closed the place out. Two a.m. After that, I could tell Joe wasn't quite himself."

"What do you mean by that?"

"Well, he was real down. I think it'd been a rough weekend with the holiday. He and Sheila weren't getting along. He didn't see his kids. I felt bad for him, you know? I think a lot of the times people just make assumptions about Joe. He's got a bad reputation."

"Objection," I said. "Is there a question in there?"

"Mr. LaForge?"

"Mr. Monroe," Jack restarted. "Where did you go after you left Mickey's?"

"I invited Joe to come crash at my place. I don't know. Just the thought of him heading back to that hotel room alone kind of depressed me."

"Did he accept your invitation?"

"Yes. He did. My place is only about a five-minute walk from Mickey's. I'd thrown back a few. Joe hadn't, I don't think. But that was for show. Ya know? I don't think he wanted it getting back to his kids that he'd been hitting the hard stuff. Which I can understand. It wasn't too cold out so we walked. I'd say we probably got to my place by two thirty in the morning."

"Then what happened?" Jack asked.

I leaned forward in my seat. Something changed in Davy Monroe's face. For his entire testimony he kept looking back and forth from Jack LaForge to my dad. Now he stared straight ahead.

"I didn't last long once we got back to my place," he said.

"What do you mean?" Jack asked.

"Well, I'd stuck to draft beer at Mickey's. I got the hard

stuff out when we got to my house. I had some good bourbon and I did a shot or two."

"And then what?"

"Joe didn't want any. He said liquor always got him in trouble. Well, he's right. Anyway, I don't remember much after that. I must have passed out. I woke up and it was daylight. Joe wasn't there and his car was gone. See, he parked at my place and we walked to and from Mickey's."

"You son of a bitch," my father muttered. It wasn't a shout, but he said it loud enough most of the jury could hear.

"Shut. Up!" I said through gritted teeth.

"What woke you up?" Jack asked.

"Somebody was pounding on my door. When I went to go answer it was the cops. Two patrolmen. Said they were looking for Joe."

"What did you tell them?" Jack asked.

Davy looked down. "I ... I told a white lie."

"A white lie?"

Davy looked back up and tears filled his eyes. This time, he kept his gaze on Jeanie in the back of the courtroom.

"I didn't know what they were there for. I didn't know about Sheila. I swear. I thought I was just helping out a friend. I told them Joe'd slept on my other couch but that he left just a couple of hours earlier. Told them to try him at his son Matty or his daughter Vangie's. He was in contact with them and I do remember Joe saying he was gonna meet over at Vangie's that morning."

My father pounded his fist to the table. I heard the courtroom doors swing open. No doubt the two local reporters who'd bothered to cover this trial were off to file a story. Davy Monroe, my father's alibi witness, had just gone south.

Chapter 34

JACK ASKED JUST two more questions of Davy. He pinned him down to the prosecution's timeline. Davy reiterated that he and my father arrived at his place no later than twenty minutes past two that morning. And Davy stuck to his guns that he blacked out pretty much right after taking his second shot of bourbon some twenty minutes later.

It put my father in the wind at least an hour before Claudia Christie claimed to have heard screams coming from his hotel room. The Harmon Arms was only four blocks from Davy Monroe's house.

"I have nothing further at this time," Jack said.

I asked for a short recess hoping I'd have that time to get my father under control. He seethed beside me. Judge Castor denied my request.

Livid, I walked up to the lectern.

"Mr. Monroe," I said. "You just indicated you told the police that you were absolutely sure Mr. Leary didn't leave your home until eight o'clock the next morning, isn't that right?"

"I told them that, yes," Davy said.

"And not just once. You were then visited by Detective Megan Lewis on December 4th in the morning. May I show you your statement?" I asked.

"Objection," Jack said. "The witness hasn't claimed to have forgotten what he told the police."

"Sustained," Castor said. "Ms. Leary, you may ask the witness what he said."

"Mr. Monroe," I said. "What did you tell Detective Lewis when she questioned you about the night of December 1st?"

Davy cleared his throat. "I told her Joe was with me the whole night. I told her we stayed up watching Clint Eastwood movies."

Before trial, Jack had already stipulated to the fact that the classic movie channel had indeed run an Eastwood movie marathon that night and into the next day. I'd never in my life been more glad Tori Stockton worked for me. She'd been the one to secure that particular admission of fact. I left it there though. I could use it in my closing argument. Better to let that detail lie and hope that Jack forgot about it for now.

"So you admit that you lied to the police?" I asked.

"Yes," Davy said. "I'm sorry for that. I thought I was doing a favor for a friend. I didn't know Sheila Brewer was dead at the time."

"Excuse me?" I said. "You didn't think she was dead when you spoke to the two patrolmen on Monday morning, right?"

"That's right."

"But you had been told the police thought Sheila was dead Tuesday morning when you spoke with Detective Lewis, isn't that right?"

"Yes," he said. "I knew what happened to her by that point."

"And yet you stuck with your story. I mean, we're talking about some favor."

"I'm sorry, what can I say?" Davy said. He was full-on crying now.

"And you spoke to my associate and me several weeks after Mr. Leary's arrest. You knew what the police were claiming about Sheila Brewer's fate then. And you told me the exact same thing. You told me the defendant had been with you the entire night, correct?"

"It's true I told you that," he said. "It's not true that it happened. I mean, I don't know if it happened. I was out cold."

"And you've met with Mr. LaForge more than once, isn't that right?"

"What?"

"Mr. LaForge has interviewed you prior to your taking the stand, right?"

"Yes."

"How many times?" I asked.

"Uh ... I'm not sure. Twice, maybe three times."

"When was the first time?" I asked.

"Um, maybe a month after Joe got arrested."

"And you told Mr. LaForge you were with Mr. Leary that whole night then?"

"I did. Yes."

"Did you meet with Mr. LaForge yesterday?" I asked, acting on a hunch.

"Yes."

"Did you call him or did he call you?"

"He, uh ... he called me to make sure I knew what time to be here. That's when ... um ... I told him I had something to confess. I told him I'd been lying this whole time. I just couldn't live with myself anymore."

"How convenient," I said.

"Ms. Leary," Castor admonished me before Jack could pop up to object.

This made no sense. My blood boiled. Jack knew a day ago that Davy Monroe was going to change his story. He had a legal obligation to share that information with me. And yet, he kept silent.

I took a breath and turned back to Davy Monroe. "I have nothing further at this time but reserve to recall this witness on rebuttal," I said.

"Mr. LaForge?" Castor said.

I thrust my shoulder out and bumped Jack as he walked past me to the lectern. Not my best moment, but I had enough of my father in me that I couldn't help it.

"What the hell is going on?" my father whispered. "You better do something."

"I'm trying," I said.

"Mr. Monroe," Jack said. "Do you understand that your testimony today puts you at substantial risk of criminal prosecution?"

"I do," he said. "But it's time I did the right thing. No matter what happens to me."

"Mr. Monroe, isn't it true that you told me you had already contacted Mr. Leary's lawyer and told her what you were going to say here today?"

Davy dropped his head. "I said that, yes."

"But you didn't?"

"No. I'm sorry. I was scared of what she might do."

Terrific. So he was lying again now.

"Thank you," Jack said. "I have nothing further."

"All right," Castor said. He looked just as angry as I felt. "I'll dismiss the jury for the day."

I kept my composure as the jury filed out. Then I exploded.

"Your Honor," I said. "I'd like to move for an immediate mistrial. The state is under a continuing obligation to disclose discoverable facts in this case. A material witness calling at the eleventh hour to substantially change his testimony and Jack LaForge doesn't see fit to call me?"

Castor stared Jack down.

"Explain yourself, Mr. LaForge," he said.

"Your Honor, Davy Monroe is the defense's so-called star witness. Counsel admits that she and her staff have been in communication with him all along. I've withheld nothing. He's been on my witness list. He's on theirs. He's been prob-lematic from the beginning and defense counsel knows it. And you heard the man. He said he'd already told Ms. Leary he was changing his testimony."

"He did no such thing," I said. "And the burden is on the prosecution to disclose that."

"There was nothing to disclose!" Jack roared. "I didn't know what he was going to say."

"Enough," Castor said. "Look, I don't know what I'm going to do with this. For now, I'm going to sleep on it. I'll take your arguments under advisement. For now, we're adjourned. And Ms. Leary?"

"Yes, Your Honor," I answered.

"Get a hold of your damn client."

He banged the gavel. It echoed through me. After Castor left the bench, and cleared the courtroom, Jack grabbed his things and stormed out of the courtroom. The deputies closed in.

"May I have a moment with my client?" I asked them.

I got a pair of solemn nods in unison. Jeanie and Tori had already cleared out. No doubt Jeanie was off to figure out a way to wring Davy Monroe's neck without getting herself disbarred.

"You fucked this up!" my father's voice boomed.

I took a step back, feeling the force of his words like a physical blow.

"Are you kidding me?"

"You told me you had Davy under control."

The deputies were still within earshot.

"Guys?" I said. "This is a private conversation."

They looked at each other. There was literally nowhere else for my dad to go. One of the deputies moved forward to cuff him.

"We'll be outside of those doors. You have five minutes."

"We'll only need one!" Dad shouted.

I waited until the courtroom doors shut and we were alone.

"That's the last time you say anything to imply I'm in the business of tampering with witnesses," I said. "You got that?"

"You put me on the stand," he said. "I'll clean up this mess."

"You're nuts."

"Davy was solid. I handed that to you on a platter with a bow wrapped around it. And you let him start flapping his gums to the enemy."

My brain started to buzz. The air felt thick as tar. I saw something sinister come into my father's eyes. He'd handed it to me? No. No. No.

"Christ," I muttered. "You put him up to this all along, didn't you? You told Davy to lie for you.'"

The moment I asked the question, I knew it was true.

"I was at his house that night. The whole night. That's not a lie."

"That's not what I asked you," I said. I knew I should quit. This was dangerous territory. I suspected my father had suborned perjury. It was witness tampering. Obstruction of justice.

I started to pace. "But you knew Davy passed out. That whole Clint Eastwood stuff. That was your idea, wasn't it? You told him to say that? He came up with that detail three days later."

My father sneered at me, nostrils flaring. He didn't say the words. He didn't have to. I knew.

"Put me on the stand," he said.

I shook my head. "I can't. Even if I wanted to. Not now." He was lying. I felt it in my bones. I could not ... *would* not risk my career by allowing him to perjure himself.

"It's my decision," he said. "And I didn't tell him to lie. What he told the cops when they came looking for me, that was on him."

"But after that. After they cut you loose. You talked to him. You tried to shore up his story. Did you threaten him before he talked to Lewis three days later?"

I shouldn't have gone there. He didn't answer but the cold look in his eyes told me all I needed to know.

"No," I said. "You've crossed a line. And now you're trying to drag me over it. I won't. I can't put you on the stand."

He looked back at the closed courtroom doors.

"Fine," he said. "Then you're fired. Freddy!" He shouted the last bit at the top of his lungs.

The deputies walked back in.

"Get me the hell out of here," he told them. "I'm ready to go."

I watched them lead my father out of the room. My knees trembled. As the heavy double doors slammed shut, I sank back into my chair and buried my face in my hands.

Chapter 35

WE MET in Judge Castor's chambers the next morning, twenty minutes before the jury was scheduled to arrive.

"You want to what?" he said, staring at my father down the bridge of his nose.

Dad pursed his lips and glared at Jack. "Do I have to do this in front of him? I know my rights."

"You don't have the right to an in-camera discussion with the judge without my presence," Jack said, refusing to even make eye contact with my father or me.

I had a headache. A huge one. At the moment, I felt like I had cause to regret pretty much every decision I'd made in my life. Each and every one of them had led me to sitting in that particular chair, at that particular time, watching my father torpedo his case and possibly my entire career.

"The answer is no," Castor said. "I haven't been thrilled with Ms. Leary's decision to represent you. But since she's not a witness in this trial, I allowed it. I'm going to do you a favor, Mr. Leary. I'm going to save you from yourself, or try to, and keep you represented by competent counsel. Is there anything else?"

His words provided a preview for what I suspected was to come. He still hadn't ruled on my motion for a mistrial. If Castor were inclined to grant it, he likely wouldn't have even entertained this conversation in his chambers.

Great. My bad day was about to get worse and then some.

"Go out there and get yourselves prepared," Castor said. "Let's see if we can get this wrapped up."

That gave me a small glimmer of hope. Maybe he was planning on granting my request. I led my father into the courtroom.

"This is bullshit," he whispered.

"Enough. You know the saying about when you find your-self in a hole? Quit digging. Let's just get through this."

"He's on the take, I'm telling you." Dad pointed toward the closed door behind Castor's bench.

"He's not on the take. You just don't like that he disagreed with you. Now I need you to sit down and shut up. I have to figure out what the hell I'm going to do to counter Davy Monroe's performance yesterday."

"I'll handle it," he said.

"You'll what?"

"Put me on the stand."

I drew in a big breath of air then slowly let it out. "You admitted to me yesterday that you conspired with Davy to get him to embellish a lie for you. Even if he did it on his own at his initial contact with the cops, you put pressure on him before he talked to the detectives. That's a crime, Dad. Not to mention how it'll make you look to them." I gestured to the empty jury box.

"They don't need to know that."

"And I have an ethical responsibility to keep you from perjuring yourself. I won't do it. I'm not putting you on."

"Screw your ethics," he said. "You never let that get in the way of what you did for those gangsters in Chicago. That's why I hired you. That's the girl I want."

I gritted my teeth to stop myself from reminding him he didn't hire me at all. And I wasn't doing this for him. I'd let my concern over Matty trump my common sense. That's the last time I'd let that happen.

"All rise!"

Castor took the bench. "I'm going to make this part short and sweet. Defense counsel's motion for a mistrial is still before the Court. While I understand the testimony we heard from the state's witness was problematic, I see no undue prejudice to the defendant. Mr. Monroe was on both sides' witness lists. Defendant has had the benefit of discovery and cross-examination of that witness. While the state is under a continuing obligation to supplement discovery, I believe that burden was met under MCR 6.201. Defendant's motion is denied in whole. What else have you got for us, Mr. LaForge? I'd like to get a sense of where we're going."

"Um, Your Honor, the state is ready to rest its case once the jury is called back."

Castor nodded. "Are you ready to proceed with your first witness?"

"Your Honor?" My father addressed the judge.

"Sit down," I whispered.

"Mr. Leary, you'd do well to listen to your lawyer."

"She's not listening to me," he said. "Put me up there. I want to testify."

My father was about to not have to worry about the verdict in this case. I was damn close to strangling him myself.

"Counsel, approach the bench," Castor said.

Jack actually shot me a look of sympathy as he met me around the tables and we walked up to the judge.

"Ms. Leary," Castor said. "I told you you needed to control your client."

"Yes, Your Honor," I said.

"It's the defendant's right to testify," Jack said.

This was worse than a nightmare. This was hell. And I'd brought every damn bit of it on myself.

"Is he set on this course of action?" Castor asked.

I looked back at my father. He was still standing, glaring at me.

"I believe he is," I said, wishing the ground would open up and swallow me.

"Very well. Call him up there after the defense rests."

"Your Honor," I said, my heart pounding out of my damn chest. "I'm going to have to ask the Court to permit my client to testify in the narrative under the circumstances."

Jack looked stunned. Castor frowned.

What I was doing was tantamount to admitting to the court and the prosecution that I knew my father was going to get up there and lie. But I had no choice. If I participated in a traditional direct examination, the risk of suborning perjury was too high. I'd done all I could for my father. He'd dragged me down far enough. I wasn't willing to lose my license to try and save him.

"Fine," Castor said. "That's your choice. Or it's his, anyway. Let's get on with this."

Once the jury was seated, Jack made good on his promise to rest the prosecution's case. I made a motion for directed verdict that I knew only had a snowball's chance in hell of succeeding. Castor quickly shot it down.

"Counsel?" Castor asked while staring at me. I thought I detected a flicker of hope in his eyes that I'd managed to dissuade my dad from what was about to happen next.

"The defense calls Joseph Leary Sr. to the stand. And we seek permission for him to testify in the narrative."

"Granted." He turned to the jury. "The defendant will testify without having his lawyer question him. Mr. Leary, come forward."

I watched in horror as my father swaggered his way to the witness stand and took his oath. He climbed into the box and straightened his tie.

"State your name for the record, Mr. Leary," the judge said. "Then you may proceed."

"My name is Joseph Patrick Leary. And I'm here to tell you people that I'm not guilty."

The jury sat a little straighter. I did the same. I couldn't stop the oncoming freight train, but I could at least try to look like I wasn't afraid of it running me over.

"I know what you all want to know. So I'll tell you straight off. I didn't kill Sheila Brewer. I wasn't anywhere near her the night of December 1st or the morning of the 2nd. I appreciate you all taking the time to listen, so I'll tell you what happened.

"A lot of what Davy Monroe had to say was right. I've known Sheila for years. Going all the way back to high school. Up until the last few years, I've lived in Delphi my whole life. Sheila was a couple of years behind me in school. Pretty girl. Quiet. She was kind to everybody. I think she maybe did have a crush on me and I was sensitive to that, but nothing ever came of it. I only ever had my eyes on Lynn Dauber. My Lynn. We got married not long after we graduated. Had five kids together. Lost a couple along the way. Miscarriages. Nearly broke Lynn, those did. But we got through."

"Your Honor?" Jack said. "Could you perhaps instruct the witness to stick with the relevant facts to the case?"

"Mr. Leary," Castor said. "Do you understand the objection?"

My father looked down. There were tears in his eyes. "I'm sorry. No. I know what he means. You want to hear about Sheila."

He looked back up, making eye contact with the jury. They were hard to read. Every single one of them was paying attention though.

"So yeah," Dad said. "After I lost Lynn and the kids grew up, I didn't have a whole lot tying me here to Delphi. I did like Davy said and went down to Florida with a woman I started to care about. That lasted a while. Eventually, I found my way back to Michigan. Was living in Jackson most of the last two years. It was close enough where I could keep tabs on my kids but far enough I wasn't in their way, you know what I mean. It gets like that when you get old and your kids grow up. They don't need you. And I suppose that's what we all want.

"Anyway, I did stay in touch with Davy Monroe. Everything he said was true as far as that goes. I think he worried I was lonely. What he didn't tell you is that it was his idea me getting together with Sheila. He set it up."

I wanted to shoot him. It was another significant detail my father had failed to mention to me. So I immediately wondered if this would be the first of his lies.

"It was good to reconnect with her. She was still just as pretty and as nice as I remembered. She was easy to talk to. We liked some of the same things. Usually, when we went out, I'd meet her out of town. Either in Jackson or at some halfway point between there and here. A lot of that was her idea. She's got a real nosey family. Hell, she kept telling me how she couldn't stand how much they butted into her business. So she wanted us to just be secret. She knew how the town liked to gossip and she was a real private person. She didn't want everyone knowing her business until we figured out if our relationship was going somewhere, you know?

Anyway, it didn't. Not really. And I'm ashamed to admit that now.

"At the end of last summer, I kind of knew we'd reached a natural end to things. You see, Sheila, I think, was looking for something more than I could give her. I couldn't marry her. That's why I was trying to explain about my sweet, Lynn. In my heart, Lynn's my wife. That's forever. If Sheila wanted me to marry her, I just wasn't in it for that. So I told her. I thought I was doing the right thing. Not leading her on. You know. I'd say that was a week or two before Thanksgiving. I took her to one of her favorite places to eat. The House of Waffles over on M-50. Told her it was time to go our separate ways.

"The thing is, she was fine with all of it, I think. As far as I knew anyway. And that's the last I saw of her. That's the truth, the whole truth, and nothing but.

"As far as what else Davy said, well, yeah. We did meet at Mickey's the night of the first. And he did invite me to crash at his place. I was kind of feeling sorry for myself on account of not getting an invite to my daughter's house for Thanksgiving. Davy was a good friend. Was. And we stayed up watching those spaghetti westerns. That's the truth. Neither one of us fell asleep except maybe to doze off here and there and not until way later in the morning. He might have been asleep when I left but not during the night. Not when that maid said she heard stuff at that hotel. I wasn't there. Yes. That was my hotel room where they found whatever they found in it. But I hadn't been there since early the morning before. So it wasn't me. I wasn't with Sheila Brewer that night. I was at Davy Monroe's house. Period. And I hadn't seen Sheila Brewer in days. I don't know how her stuff got in that room. I did meet with her there a couple of times earlier that month. But not after our meeting at the waffle place. End of story."

The room fell silent. My father nodded, satisfied with himself.

"Is that the end of your statement?" Castor asked.

My father scratched his chin. "Yeah. That's my truth, Your Honor."

"Mr. LaForge?" Castor said.

Jack buttoned his jacket and made his way to the lectern.

"Mr. Leary, isn't it true that you lied to the police on December 1st? You told them you hadn't seen Sheila in weeks."

My father squirmed in his seat. "I was confused."

"By what?" Jack asked.

"Well, I thought they meant had I seen her that day," he said.

Jack pulled a page from the police report that had already been admitted into evidence.

"Mr. Leary, I have a copy of the signed statement you gave to the police. Would you like to review it? May I approach?"

"Go ahead," Castor said. On his way, Jack placed a copy of the exhibit in front of me. I didn't need to read it. My father read the statement then looked back up at Jack.

"Does that refresh your recollection as to what you actually told the police on the morning of December 2nd?"

"Kind of."

"Would you like me to read it back to you?"

"You can if you want," Dad said.

"When asked when you last saw Sheila Brewer, you said, 'I haven't seen that woman since at least six weeks.' But that was a lie. You just testified you had lunch at the waffle place with her three days before she was murdered."

"Who even says she was murdered?" my father said. "You've got what you say is blood in that room. I don't know how it got there. Sheila maybe put it there. Maybe she was lying to me about how sore she was about me wanting to break things off. You all keep saying she's dead, I don't buy it."

"Mr. Leary," Castor said. "You will answer the questions asked of you."

"You lied to the police about the last time you saw Sheila Brewer, didn't you?" Jack asked.

"It wasn't a lie. I just got my dates wrong. It wasn't like I was marking all of this in a calendar. It felt like weeks, that's all."

"Mr. Leary, you lied. You said weeks, but it was really days, right?" Jack asked.

"Your Honor," I said. "The question has been asked and answered. Just because Mr. LaForge doesn't like the answer doesn't matter." Though I'd waived my direct exam, it didn't stop me from objecting on cross.

"Sustained," Castor said. "Move on, Jack."

"And that's not the first time you've given a false statement to the police to cover up your own misdeeds, is it, Mr. Leary?"

"Objection," I said. "Counsel is testifying. And there's been no offer of proof on any prior statements."

"If you'll allow me," Jack said. "I'm getting to that."

"I'll allow it," Castor said.

"Mr. Leary," Jack said. "On second thought, I'm glad you brought up the issue of your late wife. Can you tell me how she died?"

"Objection," I said, my heart racing. "This isn't relevant."

"Your Honor," Jack said. "Counsel for the defense doesn't get to have it both ways. She wants an offer of proof on a prior false statement, I'm laying that foundation now."

"Go ahead," Castor said. "But get to it. The witness may answer."

"Repeat the question," my father said. He went very still,

his expression cold. I knew that look. It's the one he wore just before he was about to explode.

"Mr. Leary, will you tell the court how your first wife passed away?"

My father picked at a piece of lint on his tie. His eyes were glassy when he looked back up. "It was a car accident."

"So, you were in the car with her when it happened."

I heard Jeanie swear under her breath behind me. I went cold as ice. No. This wasn't happening. Not now.

"And you gave a statement to the police in the aftermath of that tragedy as well, didn't you?"

"Yes." My father hissed the word like a snake.

"You told the police your wife was driving that day, isn't that right?"

"I'm not the only one who told them that, you son of a bitch, my Lynn told them that."

"Mr. Leary," the judge said. "You will treat these proceedings and the prosecutor with respect."

"So you did, in fact, file a sworn statement with the police incident to that car accident that she had been driving?" Jack pressed on.

My father looked at me. There was nothing I could do. He'd walked right into the trap I'd begged him to steer clear of. The moment he took that stand, his credibility was at issue. I couldn't breathe. I saw stars. The only thing keeping me from crawling under the table was the knowledge that none of my siblings were in that room. Joey would have vaulted over the gate and tried to choke my father. I knew it.

"I told them the truth," my father said. "Lynn was driving."

"Only, you've changed your story since then, haven't you?" Jack asked.

"Objection," I said. I didn't even know what grounds I'd

used when I popped up. But I couldn't stay seated a second longer.

"Your Honor, again this question has been asked and answered. The witness testified he told the police what happened twenty years ago and he's said the same thing now."

"Counsel, approach the bench," Castor said through a clenched jaw.

I was shaking when I got there. Sweat poured down the back of my neck.

"What the hell's going on?" the judge asked.

"Your Honor," Jack said. "It's come to my recent attention that the defendant filed a false police report incident to his wife's fatal car accident. Cass, I'm sorry. I know this is personal for you. But that's exactly why you shouldn't have gotten involved."

"Prior bad acts aren't admissible," I said.

"Credibility is," Jack said. "Your father's veracity and his history of lying to the cops to cover up his crimes is. I'm truly sorry for what this is doing to you and your family."

Castor dropped his head. When he raised it, his face looked worn and haggard. It didn't make me feel a bit better that I had his sympathy.

"He's right," Castor said even though I already knew it. "If Jack's got proof that the defendant filed a prior false police report, it's coming in. I can't stop it and I won't. We done here?"

Jack nodded. I balled my fists. There was nothing for me to say.

I tried to make my face a mask of indifference. Each member of the jury tracked my movements as I made my way back to my table. Jeanie leaned in and put a hand on my shoulder. I knew this had to be hollowing her out as much as it was me.

"Mr. Leary, isn't it true that you in fact were driving and caused the accident in which your late wife perished? The statement you and she gave to the police was a lie, wasn't it?"

My father white-knuckled the microphone. "That's not true," he said. "Lynn was driving. I'll take that to my grave."

Jack tried a few more times. My father stuck to his statement. I objected on the ground of badgering. Castor sustained.

Jack continued his questioning, hammering my father on his whereabouts the morning of December 2nd. He pinned him down that room number seven was registered to him and that he'd given Sheila a key.

Finally, he finished his questions for my father. He left the stand and came back to the table. I kept my neutral expression in place. When I glanced behind me, I saw Jeanie had left. I didn't even need to ask. No doubt she was on the way to get ahold of Joey and Vangie to brace them for everything that had happened today.

Then there was nothing left to do. I called the hotel manager. He admitted that he'd seen Sheila Brewer come and go with my father in the weeks prior to November 30th, but not during that week. He'd seen her use that key to let herself in once before my father arrived.

It was thin, but it was something. And it was all I had left.

I felt numb as I stood at the defense table next to the man I wanted to kill. I did the only thing left. I rested my case.

Castor glanced at the clock. It was only two thirty in the afternoon.

"Mr. LaForge?" he asked.

"Your Honor, the state has one rebuttal witness. We'd like to recall Davy Monroe to the stand."

"All right," Castor said. "Let's take a ten-minute recess and you may get to it."

I don't remember the judge banging his gavel or the jury filing out. I don't remember even walking out of that court-room. One of the deputies brought my father and me to an open conference room beside Judge Castor's chambers.

I turned to my father. I had no tears to cry. He straightened his back. I closed my eyes and took a breath to steel me for what I had to say.

Chapter 36

"TELL ME," I said.

"Tell you what?" my father asked, his voice dripping with venom.

"What is Davy going to say about the accident with Mom?"

"Who knows? He's a lying weasel. Haven't you figured that out yet?"

"Was it you?" I asked.

"I didn't kill Sheila Brewer."

I smacked my palm to the table. "I'm not talking about Sheila Brewer. You want to know what? In spite of all of this, I actually believe you about her. I must be insane. Like I've got Helsinki Syndrome or something where you're concerned."

"Don't be so melodramatic," he said.

"Were you driving that car? The day Mom died. It was you, wasn't it?"

"You know what your mother told the cops. Why are you even asking me this?"

I shook my head. "You were drunk. That's what it was. You had two DUIs. She knew if you got a third you'd get real jail time. You'd lose your job and despite every other awful thing you did to her, at that time you were paying the bills."

He sat silently staring at the wall.

I started to pace. My chest tightened. "She knew she was going to die. Did you know I talked to one of the nurses who was in the room with her that day? Years later. She said she'd never seen someone so brave. But Mom knew she was going to die. So she lied for you. She lied because she knew we'd lose two parents that day. She was delusional. She thought you'd step up. After all of it, she still loved you. She still tried to protect you. And here I am ... this whole time ... I'm doing the same thing."

That was the harshest truth I'd ever uttered. It slammed into me like a thunderbolt. She protected my father. She always did. And I'd fallen into the same, destructive pattern. I'd strained friendships, risked my career, all to try and save this man. The irony was, now I had no choice. I had to see this trial through, no matter what.

"You killed her," I whispered. I squeezed my eyes shut tight. "None of us wanted to believe it. We believed what Mom told the cops too.'"

"Listen to me," my father said through pursed lips. "Davy Monroe is lying. It happened just like I said. We went to his place that night. And I stayed there the whole night!"

"You told parts of the truth. The parts that suited you."

"Someone is framing me," he said. "You tell that to the jury."

"We have no proof of it," I said. "And you've been caught in lie after lie after lie. Now the whole town knows it."

"I didn't kill Sheila Brewer. Something's not right about all of this. I told you, Sheila wanted to disappear. She hated her life. Hated her meddling cousins. That's what I was for her. A big middle finger to them. I don't know how she did it, but I swear this is a setup."

"You sound insane right now." I backed up until I hit the far wall. I was suffocating. I couldn't be in the same room with him a second longer.

He may not have killed Sheila Brewer. Or maybe he had. But his veil of lies had been lifted once and for all. My mother had let them destroy her. After today, I knew I would never let them touch me again.

Chapter 37

DAVY MONROE RETOOK the stand just past three. Jack kept his questions plain and short. Their impact was devastating.

"Mr. Monroe," Jack said. "Did you ever have occasion to discuss the circumstances of the death of the defendant's first wife?"

Davy shifted in his seat. "Lynn. Her name was Lynn. And yes. We talked about Lynn."

"Can you tell me what the defendant said about her accident?"

Davy's nostrils flared. He gave me a pained expression. "Cass, I'm sorry."

"Mr. Monroe," the judge intervened. "Please answer the question."

"Joe was torn up about Lynn. He loved her more than anything. And she loved him too. But they were no good for each other."

"Mr. Monroe," the judge said sharply. "You were asked a simple question. Has the defendant discussed his late wife's accident with you?"

"Yeah," Davy said. "A few years back. Oh. Maybe ten years ago. Actually it was right around the tenth anniversary of her passing. Joe and I got together. He was real torn up. I'd been with him plenty of times on that day. It was a rough one for him. Same as Lynn's birthday. But that one seemed to hit him extra hard. By then, both of his daughters were gone and he wasn't getting on so great with his sons. Anyway, Joe said, Davy, I gotta tell you something but you gotta swear never to tell a soul. He said it was eating at him so that he didn't think he could get clear of it anymore. We were in the car at the cemetery. He wanted to go visit Lynn but he couldn't bring himself to get out. He just broke, you know?"

"Go on, Mr. Monroe," Jack said.

"Joe told me it was him. He said it was his fault. That he'd been the one driving and it was killing him to live with that."

"Let me get this straight," Jack said. "You're telling the court that the defendant admitted to being behind the wheel the day his wife was killed?"

"Yes," Davy said. "He said he'd told her he was sober. Told her this time was different. He thought he had a handle on it. But that day, it was raining. The roads were slicker than he realized. He put the car in a ditch and they were both thrown from it. He told me he came to and found Lynn lying in that ditch. He held her until the ambulance came. Before they did, she told him not to worry."

"Objection," I said, feeling like a robot. "Mrs. Leary's statements are hearsay."

"Your Honor," Jack said. "I believe Lynn Leary's roadside statements fall under an exception as a dying declaration."

Castor took a deep breath, then agreed with Jack.

"Mr. Monroe, what else did the defendant say?"

Davy shrugged. "He was broken up. He said it over and over. He said it was him the whole time. His fault. He only went along with the lie because it's what Lynn wanted. He said he told the cops it was her. She backed that up when they questioned her just before they took her into surgery. She died on the table, I think. They never charged him with anything. I thought he was going to kill himself that day at the gravesite. I was scared for him. He told me Lynn's last words to him were to take care of the kids. She told him to earn it and take care of them."

I blinked back hot tears. Blood welled in my palms where I dug my nails in. But I stayed motionless, my face blank.

"Mr. Monroe," Jack said. "Thank you. I have nothing further."

"Ms. Leary?" Castor said.

I rose slowly. "Mr. Monroe," I said. "How much had you been drinking that day at the cemetery when these alleged statements were made?"

Davy rubbed his hands together. "I had a few."

"Did you have a flask in the car?" I asked, knowing damn well at that time my dad always kept one on him. He liked his whiskey.

"Yeah," he said. "Joe brought one."

"Whiskey, right?"

"Yes."

"How many shots did you take?"

"I don't know, a couple."

"And how many did you watch my father take?" Davy looked at the judge. Castor would provide no help.

"I don't know," he said. "But I watched him drain the thing."

"So, he was drunk," I said. "And as you stated, wracked with grief when he supposedly made these statements."

"Yeah. Yes."

"And you were also drunk," I said.

"Yes. I'm ashamed to admit it now. But yes."

"Thank you," I said. "I have nothing further."

Davy Monroe left the witness stand and I rested my case. I could almost feel the dying embers of all the bombs that had gone off in that courtroom that day.

Chapter 38

By the time I walked into my office, it felt as though someone had taken a sledgehammer to my head. Miranda stood in the doorway, ready to take my bag from me. She did that, and also wrapped her arms around me.

"I love you, Cass," she said. "I'm so sorry."

Not that it surprised me, but the news of what happened in court today had obviously already seeped its way through town. My brother Joe's truck was parked at an odd angle in front of the building.

"Jeanie's got 'em all upstairs," she said.

"Suppose it's best to just rip the Band-Aid off," I said.

"One fell swoop," Miranda smiled. "It's gonna be okay."

I refrained from asking her how. In my heart, I knew the answer. It would be okay because somehow, some way, I'd make it okay. For now, I was just bone tired.

I practically crawled up the stairs and into the conference room. Joe was pacing a blazing path in the carpet at one end of the room. Vangie sat at the table with her face in her hands, crying. Jeanie sat beside her, rubbing her back.

Joe whipped around when I came in. His eyes were bloodshot, his color ashen.

"He did it," Joe said.

"Did what?" I said. "Killed Sheila Brewer? Killed Mom? Lied about all of it? None of it? Single-handedly ruined my career?"

"Sit down, Cass," Jeanie said. "You look like you're about to drop."

"Is he lying?" Vangie asked. "Davy Monroe?"

I flapped my hand in defeat. "I don't know anymore."

"I filled them in on what I could," Jeanie said.

It was then I noticed the hole in my wall beside the bookcase. I had no doubt my brother had made it with his fist.

"I did what I could," I said. "I never should have gotten involved in the first place. I should have trusted my instincts."

Joe froze. His face contorted with anguish. "I'm sorry," he said. "I pushed you into this as much as anyone else. Or at least, I didn't put up enough of a fight to stop you. I was worried about Matty."

"We all are," I said.

"This is going to destroy him," Vangie said. Something shifted inside of me when she said it. A dam burst. A wall fell. I lifted my head and looked her straight in the eyes.

"Then he'll be destroyed. I'm sorry, but helping him as much as I have has only made things worse. Either he stands on his own two feet or he doesn't. He's not responsible for Dad. And he's not Dad. I'm done chopping off pieces of myself to try and fix things for him."

Joe slid into the chair beside me. "That son of a bitch. He killed her. He drove her straight into that ditch and let us believe it was her fault."

"Yep," I said.

"I should have known. But ... she lied too."

"Yep," I said again.

I was numb from it. The lies. The dysfunction.

"Do you think he killed that other woman?" Vangie asked. I couldn't help it. I was spent. I first answered with a bitter laugh. Finally, after a full minute, I settled.

"You know," I started. "Of that crime, I actually think he's innocent. And I don't even know why. Just an instinct. He's lied about everything else. But I don't think he's lying about that. Something doesn't sit right with me about Davy."

"Me either," Jeanie said with an edge to her tone. "That little weasel."

The one thing I hadn't and couldn't tell them was how Dad admitted to threatening Davy and getting him to embellish his statement after he was arrested for obstruction. After everything that happened, I would stay true to my ethical obligations if it killed me.

"He's not returning my calls," Jeanie said.

"Something happened," I said. "I don't believe Davy Monroe just suddenly had a change of heart or grew a conscience. But I don't know. I'm just tired. And I still have a closing argument to deliver in the morning."

"They'll convict," Joe said.

"The odds are not in Dad's favor," I said. "He's been caught lying up and down. His alibi was blown to bits. The only shred of hope he's got is if the jury doubts whether Sheila Brewer actually died in that room. It's the thinnest of threads. Jack put on a good case with the physical evidence. I poked a few holes. Raised a few questions, but in the wake of every lie Dad told, I doubt it will matter."

"Good," Joe said. His upper lip twitched and he curled his fists. I put a hand over one.

"Easy," I said. "You're already cutting into my drywall repair budget, brother."

"I mean it," he said. "Whether he killed poor Sheila Brewer or not. He killed Mom. It'll be karma that gets him even if it's not true justice."

"You can't really mean that," Vangie said. "I mean, I hate him for Mom. But if he didn't really kill Sheila, then this is wrong. I should know."

That she should. My sister knew exactly what it was like to nearly go down for a murder she didn't commit. It would haunt her and me for the rest of our lives.

"We've all done everything we can and more," Joe said. "For Matty too. Cass is right. If he uses this as an excuse to not follow through on his treatment, that's on him."

"It's not the end of the world," Jeanie said. "If he's innocent, then there's someone else out there who knows what really happened to Sheila Brewer. I'm not done with Davy Monroe. He knows more than he's telling. That was hatred I saw in his eyes today no matter what sentimental shit was coming out of his mouth."

I raised my head. Jeanie had hit on something that had been bothering me all day too. There *was* something cold about Davy today. It was hardly much to go on. And I knew I shouldn't care. Still, there was a justice warrior part of me that didn't like what went down. It's just my sword felt extra heavy today and I just wanted to lay it down.

"That's enough," Jeanie said, watching me. "Cass needs to decompress. You'll all have the rest of your lives to figure out how to deal with what your father did. In the end, it doesn't change anything. You knew what he was. And you've all survived it. This doesn't touch you."

"Except for Matty," Vangie said quietly.

Jeanie went to her. She put her arms around Vangie's shoulders and kissed her on the head.

"I love you, kiddo," she said. "And Matty's a grown-ass

man. His life is his own and no one else's. The day he under-stands that is the day he'll get better. So all of you quit beating yourself up over him."

Joe rose. He held out his hand and Vangie took it. He shot me a look over her head. I found a smile for him and got to my feet.

I hugged my brother. I hugged my sister. But I was damn glad to watch them leave for once.

Chapter 39

I WAS STILL at my desk near midnight. I needed the quiet solitude. I texted Vangie and told her not to expect me back at the house until after court tomorrow. In all likelihood, the jury would have the case by noon tomorrow. For now, I tried to carve out what little peace I could.

I kept a single picture of my mother in one of my desk drawers. It wasn't even a very good one. It was just the two of us when I was maybe eight years old. We sat on a bench at the zoo. My feet dangled, too short to touch the ground. She held my ice cream for me as I sat on the metal sculpture of an elephant and squinted at the camera.

I kept the picture because I remembered the day. It was just the three of us, Joe, Mom, and me. It was Joe who took the picture. A few minutes later, I'd done the same while my brother sat on that same elephant. Whoever thought to make a metal sculpture for kids to sit on under the hot sun? I remembered my mother had sat on it first for a moment so we wouldn't burn ourselves.

I closed my eyes. I missed her. I loved her. But I was so

weary of all the lies she'd spun to protect my father. It was in my DNA to carry on the tradition, it seemed. The protection part.

"Cass?" Tori's soft voice pulled me out of my head.

"Hey," I said. "I didn't realize anyone else was even here."

She smiled and came in. I gestured toward the chair next to my desk.

"I was just organizing the trial folder again. Making sure everything's tabbed the way you like for closing."

I laughed. "Thanks."

"We're going to lose tomorrow, aren't we?"

I took a breath then let it out. "Yes. We probably are. And if you don't mind, I'm so sick of talking about it."

She waited for a beat. Then she placed a thin file folder on my desk. "I think we're coming close on Alicia Romaine's birth mother."

That gave me pause. DNA. Alicia wanted to use hers to expand her family. I currently wished I could change mine.

"Most of the names your friend Newt gave us didn't pan out. Either they didn't return my calls or their mothers didn't have the right age or geography to be good candidates. But then this lady called. Her name is Beth Chase."

"Oh?" I took the file. Tori had made meticulous notes of phone conversations she'd had. She'd made big red cross marks through most of the names Newt gave me. These were other daughters of Marilyn Evans and their children. She had highlighted Beth Chase's name.

"What did she say?" I asked.

Tori shrugged. "She remembers an aunt, a sister of Patricia Evans's, Newt's wife. She dropped off the grid from the family about thirty years ago, she said. She said she always heard she was a runaway."

Scowling, I looked harder at Tori's notes. She'd printed a family tree detailing Marilyn Evans's immediate family. She'd drawn exes through those members and branches we'd already ruled out. But she'd drawn in a new level with a question mark through it.

"Rhonda Evans?" I asked. "Newt never mentioned her."

"It's possible he never knew about her. This cousin, Beth? She said nobody talked about Rhonda after she went AWOL. She never really knew why but always assumed she must have gotten into drugs or something. Being a runaway."

"I'll ask Newt about her," I said. "When I get out from under all the rest of this."

"He's left a couple of messages for you with Miranda," Tori said. "I tried returning one yesterday but he really seems partial to you."

I sighed. "He's a sweet old man," I said. "Bored out of his mind though, I think. See if you can get this Beth Chase to come in and talk to us."

Tori nodded. "I'll take care of it. In the meantime though, you should try to get some sleep. Really. If you don't want to go to Vangie's, I mean, I totally get that. Why don't you come crash with Miranda and me?"

I gave her the warmest, albeit weariest smile I could. "I appreciate that. I really just want to stay here. You know, when we bought the place I thought that stall shower off Jeanie's office seemed insane. Now it's probably my favorite thing about this place."

"Suit yourself," she said. "I'll be here first thing in the morning."

"Thanks, Tori. I don't know what we did around here before you came along. If I haven't said how much I appreciate you lately, I'm sorry."

"You have, don't worry. And it goes both ways. I just hope I can be half as good an attorney when the time comes."

Then she left me in the quiet. I closed the file on Alicia Romaine's DNA and tried not to feel the weight of my own.

Chapter 40

My father and I walked into a tightly packed courtroom on the morning of April 8th. He had nothing to say to me. To everyone watching, I knew they saw a stoic, maybe even proud man bravely awaiting his fate. I knew better. The man seethed with rage, barely contained beneath the surface. Though he wouldn't talk to me, I made him listen.

"You'll sit there," I said. "Quietly. Respectfully. Keep your hands folded and resting on the table. Who knows, maybe some of them will think you're praying. It wouldn't be a bad idea if you tried."

Joe and Vangie came. I couldn't stop them now. Proofs were closed. There was no possibility of either of them being called as witnesses.

"I know you hate him now," I whispered a warning to them before they entered the courtroom. "You just can't look like it."

Fractured, frazzled, furious, and fatigued, the remains of Clan Leary walked into that courtroom as I prepared to deliver my closing argument.

With the burden of proof on his side, Jack LaForge went

first. He was a good lawyer. Though I hadn't seen it on display as much in this trial, he was a masterful litigator. Neutral in both appearance and demeanor, Jack knew how to talk to a jury, to simplify things without making any of them feel as though he were talking down to them. An everyman, he wore suits he got at what was left of the mall. Always red ties and polished shoes. He was your dad, your brother, your husband. And in this case, he felt as if he had all the evidence on his side. He laid it all out to simple, devastating effect.

"Ladies and gentlemen," he said. "There are a lot of unknowns in this trial. I'll admit that. We don't know exactly what happened to Sheila Brewer in her final moments. But what we do know is devastating.

"She cared about the defendant. Trusted him. But she also cared what other people thought of her. She'd been hurt before in love like all of us have. She wasn't ready to bring the defendant fully into her life. Why was that, do you think? I think it was because in the back of her mind, Sheila Brewer knew there was something untrustworthy about him. Maybe on some level, she sensed he was lying to her like he's lied to so many other people in his life.

"What we do know is that Sheila Brewer's end was cold and violent. She was left to bleed out almost eighty percent of her blood volume. Then she was thrown away like garbage."

"Objection," I said. It was unusual for me to do that. It was also against a sort of professional courtesy.

"Not a shred of evidence has been presented detailing what, if anything, happened to Sheila Brewer's body," I said.

Castor let out a sigh I hoped he'd reserved for Jack.

"Stick to the admitted evidence, counsel," he said to Jack.

Jack cleared his throat, his flow disrupted. That told me he'd planned a whole theme around the "discarded like garbage" image. I had to take my victories where I could now, though it gave me no satisfaction whatsoever.

"The truth is in her spilled blood. It's in her belongings left in that dreary hotel room. It's in the literal cries for help she uttered that went unheeded for so long. Heed them now. I beg you.

"The defendant is a liar. He lied to the police about where he was the night she disappeared. Only a guilty man would do that. He tried to get his friend to lie for him about his alibi. And he has a history of disrespect and lies to law enforcement going back nearly three decades.

"The defendant has even lied to his own family about the most horrific moment in their lives. He's responsible for what happened to the mother of his children and committed the most unconscionable act of having her lie to cover up for him on her literal death bed.

"Only a guilty, irredeemable man would do that. We have proven beyond any doubt that Joseph Leary is guilty of killing Sheila Brewer.

"Be her voice now. We have proven to you that Joseph Leary is a liar and a killer of women. It's up to you to bring him to justice and finally answer Sheila Brewer's cries for help with your verdict. Thank you."

Jack paused for a moment, nodded his head, then walked back to his table.

"Ms. Leary?" Judge Castor said.

"Ladies and gentlemen," I said. "My father is a bad man. He's led a life full of mistakes and regret. He may be judged for them. But as much as you may wish to punish him for the choices he's made and the people he's hurt, your job is to look at the facts presented, the evidence before you, and determine whether the state has met its burden of proof.

"They have to prove that my father willfully took Sheila

Brewer's life. And they must prove that beyond a reasonable doubt.

"The state cannot even prove that Sheila Brewer is dead. There is no body. There is blood. But you should have questions, doubts, a need for more answers.

"If Sheila Brewer was killed in that hotel room and then moved, why is the blood concentrated in that one spot? You heard the state's expert. To have suffered a wound of that nature, there should have been a blood trail leading out of the room. There wasn't. They have no answers for that.

"Mr. Leary has been consistent about his whereabouts the night whatever incident happened in room number seven. He wasn't there. Davy Monroe's testimony is a hot mess. I'll give you that. First he swore Mr. Leary was with him. Then he changed his mind. Again, more questions than answers.

"But here's what's not in dispute. There is no dispute that Mr. Leary was at Mickey's bar until the early morning hours of December 1st. There is no dispute that he went home with Davy Monroe after the bar closed. There is no dispute that he was not seen at Harmon Arms after the morning of the 30th. His bed there hadn't been slept in or disturbed in any way. The towels were clean as the maid left them the day before. It's unfortunate that we have no security footage from the corridor near room seven, but we have something else. You saw Mr. Leary leave in his car late Saturday morning. And he never came back. He wasn't there.

"You have more questions than answers. Any one of them raises reasonable doubt over the elements of murder.

"I agree with Mr. LaForge. Sheila Brewer deserves justice. Whatever may have happened to her, if she were mistreated or injured, someone should be held accountable. But the law is clear. You'll be instructed on it by the judge. The weight of the evidence lies heavily in the defendant's favor. The state cannot prove a murder took place. And they cannot prove that the defendant was anywhere near room number seven if it even happened. The only proper verdict in this case, despite whatever personal feelings you may have toward Joseph Leary, is not guilty.

"Thank you for your time, your patience, and your dedication to fulfilling your duties here today."

I squared my shoulders and walked back to the defense table. My father gave me a subtle, satisfied nod. It took everything in me to return it as I took my seat.

Chapter 41

THERE WAS no quick and easy verdict that afternoon. Deliberations went well into the dinner hour before they broke for the evening. There was nothing more I could do for myself or my family but work.

At my instruction, Tori set up an appointment for me to talk to Beth Chase. Beth was surprisingly eager to meet with me face to face. When we floated the idea past Alicia, she wanted the same. So at eleven o'clock the next morning, I would meet both women together.

I called Mara Brent's office just before they arrived.

"I didn't expect to hear from you this week," she said.

"Just trying to stay busy."

She paused for a beat, and then, "I'm the same way during deliberations. I just can't imagine what you must be going through considering it's your own family."

I laughed. "My family is ... prone to this kind of drama."

"Mmm," she said. "Well, I hope it works out for you. Whatever way this goes down."

"Thanks," I said. I didn't know Mara Brent well, but her sentiment seemed genuine and heartfelt. I appreciated it.

"We may have a lead on Alicia's mom," I said. "It's a thin strand, but Alicia agreed I should give you a call. My contact within the Evans family gave us something that panned out."

"Oh?"

I gave Mara the highlights of Tori's communication with Beth Chase. "The woman, Chase's aunt, would have been about the right age, and her falling off the family grid more or less tracks with the time frame of Alicia's gestation and birth."

"Wow," Mara said. "Can you share her name?"

I hesitated. "Not yet. The cousin is coming in with Alicia to meet with me in a few minutes, actually. Let me field this one. I don't think the cousin knows anything about this woman's current whereabouts but it's a start. I'll give you a call back."

I could hear Mara's breathing change and sensed she didn't like my answer.

"Look," I said. "It's better you let me take the lead on this. You're not law enforcement exactly, but you're in this in an official capacity. I'm not. I don't know where this is going to take us yet. Nothing I do needs a warrant. It's still my case, not yours."

"I get it," Mara said. "And you're probably right. I'm just ... well ... I'm not great at group projects."

This got a laugh out of me. "Fellow control freaks unite."

"Something like that."

"Listen," I said. "I have a strong feeling that this woman we're after doesn't want to be found. If we're right about the circumstances surrounding Alicia's conception, I don't blame her. I don't want to do anything too heavy-handed yet. For all we know, this is a setup. The woman may very well be in contact with the cousin already and she's sending her in for recon. If she catches wind of what we know, or that there's a curious prosecutor on the other end of this ... well ..."

"I get it. I get it," Mara said. "You're right. And I do trust you. You've been straight with me from the beginning when you didn't have to be. So has your client. She's remarkable, really."

"She is that," I said. "So just sit tight and I'll give you a call as soon as I know more. Deal?"

"Deal," Mara said. "And Cass ... I really meant what I said about your family and your verdict. I can't imagine what ... but just know you can call me if you need a favor. Heaven knows I'll owe you one after this."

"Thanks," I said. We said goodbye and clicked off. I had just enough time to gather my notes before Alicia and Beth Chase arrived. Separately, but within thirty seconds of each other.

I had Miranda show Alicia in first. She'd made a stunning transformation since the last time I saw her just a few weeks ago. Alicia had delivered her baby, a little girl, just two weeks prior. Though I could see the hallmarks of her sleepless nights, the woman positively glowed with the blush of new motherhood.

"Look at you!" I said smiling. I came around my desk and gave her a hug.

"How's the baby?"

"She's great," Alicia beamed. She produced a picture of her on her phone. In it, Alicia held a little pink bundle. The baby kept a tightly curled fist near her chin but stared straight at the camera with a pair of luminous, brown eyes.

"She's a beauty," I said.

"We named her Aniyah," Alicia said.

"That's beautiful," I gasped. "I can't wait to meet her sometime."

Alicia sat in one of my leather chairs along the back wall

of my office. This meeting needed to take place without the formal auspices of my giant, cherry wood desk.

"You ready for this?" I asked.

Smiling, Alicia gave me a nod. "All information is worth having as far as this goes," she said.

I admired her strength and told her so. Then I called down to Tori and told her to bring Beth Chase up to meet with us.

Alicia's hands trembled as she got back to her feet. My office door opened and Beth walked in. She had a nervous smile of her own, lighting a pleasant face with round features and dyed red hair that she wore in a short bob.

"Beth?" I said, extending my hand. "I'm Cass Leary. And this is my client, Alicia Romaine."

Beth froze for a moment, her eyes taking in every detail of Alicia. Then she blinked hard, fighting back tears.

"You ... I didn't know what to expect. But you look just like my Aunt Rhonda."

The words hit Alicia Romaine like a bullet to the chest. She took a step back; her hand fluttered to her heart. For a moment, I worried I'd made a huge mistake having her here for this. I should have met with Beth first.

"Let's sit and talk," I said.

Alicia nodded, her head moving in a circle. Then she sat back down and grabbed a tissue from the box I kept on the nearest end table.

"I'm sorry," Beth said. "I didn't mean to upset you. I swear I didn't walk up here thinking I'd react like this. But Aunt Rhonda, she was close to me and it's been so long since I've seen her. I thought maybe I'd forgotten what she looked like. But it's uncanny."

"Let's start from the beginning," I said.

"The DNA," Beth said. "Tree of Life. Did you know one

of the reasons I submitted mine is because I wondered if I might find Aunt Rhonda through it. This is the last thing I expected."

"Alicia," I said. "Are you okay?"

She nodded. "I just ... you know this isn't even about my birth mom," she said, gesturing to Beth. "Why I'm crying, I mean. It's just. It just hit me all of a sudden. We're related. Whether Rhonda is really my mother or not. We're cousins, aren't we?"

Beth smiled. She held her hands out and Alicia grasped them. "We are. Wow. Yes. We are."

"So tell us about your family," I said. "What you know of Rhonda Evans."

"Well," Beth started. "My mom, Janelle Evans Chase, and her were sisters. Though my mom was the second oldest of Marilyn Evans's children. She was something like twenty years older than Rhonda. They weren't very close growing up, obviously. My mom had moved out of the house long before ... um ... she did. My mom would be seventy-three if she were alive."

"I see," I said. "But you knew Rhonda. I have to admit. I've spoken to other members of the family, but no one has yet mentioned her."

I decided to keep my conversations with Newt out of it for now. I wanted to make sure Beth's story was consistent with what he told me and vice versa. I did the family math in my head. He would be Beth's uncle by marriage, but if I understood correctly, his wife had been the oldest sister. They might not have known each other well at all. Patricia Evans, Newt's late wife, would have been something like twenty-four years older than Rhonda.

"I didn't actually meet Rhonda or at least have any solid memories of her until I was maybe eight or nine," Beth continued. "She stayed with us for a little while. She and her mom, my grandma, weren't getting along at the time. Rhonda was just the coolest person to me. I guess she would have been sixteen or seventeen years old. She was so pretty. She had this big hair and wore what I thought were the best clothes. Though now we'd cringe. We're talking early eighties fashion."

I smiled. "I can imagine."

"Do you know what the trouble was with her mom?" Alicia asked.

"I don't know," Beth said. "My mom wasn't real specific. She was kind of annoyed with Rhonda. And it caused friction with my dad having her live with us, as you can imagine. She was such a free spirit, my aunt. She had her own car. It was this red Volkswagen Bug, of all things, with stickers all over it. That stuck out to me. Just having that kind of freedom. But she and my mom got into it a few times. She stayed with us for a summer, I think it was. Then she was just gone."

"She ran away?" I asked.

"I don't know. It was more that my parents had their fill. My understanding was that she went back to live with my grandma."

"This would be Miss Marilyn ... er ... Marilyn Evans?" I asked.

Beth cocked her head for an instant. "Uh ... yeah. Grandma Marilyn."

"Did you keep in contact after that?" I asked.

Beth shook her head. "Not at first. She sent me letters though. Birthday cards. She sent me candy on Halloween. Then it was postcards. She just asked how I was doing and would always tell me how pretty and smart she thought I was. That was nice. I didn't come here to dredge up all my own family problems, but I didn't get a lot of validation like that from my folks. So it was nice. I idolized Aunt Rhonda."

"When did you see her again?" I asked.

"She came to visit us again. It was the summer I turned thirteen. So let's see, Rhonda was probably nineteen or twenty at the time. She was different then. She seemed sad. Moody. Not at all as fun and free-spirited like I remembered. But I was a pretty sullen teenager myself at that point. I remember I got mad at her because she got into it when my parents were yelling at me about something. I don't even remember what. I think it was some show or party I wanted to go to with my friends and they said no. I remember Rhonda said I didn't know how lucky I had it and that I should listen to my parents. It stung."

"It's tough watching our kids grow up, I imagine," Alicia said.

"Right," Beth said. "I have a different perspective now, having teenagers of my own. Anyway, I never saw her again after that visit."

"Did something happen?" I ask.

Beth's face changed, growing darker. "That's what I never knew. We never saw her again. She just completely fell off the face of the earth, as far as I know. The letters and cards stopped coming. We lived near Columbus. My mom's family was all the way up near Grand Rapids. Dad always called them our weird Michigan relatives. We were closer to my dad's family than my mom's. We never really went to family stuff on the Evans' side. That's the other reason I submitted to Tree of Life. I know so little about them. My mom wasn't super warm to Grandma Marilyn either."

"Did you ever ask about Rhonda?" I asked.

Beth nodded. "A couple of times. My mom seemed unconcerned. She'd say, oh, she's off saving the rainforest, or something flippant like that. I asked my grandma one time and she said something that shocked me a little. She told me not to talk about her. I asked her why and my grandma got this teary-eyed look but she turned her back on me and walked out of the room. My mom told me not to upset Grandma because she was getting old. I just left it."

"That is strange," Alicia said.

It was strange to me too. Newt had never mentioned Rhonda or any falling out she had with Marilyn. I wondered if his wife Patricia had been under a similar embargo about talking about her. Was it possible he didn't even know as much as Beth did about her?

"Then I got this." Beth reached into her purse. She pulled out a crumpled letter on blue-and-white stationery.

A quick look of fear from Alicia, and I took the letter from Beth. I opened it carefully. In a scrawling hand, Rhonda Evans had written a simple note.

"I love you, kiddo. You're going to do great things one day. Keep writing. Your words will touch people's hearts. Talk to you soon, Love, Aunt Ron."

She'd drawn hearts beneath her signature. A faded strip of stiff, rectangular paper fluttered out. I picked it up off the ground. The paper contained three pictures of two young girls, one about nine years old, the other a teenager. I immediately recognized the child as Beth. My heart stuck in my throat as I studied the older girl. Beth was right: if this was Rhonda she was the spitting image of Alicia Romaine.

"That was from the first summer when Rhonda stayed with us. We had it taken at the county fair. I didn't even know she kept it," Beth said.

Alicia took the letter and the photo strip from me. Her hand went to her face as she saw the uncanny resemblance between her and the girl in the photos. Then she read the letter.

Alicia let out a breath, closing her eyes as she held the letter to her chest. "She was saying goodbye," she whispered. "The date on this letter is less than a month before I was born."

Chapter 42

ALICIA AND BETH talked for another hour, sharing family memories, laughing at each other's stories. I left them to it as I recorded what I could about Rhonda Evans. There were still so many unanswered questions. But I felt sure in my heart we'd found one huge piece of Alicia Romaine's family puzzle. We had a name. We had a timeline. I just prayed my suspicions weren't true and that Rhonda Evans was still very much alive somewhere.

Alicia and Beth made plans to keep in touch. Beth agreed to bring her husband and sons to the Romaine's coffee shop next week. As they left, Alicia gave me a knowing glance. At some point soon, we'd need to question Beth about who Alicia's father might be. Not yet though. There was still an active rape investigation in Maumee County that it could impact. I would touch base with Mara Brent again as well.

In the meantime, I left a message for Newt. I wasn't sure yet what I'd say. Now that I knew what Rhonda looked like, I really wanted to take a look at those photo albums he had. They could give us an even bigger clue as to what might have happened to Rhonda and when. She would have friends.

Yearbooks. Someone out there knew something about what happened to her. And as much as it could bring Alicia Romaine closure about her mom, it might also lead us straight to a killer.

I had the phone in my hand, ready to dial Newt's number. I didn't get the chance. I glanced at my phone. It was three o'clock in the afternoon when Tori came to my doorway, her expression dour.

"What is it?" I said.

"The foreman just reached out to the judge," she said. "There's a verdict in your dad's case."

Her words left a hollow pit in my stomach as I dropped my phone to the desk.

Chapter 43

JOE AND VANGIE arrived at the courthouse when I did. Joe's face was hard as steel. Vangie looked like she was barely holding it together. Again, I counted my blessings that Matty wasn't here. He had ten more days on his ninety-day rehab stint and was doing well, from what I knew. Whatever happened here today, I just prayed it wouldn't derail his recovery.

"Come on. I can give you guys ten minutes if you don't let on I'm the one who arranged it."

I looked up at one of the strapping deputies who'd been assigned to guard my dad all week.

He gestured toward the open doorway of the empty conference room beside Judge Castor's courtroom. The service elevator opened behind him and two more deputies brought my dad in, still in chains.

"Thank you," I said. "You're one of the good ones."

He shot me a wink and I jerked my chin at Joe and Vangie. Looking stunned, the pair of them filed into the conference room while the deputies led my father in behind me. This favor didn't allow us complete privacy. One deputy stood sentry inside the room while the other two took posts outside the door.

"What do you think this all means?" my father asked.

"They took their time," I said. "The jury deliberated for a day and a half. It could mean anything. And we'll know one way or the other any minute."

If he was nervous, he didn't show it. My brother turned to him. His granite jaw twitched.

"It doesn't matter," Joe said. "Whatever happens in there, whether you killed that woman or not, I hope they lock you away forever for what you did to Mom."

The deputy at the door had the decency to look away.

"Joe, stop," Vangie said. "What's the point now?"

"No," my dad said. "You came in here to have your say. So say it."

"You killed her. You might as well have murdered her. And you let us believe it was her mistake. You deserve to rot for that."

"It was her wish," my father said, keeping his voice low and steady. "She asked me to do it. For you. For all of you. She didn't want you to hate me."

"You got us to do that all on your own," Joe said.

"She wanted to give you a chance," Vangie spoke up. "She thought you'd turn your life around after she died. That's what it was, wasn't it?"

My father went mute. Vangie was right.

"It doesn't matter," Joe said. "Not to me. You're dead to me."

My father raised a hand. His handcuffs rattled and he scratched his chin. "You think you're a saint, son? How many hearts have you broken? Where's Josie, Emma's mom, right now? You ruined that girl when you got her pregnant."

"Joe!" I grabbed my brother by the shoulder. The deputy

moved forward. A gesture from me and he stood down.
For now.

"Don't," I said. "He's just trying to goad you. He's good at it. Don't give him that power over you anymore if you really want him to be dead to you."

"And what about you?" my father asked. "You've always thought you were better than me."

"Stop," I said. "You know what? I don't even blame you for lying about that car accident. I believe you that it was Mom's last wish. That was like her. Always trying to cover up your sins to protect you. I've been doing it too. Here. This whole trial."

"You know I didn't kill that woman!" he shouted, showing the first signs of cracking.

"Yeah. I actually do. Only you've told so many lies they're finally catching up to you."

"It's Davy," he said. "Look into it. Have your cop lover do his job and investigate him."

"My cop lover?" I put a hand up. "I'm not going to even dignify that with a response. I've been the biggest idiot of all in this. I did this for Matty, not you."

"I thought he was over it," my father said. "Guess I was wrong."

"Over what?" I said.

My father looked over his shoulder. "Not with him in here. This is a privileged conversation."

"Not with all of us here," I said. "If there's something you want to say to me in confidence, I'm afraid everybody else has to leave."

"No," Joe said. "No way I'm leaving you alone with this asshole ever again."

My father pursed his lips. "Fine." He leaned in close, waving me forward.

"Oh for Pete's sake," I said. I leaned forward so he could whisper in my ear.

"I had a thing with Kim Monroe, Davy's wife."

"You what?" I asked. "And you're just now telling me this?"

"Respect for the dead," my father said. "I'm an honorable man, whether you believe it or not."

My jaw dropped. I shook my head. Joey's nostrils flared and he curled his fists at his sides.

"When?" I asked.

My father shrugged. "A long time ago. After your mother. Maybe seventeen, eighteen years ago. You two were out of the house. And things weren't great between Davy and Kim at the time. She was about to throw him out for drinking."

I sputtered. "So she thought *you* were a better alternative?"

"I was on the wagon. She came to me for advice. One thing led to another. It was brief. Only a couple of weeks before we both realized it was a bad idea. No one knew. Kim took it to her grave. But I've had a lot of time to think in here. Maybe she told Davy. Or maybe he found out some other way. Whatever it was, he's trying to screw me now and he thinks he's got a reason. If I could just talk to him ..."

My brother stared hard at me. I couldn't tell if he'd overheard my father's little revelation about Kim Monroe or not. Did it matter?

"You know?" I said. "In the end, it's your narcissism that'll be your undoing. Not your drinking. And not even your lies."

He scowled at me. We sat in silence for a moment. "But you'll look into it?"

I hadn't spoken to Eric since right after the trial started. I had no idea whether the department would pursue Davy

Monroe for obstruction of justice. Regardless of the lies my dad told, I knew they probably should.

"I'll pass the information along," I said. "But it's not up to me."

"We'll appeal," Dad said, once again missing the ever-loving point. "If they convict me, I want you writing it up by the end of the day."

"Like hell she will!" Joe said. He lost it then. He vaulted over the table and lunged at my father.

Vangie cried out. I pulled at Joe's shirt.

The deputy moved with the force of a freight train and shoved my brother back against the wall.

Joe had gone feral. His eyes glinted and spit flew out of his mouth.

"Enough!" I said.

"We're done, Joseph," my brother said, refusing to call our father Dad anymore. "Cass is done. Call someone else to clean up your messes from now on."

My father sat back and smirked. In another second, the deputy would have to hold me back right along with Joey.

There was a sharp knock on the door and another of the deputies opened it.

"They're ready for you all now," he said.

My heart flipped. This was it.

My brother composed himself. My father rose and let the deputies lead him into the hallway. I took my brother and sister by the hand and the three of us walked into Judge Castor's courtroom together.

Chapter 44

TIME NEVER MOVES SLOWER than waiting for a jury to file in. It doesn't matter how well you think you've presented your case. It doesn't matter if it's a civil or criminal trial. The simple sounds, papers rustling, the faint coughs of a handful of people in the gallery as they shift nervously in their seats, the echoing footsteps of the bailiff and then the jurors themselves as they file into the courtroom and hand over their power. It all fades away under the pounding of your heart.

It's a myth that you can read something in their faces. I've won and lost trials from jurors who made eye contact with me or avoided it when they took their seats and waited for the judge. I've seen them smile, glare, and even shed tears whether they've handed me victory or defeat.

I could not read them that day either. I could only stand beside my father as they stood in unison and Judge Castor took the bench.

"Ladies and gentlemen of the jury, have you reached your verdict?"

"We have," the foreman said. It wasn't who I expected.

This was juror number eight, a middle-aged woman who worked in a candy shop on the other side of town.

She handed her verdict form to the bailiff, who brought it over to the judge. Castor's face was similarly unreadable as he looked it over and handed it to his clerk. She waited a beat as the court reporter repositioned her fingers on her keyboard.

"You may read the verdict into the record," Castor said.

My father took a breath. Then he slipped his hand into mine and squeezed. He was shaking. His bravado fell away. He became a human being, only it was far too late now. Still, I felt my mother there that day, which made me sad. Despite all of his faults. His lies, his deceit, his unforgivable sins. She loved him. It was her downfall.

"In case 19-3402-FY, the People of the State of Michigan versus Joseph Patrick Leary, we the jury on count one of the complaint, murder in the first degree of Sheila Ellen Brewer in violation of MCL 750.316 find the defendant, Joseph Patrick Leary, guilty as charged."

I heard a rushing sound as my heart began to beat again. My father's grip tightened, cutting off the circulation to my fingers.

The judge asked the members of the jury if their verdict was unanimous. It was. When polled, each and every juror answered in the affirmative.

My father crumpled beside me. I heard the heavy court-room door open and close. I didn't have to turn my head to know it was my brother Joe who had left. He had seen what he came here to see. He didn't make idle threats. As that door slammed shut, I knew he'd walked out on Dad for the last time. The question was, would I?

"Son of a bitch," he muttered. He said it over and over again as the jury was dismissed. I stood mute, bearing the bone-crushing grip of my father.

Jack turned to me; his expression was pained. I was grateful for that in the end. No matter what else happened here today, my family would never be the same.

But I'd done all I could for Joe Sr. He may be innocent of this crime, but his actions had sealed his fate, not mine.

When the deputies came to take him back to his cell, he dropped to his seat, his face ashen. He was sweating.

"Joe?" one of the bailiffs said. "You okay?"

"He's hyperventilating," I said. "Dad ..."

I stopped myself. In my mind, I heard myself say that it was going to be okay. I know it's what he wanted to hear. He begged me for it with his eyes. Dammit if my heart didn't break a little for him. Even after everything that happened.

"You'll do what I asked?" he said. "Talk to your friend. Tell him what I told you. Look into it. I swear. You have to have them look into it."

"I'll tell them," I said. I left out the rest of it. I could make no promises it would do any good.

The judge set sentencing for one week from today. A formality. My father had just been convicted of first-degree murder. It carried a mandatory life sentence with no chance for parole.

As they led my father away in chains, he looked back at me one last time and flashed the smile that used to melt my mother's heart. For me, I could only feel the cold.

Chapter 45

"Don't worry about Joe," I told Vangie. He'd been her ride to the courthouse. I took her out the back way. Not that my father's case had garnered much more press than local news and an MLive reporter, but Vangie herself was a bit of a local celebrity now for her own recent legal entanglements.

"I'm not worried about Joe," she said. "But I think somebody needs to tell Matty before he gets out of Maple Valley. I don't know. I think it's a safer environment for him there. Better he has the support of professionals as he tries to process everything."

"Agreed," I said. "I'll make arrangements to see him sometime tomorrow."

"No," she said. "I didn't mean you. I meant me. Let me do it. He's ... Cass ... don't take this the wrong way. But he worries about disappointing you more than he does me. It can be a trigger for him."

I damn near slammed on the brakes when she said it. "I'm a trigger?"

"Cass, I said don't take it the wrong way. It's not a bad thing. He loves you. He wants you to be proud of him. He needs people in his life who hold him accountable like you do. But for this one, I think maybe it's better if he hears it from somebody he won't feel bad about falling apart in front of."

My head started to pound. "Fine," I said. "Be my guest. It'll be one less thing on my plate."

"I love you," Vangie said. I'd just pulled in to her driveway. It had been my driveway too for the past six months. I was grateful, but the thought of spending the night here later felt stifling. My office couch was looking better and better.

"I'll see you later, okay?" she said, leaning in to hug me. "Will you at least have dinner with Jessa and me? She misses you. The dogs miss you. Then if you wanna disappear, I totally get that."

Looking at my sweet sister's face, I felt guilty. "Yes," I said. "You, Jessa, and the dogs are about all the family I can handle tonight. Thanks. You want me to pick up Louigi's?"

"Sounds great," she said. "And take a few days off after this if you can. You deserve it."

I could see the rest of her thoughts written on her face. To her I know I looked like hell.

I hugged my little sister one more time then drove back to the sanctity of the Leary Law Group building. Tori, Miranda, and Jeanie waited for me in the lobby. They were as much family to me as anyone who shared my blood.

"Tough break, kiddo," Jeanie said. "Though I can't say it was a shocker. Old Joe's been shooting himself in the foot since day one."

"I know. He told me today he had an affair with Kim Monroe something like fifteen years ago. He's wondering if Davy found out about it and that's why he turned on him on the witness stand."

"Sheeit," Jeanie said. "Fat lot of good that little nugget does him now. You could have cross-examined Davy with it."

"Do you really think it would have helped?" Miranda asked.

Jeanie and I looked at each other. We answered in unison. "No."

Still, it illustrated my problem from the beginning. I'd been hamstrung by my client's lies from the word go.

"If you feel like working," Miranda said. "Mara Brent has called a couple of times."

I took the pink messages from Miranda. "Thanks," I said.

"Unless she's calling to gloat," Jeanie said wryly.

"No," I said. "That isn't the vibe I've gotten from her at all. Alicia wants me to share what we learned about Rhonda Evans. She's ready to let that investigation go forward, no matter what it brings."

"Hmm," Jeanie said. She shook her head. "Fathers. Lately all they are is trouble."

I couldn't argue. I climbed the stairs and retreated to my office. I kicked off my heels and put my feet up on the desk as I dialed Mara Brent's cell number. She answered on the second ring.

"You holding up okay?" she asked.

I sighed. "So the Delphi rumor mill has already spread across the Ohio border?"

Mara laughed. "Small world, Cass. And I'm sorry. For you and your family."

"I appreciate that," I said. Mara's voice held genuine concern.

"Listen," I said. "We should probably meet about all of this, but I'm planning on hiding in a cave for a few days."

"Ah," she said. "Post-trial hermit plan. I know it well."

"I just wanted to pass along a few things we've uncovered on Alicia Romaine's paternity search. She's okayed me talking to you."

"Oh?" Mara said. I heard her chair squeak which told me she must have sat upright.

"We think we've cracked who her birth mother was. There's a woman by the name of Rhonda Evans who lived in Kentwood, Michigan. Just south of Grand Rapids. She was Marilyn Evans's youngest daughter. She'd be about fifty-one now. As near as I can figure, she lived in Kentwood her whole life. It tracks with where Alicia was born. Rhonda had a brief stint in Columbus, Ohio when she was nineteen or just twenty. Some trouble at home and she went to live with Beth Chase, the daughter of her second oldest sister. We met with Beth. She's the one who filled all of these blanks in."

"It tracks?" Mara asked. "This Rhonda Evans?"

"It does. I mean, I've still got to work a few angles on it. This isn't confirmed, of course. But Rhonda is the best candidate we've found. Beth said she basically dropped out during the time frame Alicia would have been gestating. And Beth got a letter from her dated just before Alicia would have been born. It was a goodbye letter. As far as I know, no one in the family had any contact with her after that."

"Do you have any information like a social security number, work history, anything like that?" Mara asked.

"No," I said. "But I've told you about my contact within the family, Newt. The one married to the oldest sister, Patricia. He still lives in Marilyn's, the grandmother's, house. I got the impression the sisters gave him some friction about that, but he cared for old Marilyn in her final illness. Anyway, with the trial and everything, I haven't had a chance to touch base with him about Rhonda. I'm not sure he ever even knew her well. But if there are any records left on her, Newt would likely be the last one to have access to them."

"Good," Mara said. "Keep me posted with whatever you find out. I have a few favors I can call in. If this Rhonda Evans was a runaway or had some family trouble, maybe some of it made it into the legal system. Even if she was a minor, I think I can pull some strings and see what's what."

"That'd be great, Mara. Thank you."

"It's my pleasure," she said. "Maybe between the two of us we can get some justice for Denise Silvers or closure for Alicia Romaine. Even if it's more than she bargained for. You could use a win."

I paused. It was odd to think of tracking down Alicia's possibly homicidal birth father as a win. But I suppose in a way it was.

"It would be nice for things to feel right with the world for a change," I said.

"Let me know what you find out," Mara said. "I'll do the same."

I hung up and pushed myself away from my desk. I knew I should try to track down Joe. I should check in with Vangie and see if she ran into any trouble getting permission to visit Matty tomorrow. There was a string or two I could pull there myself.

Instead, I turned as Jeanie came to the door. She held two Styrofoam cups in her hands and I knew they contained something far stronger than coffee.

"Bless you, woman," I said. Smiling, she came in and gave me both cups.

Irish whiskey. The good stuff. I downed them both. She produced the bottle and filled one of the cups again and took the other for herself.

"Cheers, kid," she said. "And to hell with the rest of it." Smiling, I touched my cup to hers.

Chapter 46

I woke with a bear of a hangover the next morning. Jeanie and I killed the bottle of whiskey together. I slept on my office couch, she was camped out on the floor snoring.

When my phone rang beside me, it felt like my skull turned to glass and shattered. The thing vibrated off the table and hit the floor. Jeanie snored straight through it.

I checked the caller ID. It was Vangie.

"Terrific," I muttered. Fur had grown on my teeth overnight. I smelled bad.

"Lord," I whispered as I found my feet and got up.

Mistake. I sank back down to the couch.

"Jeanie!" I whispered. It was seven o'clock in the morning. Miranda and Tori would be here within the hour.

Moaning, she rolled to her side. She opened her eyes. For an instant, she didn't seem to recognize me. Then clarity came back and she sat bolt upright.

"We good?" she asked, her tone more clear and bright than I could muster.

She was on her feet, finger-combing her short hair and straightening her jacket.

"How the hell do you do that?" I asked. I swore, if Jeanie had to walk into court in five minutes, she'd have been knife-sharp. And yet, I knew she drank me entirely under the table last night.

"You look awful, kid," she said.

"That's your fault. You're a bad influence, Jeanie Mills."

Smiling, she held her hand out to mine. "Go grab a shower. I'll tell Miranda to bring you a change of clothes on the way in. I'm guessing you don't feel like facing the family firing squad."

"You guessed right. I'm gonna be in trouble as it is. I promised Vangie I'd eat dinner with her and Jessa last night."

Jeanie waved a dismissive hand. "She'll understand. She's just worried about you. Miranda will smooth things over for you. And that's about enough crying in our cups for a lifetime. You need to get back to work."

She was right. But first, I needed a damn toothbrush and shower.

I disappeared into the second-floor bathroom and took care of it. By the time I finished, Jeanie had set out an emergency change of clothes courtesy of Tori. It wasn't pretty. Track pants and a University of Michigan tee-shirt. But it was clean and I could go incognito on the way back home.

"When the hell is your new construction gonna be finished, anyway?" Jeanie said. She waited for me downstairs in the lobby with two fresh Styrofoam cups. This time, filled with coffee. "Do I need to go medieval on some contractors?"

"Not yet," I said. "They were delayed a couple of weeks. Some trouble at the lumberyard. But they're pouring the foundation the day after tomorrow."

"Good," she said. "Whatcha got planned for the day?"

I filled her in on my conversation with Mara Brent.

"I need to call my buddy Newt," I said. "See what he knows about Rhonda Evans."

"Fine," she said. "Then your ass is outta here. I insist. Take a four-day weekend. Get outta town. I don't care where. Don't answer the phone to anyone named Leary for at least twenty-four hours."

"That, my friend, sounds like heaven." The coffee tasted like heaven too as I made my way back to my office.

I got out a pen and notepad as I dialed Newt's number. I couldn't help but smile when he answered with his usual, "Hallo, dare!"

"Hey, Newt," I said. "It's Cass."

"Haven't heard from you for a while. Was about to send out a search party. You okay, honey?"

He sounded just like my grandfather. It was nice. But no sooner had I thought it than my actual family reality dragged me down. I wondered what Grandpa and Grandma Leary would have made of my father's current mess.

"Just busy," I said. "But I think I may have made some headway on your family front. I met with one of Marilyn's granddaughters. Janelle's daughter? She was one of the names you gave us though her number had changed. Took some doing to track her down. She also popped up on that ancestry site as one of my client's cousins."

"Huh," he said. "You say her number changed? That's odd."

"It's okay. She was very helpful. She had some information about another sister. Miss Marilyn's youngest. Rhonda? You hadn't mentioned her. I was wondering if maybe she was out of the picture before you and Patricia married."

"Rhonda? Marilyn didn't have a daughter named Rhonda."

I paused. "I saw a picture of her. And one of her letters.

She and Beth Chase were close for a while. Rhonda actually stayed with her family one summer probably thirty-five years ago. Beth said she believed Miss Marilyn and Rhonda had a falling out."

"Rhonda?"

"Yes," I said. Newt sounded confused. Then he shouted into the phone loud enough to make me jump.

"Oh, you mean Bean!"

"Bean?"

"Yeah. Miss Beanie. I did tell you about her."

I flipped through my notes to the ones I'd taken months ago when I first contacted Newt. Then I looked at the family tree Tori drew up.

There was no Rhonda listed on Newt's notes, just on Tori's tree. But I had written a note about Bean. It was hard to read my own handwriting, but it looked like I'd written she died as an infant.

"Newt," I said. "I thought you told me Bean died before her first birthday."

"I don't think I said that," he answered. "Miss Marilyn had a baby before my Patricia. First one was stillborn. That was the story I was always told."

My head pounded even louder. We'd had so many conversations and Newt rambled on during most of them. It was no wonder I didn't track that story. "So Bean wasn't the stillborn baby? She was another sister?"

"Yeah," Newt said. "Haven't seen her in a real long time. Only met her once or twice actually. She was a wild one. Incorrigible."

"Newt," I said. "Beth Chase says that my client, Alicia, is the spitting image of Rhonda Evans. Er … Bean. Do you think you've got anything Miss Marilyn might have kept about her? A birth certificate. Photo albums. It would be of

tremendous help if we could find out what happened to
her."

Newt got quiet. I could hear him breathing through the
phone.

"Patricia didn't talk about her much."

"That tracks with what Beth said about her mom, Janelle,
and the one time she asked her grandma, Miss Marilyn. She
said her mom always changed the subject."

"Well, ain't that something," he said. "You know, that's
pretty much how Patricia was about her. Though I can't say I
did a lot of asking. I'm afraid I don't know Beth Chase or her
mama well at all. I mean, I know Janelle's dead."

"That's okay. I'm more interested in trying to find out
whether Miss Marilyn might have kept any of Rhonda's, er ...
Bean's things. Would you mind taking a look?"

"Why, sure," he said. "Tell you what. Give me a day or
two. Then I'll bring them to you. It's high time I took you out
to lunch, little lady. It's been a real treat helping out. I just
hope I can come through on this."

"Newt, that's not necessary."

"I insist. I got me a doctor's appointment in Ann Arbor on
Monday. Arthritis. They're maybe gonna give me a new right
knee. Aw, hell, you don't need to know that. What's say we
have lunch after? I'll meet you halfway to Delphi. Isn't there a
diner off M-50 near there? Doolittle's?"

"Sure," I said. "It's called Dooley's. Yes, it's right off
M-50."

"Perfect. I'll put it in my GPS. How the hell we ever
found anything without those things. I'll bring you whatever I
find on Bean. Seems to me there's at least some school stuff.
Miss Marilyn saved all that crap. I'm pretty sure I know
where Bean's box might be."

My pulse quickened. We were getting somewhere.

"Great," I said. "Bring it with you if it's not too much trouble."

"Feel like the Hardy Boys and Nancy Drew," he said.

"Me too," I smiled.

"All righty," he said. "See you in a couple of days, Nancy Drew."

When we clicked off, I left a message for Alicia. I wouldn't tell her the details until after I met with Newt. But for the first time in ages, I felt like I might pull out a win.

Chapter 47

Saturday morning, I rode up the dingy steel elevator to the third floor of the Delphi Public Safety Building. I insisted on meeting Eric in his office as he was covering the weekend shift.

"It's like a tomb in here," I said. The detective bureau was set up like a bullpen. The junior detectives and those working property crimes occupied the cubicles in the center. The senior homicide detectives, of which Eric was one, had the bordering offices with the window views overlooking the parking lot and trash bins. The lieutenant had the corner office with the view of downtown Delphi in the distance.

"I like it this way," he said. "It's quiet. I get most of my stuff done."

"I wondered why you were giving up your weekend."

It was good to see him. I didn't like being at cross purposes with a man I considered a dear friend. Eric stood in the doorway, lips pursed as he decided whether to break into a smile.

"Come on in," he said. "I'll give you the grand tour."

I hadn't actually been inside Detective Wray's office yet. When we met on official business, it was generally at the coffee shop kitty-corner to the courthouse. When it was informally, he preferred Mickey's bar.

"I like what you've done with the place," I said.

Eric's paneled walls were sparse. He had a few federal commendations from various task forces he served on. In the corner, I spotted a box of plaques and a silver platter. I leaned down and picked one up. The engraving in the pewter recognized Eric for his service in the vice-narcotics unit before he moved over to crimes to persons.

"Have a seat," he said, clearing a chair for me in front of his desk. It had previously held stacks of file folders.

"We're still digitizing a bunch of the older stuff," he said. "Sorry things are kind of a mess."

"You're like me," I said. "Something tells me you know where to find every scrap of paper in here."

He smiled. Eric had few framed pictures on his desk. I spotted one of him with his father on a fishing trip. Eric was younger, his hair darker and his face thinner. I'd never realized how much he resembled Kevin Wray. I remembered Mr. Wray as a hulking, serious man. He ran an auto body shop on McCallister street. Wray's Body Shop. His father before him started the business. I knew Eric's becoming a cop had been a blow to the family.

The other photo was taken on Eric's wedding day. It was shoved in the corner on the credenza behind him, almost as an afterthought. In it, he looked like how I remembered him from high school. The rugged, athletic cool kid with spiky dark hair and a dashing smile. Back then, I didn't think he'd ever give me the time of day. Now though, it was as if we were two different people, and yet exactly the same.

"I'm sorry about your dad," he said. "I really do mean that. How's Matty taking it all?"

I shrugged. "I haven't talked to him directly. He's still at

Maple Valley for another few days. Vangie said he seemed pretty level. He's got a plan to live in a sober house for a few months."

"That's great," Eric said. "He's never done anything like that?"

I shook my head. "No Leary has ever done anything like that. I'm hopeful."

"I'm not sure if this is what you wanted to talk to me about, but the department isn't going to pursue the issue with your mom's accident."

I took a breath. To be honest, I hadn't really given thought to that aspect of my dad's many bombshells.

"Thank you," I said. "I think. I don't even know why I'm saying that. He killed my mother. I should want justice for her. I mean, I do ..."

"It's complicated," he said. "By all accounts she'd forgiven him. And was more worried about what happened to him than herself."

"That was always her downfall."

"Don't let it be yours," he said, leveling those piercing eyes at me. He didn't break his gaze even as I tried to lighten the mood with a smile.

"I know," I said. "Lesson hard learned. Except for one thing. One last promise I sort of made."

Eric's eyes narrowed. "Why do I already know I'm not going to like this?"

"Davy Monroe," I said. "Can you share with me what's happening to him?"

Eric raised a brow. "What do you mean?"

"He made false statements to the cops. Are you pursuing an obstruction of justice charge?"

"That's going to be up to the prosecutor's office," he said.

"Don't give me that. I know if you wanted to push it, you could."

He folded his hands and rested them on his desk. "We still don't know what happened to Sheila Brewer."

"Exactly," I said. "Whether you believe my father was truly guilty or not, there are still some unanswered questions. Is her family pressuring you to pursue them?"

"Cass," he said. "We're getting into some dangerous territory. You know there are things I can't discuss with you. And every time we have a conversation about the Brewer case, it puts me in a difficult position."

"I know. And I'm sorry about that. Look, I'll just cut to the chase. My father told me something on the eve of the verdict that may or may not be relevant. He gave me permission to share it with you alone. He told me he and Kim Monroe had a brief affair about fifteen years ago. He didn't think Davy ever found out about it. But ..."

"But," Eric finished for me. "If Davy was looking for a reason to cause trouble for your dad, that'd be about as good a one as a man could have."

"Exactly."

"Shit," Eric said. He let out an exasperated breath and rubbed his thumb over his chin. "How do you know your dad isn't lying about that? With his track record ..."

"You're right," I said. "I don't. And he might be. It's just ... something never sat right with me about what Davy did. I know you, the jury, and everyone else has their mind made up. But I believed him the first time."

"Well, I didn't," he said. "I'm sorry, but you're never going to convince me that your dad's innocent on this one. And you couldn't convince a jury either."

That wall of tension between us went back up. I hated it, but there it was.

"I know," I said. "And pretty soon I'll be done trying. I don't expect you to help me prove my dad's innocent. I'll be honest. I don't know how much farther I'm willing to go with any of this."

"Your brother Joe's already cut him off, Cass," Eric said. "You should follow him."

"I probably will. That's the truth. I'm not like Matty. I refuse to let Joe Sr.'s sins ruin my life. But I'm not talking about his sins now. I'm talking about Davy Monroe's. I believe in my heart that he knows more about what happened that night than he's telling. I *know* you're looking into the obstruction charge. You have that power. So I'm just asking ... take a harder look at Davy. What he did that night. The weeks leading up to Sheila's disappearance."

"You mean murder," Eric said.

"Fine," I said. "It's not about my dad. Not directly. Would you believe that for me, it's about Sheila?"

Eric let out a bitter laugh. "No."

"Well, it is. It's just ... it's a feeling I have about Davy. That's all. I think he's worth having another conversation with. Do what you do, Eric. Interrogate him. Charge him with the crime we both know he committed. See if anything shakes out."

Something changed in his face. It was subtle. Just the curving of his mouth.

"Son of a bitch," I said, smiling. "I think you already are."

Eric stayed stoic. I knew to quit while I was ahead.

"I'll see you around, Wray," I said.

"You're an impossible woman."

"I know," I said. I left him there shaking his head as I turned and walked out.

Chapter 48

DOOLEY'S DINER was mostly a carry-out place. They made some of the best fried chicken in Michigan. I walked in and waited for Newt at one of the only five tables in the tiny space, facing the front door.

I checked my phone. He was ten minutes late. Only one other patron sat at the counter. He was handsome, almost a Lance Armstrong doppelganger, tall, lanky, but well built, with thinning blond hair, tanned skin, and dressed neatly in blue jeans and a purple golf shirt with a collar that looked like it had been ironed.

He was currently charming the waitress who blushed as she turned away from him, her smile reaching ear to ear.

At twenty minutes past the hour, I had the feeling I'd been stood up. I checked my phone for missed calls. Finding none, I dialed Newt's number, thinking maybe he either forgot or got held up at his doctor's appointment. Either way, I could only afford to stay another twenty minutes or so myself. I had a hearing on a discovery motion at eleven o'clock and was hoping to catch opposing counsel in the hall so we could maybe settle the case once and for all.

As I waited for Newt to pick up or at least to get to his voicemail, the tanned golf shirt guy's phone started ringing. He looked at the screen, smiled, then said "Hallo, dare!

"Um ... hi?" I said.

He turned on his stool, still flashing that dazzling smile that made the waitress blush. He put his phone down and started walking toward me.

I rose and put my hand out. This was Newt?

"Wow," I said. "I guess I had a completely different picture of you in my mind. I thought you'd be ... older." The man standing in front of me had one of those youthful faces like a game show host.

"I'm Cass," I said. "Nice to finally meet you."

Laughing, Newt took my hand and shook it. "Pleasure's mine."

We said a few more awkward introductions, and Newt took his seat beside me. He had a brown accordion file tucked under his arm and he placed it on the chair next to him.

"How old are you?" I asked. I couldn't help myself.

"Sixty-one," he said.

Now that he'd said it, I could see the lines in his face that bore it out. Still, from a distance, he could have easily passed for thirty years younger.

"How's your knee?" I asked.

He extended it and I heard a loud crack. "Hopeless," he said. "They're going to go ahead and give me a new one. No more marathons for me."

Had he said that to me over the phone, I would have thought he was joking. Now, seeing him in the flesh, I knew he was dead serious. The man had the physique of a runner.

"Thanks for coming out," I said. "And I'm sorry I didn't realize that was you for so long."

"I kind of wondered," he said. "I suppose I should have said something sooner. You probably need to skedaddle."

"I have a little time yet," I said. "Were you able to bring anything interesting regarding Rhonda Evans?"

Newt looked at the file he'd brought. "I was kind of hoping you'd bring your client with you."

I sipped my coffee. "Not yet. We're still not completely sure that Rhonda is the woman she's looking for. She's had a lot of disappointment. And we don't even know if Rhonda is alive or dead. It's a lot to process."

"Understand," he said. He picked up the file and pulled out a colored stack of cardboard from a thin photo album.

"There's not much," he said. "Like I told you on the phone, Patricia and Miss Marilyn didn't talk about Bean too much. But I did find these."

He slid the stack of stiff blue paper across the table. They were report cards. He had Rhonda's grades all the way through elementary and high school. I took a glance and immediately noticed a pattern. "Bean" had been a straight-A student until her senior year in high school.

"And these," he said.

He gave me two letters. One had been torn into five pieces then taped back together. It was an acceptance letter from the University of Michigan. The other was a scholarship award letter. Bean had been offered a full ride as part of the swimming and diving team.

"Diving," I said, my heart racing. "Rhonda was a diver?"

Newt shrugged then looked at the paper. "Yeah. I can't tell you much about that though. Patricia had so many sisters, you know? And she wasn't close to Bean. Like I said, they didn't talk about her. But yeah, there were trophies and medals in the attic. Bean won a lot of championships."

"I'll be damned," I said. I knew a lot of women divers started out as gymnasts.

"Would she have been a gymnast perhaps when she was younger?"

Newt shrugged. "Could be. That would have been before my time."

"This is really helpful, Newt. All of this fits from the non-identifying information my client received. I really think we're on to something."

"But you still don't know what happened to her? To Bean?"

"I've got a colleague working another angle on that. But it would help a lot if I had a social security number. Exact date of birth, that kind of thing."

Newt opened the thin photo album. It was a baby book. I smiled as he turned the album toward me. Bean's thin plastic infant wristband from the hospital was clipped inside. All the important dates were there. Her birth date. Her immunization record.

"This is amazing!"

I flipped through the yellowing pages. Rhonda was a pretty, intelligent-looking child with dark-blonde hair and bright-green eyes. She looked so much like Alicia it startled me.

"Miss Marilyn did all of this?" I said turning page after page of Bean's accomplishments. She *was* a young gymnast. There were pictures of her on podiums collecting first-place medals. She was young in those though. They appeared to stop by the time she hit puberty. I guessed that might have been when she switched to diving.

The final layout in the book was titled "Sweet Sixteen." There was a photo of Rhonda dangling keys in her hand as she got ready to drive off. Then in the last picture she wore a peach ruffled bridesmaid's dress, standing in a row with all of her sisters. The groom was a much younger Newt. He cut a dashing figure, his beaming smile lighting up the page. He'd been underwear-model gorgeous in his youth.

The caption below read: "Neil and Patricia – June 14, 1984."

"Handsome groom," I said. "Neil. How'd you get to be Newt?"

He smiled. "Just a childhood nickname that stuck."

"Well, this is going to be incredibly helpful. I really appreciate it. Can I borrow all of this?"

He took the documents from me, slipped them back in the accordion file, and slid them across the table.

"Be my guest. I'd like to track down Bean as much as anyone. They're all gone now. All the sisters. Patricia, Janelle. Connie and Frannie both died of ovarian cancer before they turned sixty. It runs in the family. Your client should know that. I think there're tests they can do. So other than Bean, if she's around somewhere, that just leaves Lucy Ann. And she's got dementia. Poor thing. Only seventy years old."

It occurred to me that Newt at sixty-one had been something like fourteen years his wife Patricia's junior. Go Patricia, I thought.

"Can you imagine that?" he asked. "Eight sisters. All but one is still alive. Or maybe two. We don't know about Bean."

"No," I said. "That we don't." Though I wasn't optimistic based on the letter Beth had.

"Well," he said. "You let me know, will ya?"

"Of course." I tucked the accordion file into my bag. I hated to cut our meeting short, but I had to get to court.

"Newt," I said, extending my hand again. "Thank you. You have no idea what this could mean for my client."

His hand lingered in mine. His eyes twinkled when he smiled.

"For me too. Miss Marilyn didn't have much. But if there's anything at the house Bean might want if you can find her, she's welcome to it. The sisters didn't like me too much after Patricia and me moved back in with Marilyn. Then Patricia died. They thought I was taking advantage of Miss Marilyn. But it's what she wanted. Nobody else stepped up to take care of her and I promised Patricia."

That gave me another thought. "Neil ... er ... Newt ... was there an estate opened up when Miss Marilyn died? Her probate lawyer would have had to have made attempts to find Rhonda to notify her of it."

Newt shook his head. "No. Nothing like that. She put everything into a trust and left me in charge. And I never once kept anything from those girls, those who were still alive at the time. Most of Miss Marilyn's money went to her medical bills. All the personal items in the house I left for the girls to pick through. Those who cared, did. And that's what I'd like for Bean if she's still around. I'd like to see her. And if your client is really Bean's daughter, then she should come to the house and see if there's anything of Miss Marilyn's she wants. There's still some china. Her silver. Some jewelry."

"You know," I said. "That's really kind of you. I can't speak for my client on that, but I think she'd really love to see other family photos if you'd be willing to share."

"Of course," he said. "And you give her that baby book from me. It's hers to keep. I mean, unless we find Bean and she wants it."

"Newt, you've been so helpful through all of this. I really appreciate it. On my client's behalf as well. I think if she were here she'd want to hug you."

Now it was his turn to blush. "I'll tell ya what. I'll take

one from you on her behalf. If I'm not being too forward. I bet you've got a mom and dad out there who are darn proud of you, Cass. I know I would be if I were your dad."

His statement was a kindness. The sweetest of compliments, but when he said it, I felt a thousand tiny knife points slice straight through my heart. Tears welled up unbidden. I blinked hard to keep them at bay.

Newt noticed something. We rose out of our chairs in unison. His movements were awkward, but I believe heartfelt as he gave me a gentle hug.

"You're a good egg, Cass," he said. "Your client is lucky to have you."

"Thanks, Newt," I said, forcing a smile. I would not fall apart here in the middle of Dooley's Diner.

Chapter 49

I said my goodbyes to Newt with a promise I'd keep him posted if his information led us to Rhonda Evans. I was hopeful it would. And if we could prove once and for all that she was indeed Alicia's mother, even if she were no longer living, that baby scrapbook would mean everything to Alicia. At least it would be something tangible for her to hold on to.

I waved to him from the diner window as he got into his white Buick and pulled out of the parking lot.

"Do you want more coffee?" the waitress asked. I stood at the counter.

"No," I said. "I just need to make a quick call then I'll be on my way."

I sat at the counter and dialed Mara Brent.

"Your ears must be burning," she said as she answered.

"Oh?" I said.

"I was literally just picking up my phone to call you."

I checked my watch. I had maybe ten minutes to spare to fill her in. "I had a meeting with Newt Samuels. He gave me some great stuff Marilyn Evans left behind about Rhonda

Evans. Some of it fits what Alicia's birth mom reported to the adoption agency. She won a diving scholarship to U. of M. And she was a decorated gymnast as a pre-teen. I mean, it's not exactly the same ... but it's not that much of a stretch to think ..."

"Cass," Mara interrupted. "Listen, I'm in the middle of a recess, I only have a couple of minutes. But I got some new information on Rhonda too. I wanted to let you know as soon as I could."

There was an urgency to Mara's voice I hadn't heard before. It sent goosebumps racing down my arms.

"Tell me," I said, fearing the worst.

"I pulled some strings with some law enforcement contacts I have in Kent County and hit the jackpot."

"Law enforcement?" I said.

"Any chance you've got a birthdate for Rhonda?" she asked.

"Yeah. September 14th, 1968."

"Bingo," she said. "I mean, I was hoping there wouldn't be more than one Rhonda Evans in Kent County in that age range anyway, but you should never assume."

"What've you got?" A big group came in the diner and took up most of the counter. I moved away, stepping into the lobby.

"A Rhonda Evans filed a petition for a domestic personal protection order in November of 1988," Mara said.

"A *domestic* P.P.O.?" Those were reserved for restraining orders against spouses, those who were dating, shared a child in common, or who lived in the same household.

"Yeah," she said. "At the time, Rhonda Evans was living at 3514 Cedar Lane in Kentwood. The house belonged to Marilyn Evans."

"Her mother's place?" I said, puzzled. "Who was the respondent?"

I heard papers rustling on Mara's end. "Somebody named Neil Shumway. I've got a copy of the petition. Rhonda filled it out in longhand. It looks like she went to a legal clinic for help with it. It's pretty telling. She's reporting this Shumway guy threatened her. Assaulted her. It looks like it was over a pattern of years. She says she caught him spying on her in the shower. She'd wake up in the middle of the night and he'd be in her bed holding her, telling her he thought she had a nightmare. Creepy stuff. It escalated, according to Rhonda. She says he told her if she tried to tell anyone about it, he'd hurt her. She says he also threatened to hurt her mother, Marilyn. The incident that precipitated the petition is chilling, Cass. She says he followed her home from school. She had a flat tire and he just appeared out of nowhere to help her. He covered her mouth and raped her.

"Cass," she said. "I haven't shared many details with you about the other rape victims. You understand I couldn't. But the flat tire thing, it was one of my guy's M.O.s. There are at least four other victims who were profiled that way. Later the cops determined their tires were slashed."

I saw white spots in front of my eyes. Mara was still talking but I couldn't quite process the words.

Neil Shumway. Neil and Patricia. *Newt's just a childhood nickname that stuck.*

"What happened with the P.P.O.?" I found myself asking.

"Not sure," she said. "Judge wouldn't grant it ex parte, he held it over for a hearing. The petitioner never showed up for the hearing and neither did Shumway. The judge dismissed the thing."

"Mara," I said. "This Newt guy I've been talking to. Who

I just met. Jesus. His real name is Neil. I didn't know. He just told me today."

Mara went silent. Then, "Cass, is he still there with you? Where are you?"

"No," I said. "I met him at Dooley's off M-50. He left maybe ten minutes ago. I was just about to head back to Delphi."

"Cass," Mara said. "What did Rhonda Evans look like? Have you seen a picture of her?"

"Yeah," I said. "I can text you one as soon as we hang up. But she looks just like Alicia Romaine but with lighter hair."

"Wavy, not curly, light-brown or dark-blonde hair? Pale eyes? Thin?"

I could see my own reflection in the window as I stood by the door. She could also have been describing me.

"Yeah," I said.

"Cass," she said. "That's this monster's type. Every one of his victims shared those physical characteristics. I'm beginning to think Rhonda Evans might damn well have been his first victim."

I left the diner on autopilot. Mara was still talking. She described a few of the other victims her suspect preyed on. All blonde, blue-eyed, thin. I slipped behind the wheel and drove out of the parking lot. I picked up speed on M-50, my heart racing.

"I want to bring him in for questioning," Mara said. "This Newt or Neil. Can you call him back and think of a reason to set it up? I want to get a sample of his DNA"

"Mara," I said. "You don't have probable cause for that yet. We'll need more. Let me think."

"Don't go defense lawyer on me," she said, her tone clipped. "Let's just get him in. Cass, do you think he's been playing you this whole time? Oh no. Alicia."

"I never told him her name," I said. Had I?

"Just get back here," Mara said.

"On my way," I answered. Then a loud bang jolted my car and my back end fishtailed.

My phone fell to the floor of the car as I careened out of control.

Chapter 50

BLACK TATTERED RUBBER spilled across the road as my tire blew out. I skidded to the side of the road, gripping the wheel. My car came to a stop just before pitching into a deep ditch.

I slapped my palm against the wheel. I looked out of my rearview window. There was another car slowing to a stop behind me. A white Buick.

The hair stood up on the back of my neck. The car pulled up alongside me and parked at an angle, effectively blocking me from pulling back out even if I could with my shredded tire.

"Cass?" Mara was still on the line. My phone had skidded across the seat and wound up on the passenger side floor.

"I'm here," I said. "Just had a tire blow out. Mara ... call 911. Tell them where I am. Hurry!"

"What? Cass?" Mara's voice cut in and out. I started to reach over to pick up the phone. Then my driver-side door swung open. Newt stood there, grinning.

"You okay?" he asked. My heart was in my throat. I looked back at my phone. It landed screen side up. Under Mara

Brent's name, I read the call failed message. The call had dropped. I was on my own. I prayed she'd heard enough to send help.

"Neil," I said.

"Looks like you could use some help. Come on, I'll give you a lift."

My gaze traveled to his hands. Long fingers, tapered nails. They were strong hands. Had he used them to hold down countless victims as he raped them? Rhonda Evans said she'd had a flat tire. It was Newt who showed up and cornered her. It was his M.O. And I'd just walked right into it.

"I appreciate your help," I said. "It's just a tire. I already called for roadside assistance. They'll be here in a few minutes."

"Oh, that can take hours. Surely there's somewhere you need to be. Come on. I'll give you a ride into town. I'm just glad you're all right. Those blown tires can be nasty. Real glad I was right here to see it and help you out. You coulda been a goner."

I weighed my options. He was too close. Still leaning in the doorway. Morbid thoughts raced through my mind.

I thought of all his other victims. Young. Blonde or light-haired. Pale eyes. Thin.

I fit that physical description as well. Little things filtered through my consciousness. My God. Had he been grooming me? Had I fallen for it? He might have looked me up online or something ... but then, why had he pretended not to recognize me in the diner?

Goosebumps danced across my spine. I was in seriously deep trouble.

"Cass?" he said. I looked in the rearview mirror. On this stretch of country highway at this time of day, there was no one else around.

It had been a setup from the very beginning. Dooley's was out of the way. He must have circled back while I had my back turned talking with Mara at the counter and then in the lobby. He got there first. He would have known what car I drove.

If he'd slashed my tires, it meant he had a knife.

I needed a weapon. I needed to think.

"Come on," he said again, holding his hand out.

"I think I'd rather just wait. They're local boys. They know me. And I told them right where to find me."

Newt's eyes flickered. The smile on his face took on a sinister meaning. He moved with lightning quickness, wrenching my arm as he tried to pull me out of the driver's seat. He reached past me and unhooked my seatbelt. I punched him in the arm, to little effect.

"Cass," he said. "What's the matter with you?"

"You need to let go of me," I said. "Right now, Neil."

"You're acting crazy."

It was then I saw the flash of silver in his right hand. There was the knife.

Sweat poured down my neck. He gripped my arm with his free hand and yanked me out of the car. I spilled out and landed on my knees in front of him. He knelt down, holding his knife to my throat.

"I figured you'd be the type to like it rough," he said.

I screamed. It echoed across the field beside us. Someone could get lost in it. About a mile to the east, the woods came in. If he took me there. If he got me in his car.

Neil pulled me up and started dragging me toward his car.

"No!" I kicked and flailed but he was too strong for me. He was too strong for all of them. For Rhonda. For Denise Silvers. For dozens of others. He was good at this. A master. And if I didn't get my wits about me, I'd be his next victim.

He pulled me around to the other side of my car so we were down in the ditch.

"Come on," he hissed against my ear. "You know this is how you like it."

"Fuck you!" I kicked backward. The knife felt cold against my throat.

He pushed me down so my cheek pressed against the dirt. He would do it here? Out in the open?

Neil Shumway was a man out of control. More animal than man. He fumbled with his belt. I tried to rear back, hoping I could bust his nose with the back of my head. He was ready for that. He neatly dodged me then shoved me forward until I fell face first in the mud.

I saw stars. I had just enough sense to scramble up.

Neil Shumway stood over me as a dark shadow. I saw the gleam of his blade. There was nothing human about him anymore. I knew in my heart I was staring into the face of Denise Silvers and Rhonda Evans's monster.

I had one last shot. I took it. As Neil advanced, I kicked out, aiming for his right knee.

I made contact with my heel, sweeping sideways. His whole leg buckled and he cried out in agony. It seemed that part of his story was true. His trick knee, the one he needed replaced. It betrayed him now as he tried to put weight on it. He crumpled back to the ground. It was his turn to scream.

I made my move. Yelling like a hellcat, I vaulted up the side of the ditch.

There were flashing lights up ahead. It might have been the tow truck. I didn't care. I waved my arms and hollered for all I was worth.

Tires screeched to a halt. It wasn't a tow truck at all. It was a dark-gray, unmarked car, its bubble light spinning and flashing on the roof of it.

It was my turn to have my knees give out as Eric Wray came running toward me, gun drawn.

Chapter 51

Two Weeks Later ...

Alicia Romaine sat on my office couch. Terrence towered behind her, protective and strong. He didn't need to be. Alicia had shown the strength and fortitude of a lioness.

"I think I still want to see him someday," she said. She held her six-week-old baby Aniyah against her shoulder. The baby's small feet poked out from beneath a pink blanket.

"No," Terrence said. "No way."

"Not anytime soon," she said, wistfully. "I'm not ready for that yet. But someday, I think it's going to be important for me to confront him."

She leveled her gaze at me. "Cass, I'm so sorry. I feel like if I'd never started this, that man would never have come into your life and tried to hurt you like he did."

I smiled. "I'm tougher than I look. And I'm sorry too. I wish I'd have put two and two together sooner."

"No one could have," Jeanie said. She sat in the far corner of the room. "That creep was doing a damn good job trying to keep us from finding Rhonda. It was your gumshoe investigating that brought us to Beth Chase."

Alicia smiled. "I'm so grateful for that. I came here looking for family. Beth is family. Even if she's not what I expected."

Rhonda's baby book sat on the table in front of us. I hoped that Alicia could cherish it without the taint of whose hands it passed through to get to her.

"You're sure there's no doubt?" she asked.

"None." Mara stood in the doorway. We'd called this meeting so she could share an update on Neil Shumway. It was news we all knew in our hearts by now, but Mara had the science. She held the report from the blood lab. She'd managed to get it expedited.

"Shumway's DNA matches that from Denise's rape kit and at least a dozen other crime scenes. We think he's our guy."

The other truth was just as hard for Alicia to hear. Shumway was her father. There was no doubt.

But the blue-and-yellow scrapbook on the table between us was the closest she might ever get to meeting her mother in person. Working with Jeanie's private investigator and Mara's contacts, we'd learned just this morning what happened to Rhonda Evans.

"It's okay," Alicia said. "I'm ready to hear it."

"Okay," I said. "Rhonda's letter to Beth really was a good-bye. She passed away in Ingham County six months after you were born. She'd checked into a homeless shelter. She died quietly in her sleep. It was a drug overdose, Alicia. The medical examiner ruled it was accidental.

"We shared the letter Rhonda wrote in support of the personal protection order she tried to get," I said. "We're trying to figure out why Rhonda never pursued it beyond that petition. In most cases, petitioners do that when they feel backed into a corner. If Patricia and Marilyn didn't believe her, maybe they threatened to throw her out of the house again. It's all speculation, but I've seen enough cases like this to make an educated guess. For whatever reason, Rhonda felt going through with the petition was going to make things worse for her in some way. We checked it against your timeline. The petition would have been filed right around the time she found out she was pregnant with you. It looks like she chose just to run away from the Evanses instead of fighting them. Probably to protect you."

"We'll probably never know," Mara said.

Alicia nodded, tears springing to her eyes. "The thing is, I feel like I've known it all along. She was so lost. So alone. I just wonder what would have happened if she'd decided to keep me."

"Honey," Jeanie said. "She couldn't have. She did the greatest thing she could for you. She protected you. She gave you a better life. The way you're living it now in comfort and love is all she would have wanted. And I'd like to think she knows it. In fact, I know she does. I can feel the love in this room."

Terrence handed his wife a tissue. Mara was crying too.

"I'll pray for her," Alicia said, rising. She had a lot to take in. Terrence gathered the items I laid out for her. The grade cards, the baby book. No one yet knew what would happen to Marilyn Evans's house now. Someday, I hoped Alicia would have the strength to go there with Beth. Perhaps they could learn more about their family together.

"Thank you," Alicia said.

"Thank me? Alicia, I feel like I've brought you nothing but sadness."

"No," she smiled. "I don't look at it like that at all. I'm who I am today because of my mother's bravery. Corey and

Aniyah are here today because of it too. She gave me a gift. I'm grateful for that."

"That's quite a wife you've got there," I said to Terrence. "You make sure she knows it every single day."

He put an arm around her. "I know. She's an angel. A miracle."

The two of them embraced. There was sadness in Alicia Romaine's eyes, but there was joy too. She had the answers she sought. She had a new family. And she could be part of the reason her mother and other women like her might get justice now.

Mara took a seat as Terrence and Alicia left my office and walked downstairs with Jeanie.

"I see you've got another file in your hand," I said to her.

She pursed her lips and waited until we heard the front door close. "Shumway faces assault charges here. But I'm working with the local cops to have him extradited to Maumee County. I've got enough now to get a warrant issued for the attack on Denise Silvers. I'm actually planning a trip to see her to break the news to her."

I nodded. "What about the other cases?"

"We'll see," Mara said. "I'm sharing what we can. And Shumway's not talking except to say that what happened with you was all a big misunderstanding. He's framing it as a long-term phone flirtation. He's going to say you lured him to Dooley's with the promise of sex."

I clenched my fists. "My ass. And Mara, you know whatever I can do to help with Denise Silvers's case, I'm on board."

"I will definitely need you to prepare to testify. And just brace yourself for whatever craziness Shumway accuses you of."

"I will," I said. "And thank you. I think I might owe you my life."

She waved my words away. "I just wish I could have gotten that info to you before you got in the same room with that asshole. I feel like I threw you to the wolves."

"Lucky for me," I said, "I've got some fangs of my own."

It was Mara who had tipped Eric off that I might be in trouble. She called him as soon as our call dropped and told her where I'd met Shumway. He'd been racing toward Dooley's when he saw my car and Shumway's on the side of the road.

"Do you think you can get him?" I said, narrowing my eyes at her. Probable cause to arrest him was one thing. Convicting on a decades-old rape was something altogether different. He might go down for the assault on me, but he'd get out.

Mara's back stiffened. She had the cold, calculating eyes of a predator. All my competitive instincts flared. Damn. Someday I really did wish I'd get the chance to spar with her in court.

"Yeah," she said. "I think I can nail that bastard to the wall."

"I'll bring you the hammer," I said. Mara's cold eyes brightened. She reached across the desk and we shook on it.

"I'm glad you're on my side with this one," she said. "I get the distinct impression you'd be a formidable foe on the other side."

I laughed as she gave voice to my own thoughts. I walked her out. The sun was shining and I knew I was feeling the first touch of summer after the gray winter we'd just left behind.

Chapter 52

LATER THAT WEEK, Eric asked me to meet him in his office. His tone had been grim but he wouldn't tell me what it was about.

"I need to talk to you in person." It was all he would say.

I went up fully bracing for the news that something fell apart with the Neil Shumway assault case. Had he been granted bail? I'd skipped the hearing as I had my own for a client in another courtroom. Plus, I fully trusted Jack LaForge to do his job and keep Shumway in custody.

Eric sat at his desk as I walked in. His face fell when he saw me. Then he quickly brightened.

"You okay?" he asked. "I've been meaning to get down to your office to check on you."

I smiled. "I'm fine."

He frowned. "Cass, you've been through some stuff. When are you going to take some time off?"

"When are you?" I meant it as a joke. Or to give it back to him. I realized he might take a different meaning to my words. As if maybe I was suggesting we take time off together.

He cleared his throat and shuffled paper on his desk.

"I'm just glad you're okay. I'm getting damn sick of having to rescue you all the time."

He couldn't hide the smirk on his face.

"Rescue me? Seems to me I spend most of my time saving your sorry ass."

It was easy between us again as I took a seat. Eric's smile was genuine when he looked back up. Something dark flashed in his eyes that made my pulse skip. It was my turn to clear my throat and wish I had some papers to shuffle.

"Listen," he said. "I wanted you to hear this from me. And also know that I'm telling you in confidence. We aren't ready to go public with this until ..."

"Eric," I said. "Spill it."

He picked up one of the pages he'd been fumbling with and handed it to me. I scanned the numbers on it, trying to get my brain to work.

"Cell phone records?" I said, looking up.

"Davy Monroe's cell phone records," he said. "I did what you asked. We took a closer look at him. There's a particular number he's calling multiple times. Sent and received. Sometimes ten times a day. Look at the dates."

I saw what he meant. The calls became more frequent right around the day of Sheila Brewer's disappearance.

"Eric?"

"We tracked it to this little town near Nashville. Aspen Springs. It took some doing, but I went down there. Cass, this is just a podunk little nowheresville. Maybe two thousand people in the whole town. But the calls there were frequent and consistent and all the way up until last week. I followed a hunch and gave a flier to the sheriff down there not expecting to hear anything back. In fact, I think the guy figured I was crazy."

"Eric," I said. "What flier? You heard something back, didn't you?"

He chewed his lip. "Yeah. Two days ago."

He picked up his phone and swiped the screen. He handed the thing to me. It was open to a grainy video message.

"Go ahead," he said.

My fingers trembling, I played the message. It was security footage from a convenience store or a gas station. There was a woman at the counter buying snacks. The view was of her backside. But a moment later, the camera switched to the one above the door. As she exited the store, she happened to look up, giving the camera a full, unobstructed view of her face.

My stomach flipped.

"Eric."

"I know," he said. "And this is why you can't tell anyone about this yet. I don't have her in custody. I've got a crew headed down there now. The shop owner is the sheriff's brother, for chrissake. He took my flier over and showed it to him, figuring he sees pretty much everyone in town. He recognized the woman and remembered she'd been in the day before."

"When was this taken?"

He let out a sigh. "Three nights ago."

I replayed the video. Finger shaking, I hit pause again. There, staring straight up at the camera, was a very-much-alive Sheila Brewer wearing a green sweatshirt with a cat on it.

"You were right," he said. "Son of a...you were right."

I tossed Eric's phone back to him, dumbstruck.

"*He* was right?" I said. I pressed a finger to my forehead.

"Yeah," Eric said. "Friggin' Joseph Leary. The bastard was

right this whole time. And he was telling the truth. Davy Monroe's been in contact with Sheila Brewer all along. The deputies are picking him up for questioning as we speak. They're waiting for word from me that the Aspen Spring boys have Sheila down there. We don't want to risk tipping either one of them off."

"Holy shit," I said over and over.

"Exactly," he said.

"I don't get it. How? What about all that blood?"

Eric squirmed in his seat. "I don't know. Not for sure. But after this came in, I took another look at her. One of those cousins Sheila claimed to be so smothered by? She used to work as a phlebotomist before she retired. I'm having her brought in for questioning."

"And she was looking to disappear," I said.

Just then, his phone buzzed.

"Wray," he answered. His face went through a myriad of changes as he listened to the voice on the other end for a full minute. He scowled, then his face softened and he nodded. "Yeah. Copy that. Good work. I'll let 'em know."

He tossed the phone down. "They just scooped Sheila up at her hair salon. Woodbridge deputies have Davy in the back of a squad car. They said he's already copped to all of it. Crying his head off and squealing like a stuck pig. He's given up the cousin too."

"Oh my God."

"Yep," Eric said. "Damn it. Who the hell would have figured your old man was the most honest person on that witness stand?"

I swallowed hard. I had no words. And as Eric knew, that was a damn first for me.

Chapter 53

ONE WEEK LATER ...

Marbury and Madison chased a couple of mallard ducks away from the shoreline then strutted back up the hill as if they owned the place.

I supposed they did as much as I. Marby's tail had a white tip to it like a little truce flag. The ducks weren't having it and kept their distance. It was a good thing. I didn't need them camping out on my dock and pooping all over it as soon as I got it in.

The house was framed in. I stood in what would soon be my living room with a large floor-to-ceiling window giving me an unobstructed view of the lake. Jutting out on a peninsula, I could pretend I had no neighbors at all. I'd finally gotten variances from the township to merge the triple lots.

I heard him coming before I saw him. Tires crunched across the loose stone that would one day be the paved driveway curving to a circle in front of my soon-to-be four-car garage. Plenty of room to store the pontoon and the fishing boat Joe was planning to buy for him and Matty.

It would be good to have him home. Matty was living in

Saline now. He planned to stay there until the holidays. He was stronger. More solid. And the last time I spoke to him on the phone, he sounded genuinely happy for the first time I could remember since he was a kid.

My father's shadow fell long. I turned and walked up the hill to meet him.

"You look good," I said. "Lost some weight in there. You needed it."

"Yeah," he said. "Regular health spa."

"I'm glad you're okay," I said, and I meant it.

"Gonna be quite a place," he said. "You took the plans my grandpa left."

I nodded. It had always been Great-Grandpa Leary's dream to rebuild this place. Until we found the lockbox buried near the foundation, I never would have known.

"I've made a few adjustments of my own," I said. "The detached garage. And I bought the extra lots so we could have some privacy."

"My dad said he wanted that too," he said. "Never could get the township to approve his build plans though. Who'd you sleep with to get 'em to?"

He was joking. I didn't find it funny.

"Anyway," he said. "It'll be good. A place big enough for all of us. Finally. That was really their dream."

"No," I said. "Not all of us. There's no place here for you."

My father's face darkened. "Who do you think you're talking to? This is my house more than it is yours."

I smiled at that. A few months ago, I might have lost my temper and raged at him. I had none of it left for him anymore.

"It's not," I said. "That's why Grandpa left it to me. He knew I'd know what to do with it. He knew I'd take care of it.

And he knew I'd keep you away from it. That's why he didn't leave it to Matty."

"You think you're better than me," he said.

"Maybe," I said. "I know I keep trying. And the thing is, I don't want to fight with you anymore. I'm not mad at you about Mom anymore either. I should be. Joe still is. He may never forgive you. But Matty and Vangie will, if that makes you feel better."

"And you?"

"Me?" I sighed and looked back out at the water. "Me. I'm just done. Done protecting you. Done fighting your battles. Just done."

"I fight my own battles."

I turned to him. "And I and everyone else in this family take shrapnel hits every time. No more. I don't hate you. I said that. I even love you. Because Mom did. And yeah, she died because of it. But she wasn't perfect either and I know that now. I know when she fell down and got hooked on pain pills, you did try to keep it together for us. I remember that. I appreciate it. And I know in your own twisted way, you love us too. There's no place for you here. You can visit sometimes. I can't stop you. I might even open my door for you. But Delphi's not your home anymore. You were right to move on. It's time you did it again."

"I'll sue you," he said. "You know I talked to a lawyer after my dad died. He thought I had a decent case to challenge my father's will. Undue influence, he said."

I rolled my eyes. "Stop before you hurt yourself, Dad."

I reached into my back pocket and pulled out the envelope I'd saved for this occasion. I handed it to him.

My father opened it. His face changed as he read what was inside.

"What's the catch?" he asked.

"I just told you. You go back to Jackson. Or to Florida. Or wherever it is you call home."

"I was the victim, dammit," he said. "Davy and Sheila and her moron cousin framed me. All for a damn insurance claim."

I took a step toward him. "Davy and Sheila double-crossed you. When Davy got the chance to screw you over, he took it. Their stories were consistent. Won't help them stay out of jail for insurance fraud, obstruction of justice, and about ten other lesser charges, but they provided the paper trail. You masterminded the plan to defraud Sheila's insurance company. A two-million-dollar payout, right? No named beneficiary but it would have gone to her cousin as next of kin. Great way to keep her off the radar. Were you the one who floated the idea of her storing her own blood, taking it little by little until she had enough to make it look like she'd bled out?"

His lip twitched. "They can't prove any of that. Thinking about something isn't the same as doing it."

"You're right," I said. "They can't prove you acted on any of your musings. That's what'll keep you from getting charged. Lucky for you, Sheila and Davy were just dumb enough to get caught. But you miscalculated. Davy had a reason to hate you. You never figured they'd dump that blood in *your* hotel room. Or did you? Were you willing to take the risk because you thought Davy would back you up? And you thought I'd be able to fix it."

"They were caught because I was telling the truth!" he yelled. "It doesn't matter what bullshit what-ifs we discussed over a bottle of whiskey at the pool hall. I didn't act in concert."

He'd done his legal research. Of course he did.

"Yes," I said. "And I believed you all along. You seem to want to forget that. And you seem to want to ignore the toll it's taken on all of us. Damaged my professional credibility. Sent Matty into a spiral. Broke Vangie's heart. Destroyed your relationship with Joe. And then there's Mom."

"I've paid for that!" he yelled.

"You haven't. We have. But not anymore. You're free. You've got your second chance. And now you've got the means to do whatever you want with it. Just don't do it here. The condition on that check is that you get out of Delphi and stay gone."

He looked down at the check I'd just written him. I'd made it out to him for twenty thousand dollars. It was all I'd managed to save. I could make more. To me, this was a bargain.

"I'll rip it up!" he snarled.

"I suppose you could," I said. "But you won't. And I'll stop payment on it if you try cashing it here."

He folded the check and put it in his pocket, just like I knew he would.

"You're ungrateful," he said. "Spoiled. All of you."

He muttered worse things as he walked back up the hill. I shielded my eyes from the sun as he disappeared into the shadows.

Another figure emerged, passing him on the way. Marbury and Madison caught his scent and yelped with joy as Eric strode down the hill toward me.

"Everything okay?" he asked, looking back at my father. He watched with me as Dad climbed in his truck and drove away, kicking up gravel as if he meant it as an exclamation point.

"Better now," I said. "I paid him to get the hell out of town." I couldn't tell him the rest, my suspicion that my father had been at least partly in on Davy and Sheila's scheme. That had been a guess on my part. My father's reaction had just confirmed it. And like it or not, as his lawyer, I couldn't say a word, not even to my siblings.

Eric raised a brow. "You sure that'll take."

I sighed. "Yeah. For a while. He can talk a big talk but the last few months scared the hell out of him. He wants to get the hell away from here as much as I want him to. The cash just means he'll go farther."

"Leary," he said. "You have an interesting family."

"Nah," I said. "We just put the fun in dysfunctional."

He laughed at that then leaned down to scratch the dog's bellies.

"They'll always love you best," I sighed. It was true. Those two went nuts whenever Eric showed up.

"They've got good taste," he said.

He straightened and looked at the house. He walked over to one of the beams and kicked it.

"Gonna be something to see when it's all finished. Solid. Sturdy."

"New," I finished for him.

"They extradited Shumway to Ohio this morning. No bail."

"Good," I said. "That'll give Alicia some peace of mind."

"You too?" he asked. "You sure you're okay after everything that happened?"

I looked at him. He was tall, broad, handsome. A good man. A champion. I considered him for a moment, then smiled up at him.

"Eric," I said. "I didn't like it when I thought Mara Brent was flirting with you."

He opened his mouth, then froze. Then he recovered and that sly smile of his lit his face.

"Flirted?"

"Yeah."

His eyes narrowed. Some of the humor left his face. He took a breath and said something I realized later that he'd been keeping in for a while.

"And I didn't like you with Killian Thorne."

Killian, my former client, and I had briefly rekindled our affair last year. But that was over now. And I deserved what Eric had to say about it. I had a few things I could have told him about it. Instead, I took a breath and settled for, "Okay."

"And I don't like the risks you take. Or worrying about you as much as I do. Because I do. A lot. And I don't like how that makes me feel. And if you ..."

"Eric?" I said. "Shut up." I closed the distance between us. I reached up and gently pulled his head downward. Then I went up on my tiptoes and pressed my lips to his.

He felt so good. He returned the kiss. His arms came around me, protective, commanding, strong. He took my breath away as I sank into the kiss. Marbury and Madison ran in circles around us, chasing off a second family of mallards.

Heat zinged through me as we finally parted. Eric's face was flushed. His eyes sparked with mischief.

I turned and faced the lake as Eric wrapped his arms around me. He felt warm and solid as I rested my head against his chest and we watched the blazing sun dip below the horizon in the shadow of my new home. The Someday House.

Someday was almost here.

Up Next...

Cass Leary has ***many more*** cases to solve. In the meantime, don't miss Time of Justice, which kicks off a heart-stopping new series from bestselling legal thriller author, Robin James.

Hard-nosed prosecutor, Mara Brent knows her case against an elusive serial rapist should be a slam-dunk. But, a faceless powerbroker has other ideas. Unexpected bombshells at trial threaten to muddy her black-and-white conviction into frightening shades of gray. Mara suspects there's a sinister conspiracy out to torpedo the verdict... and her career.

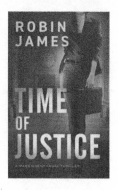

Click to Learn More

Newsletter Sign Up

Sign up to get notified about Robin James's latest book releases, discounts, and author news. You'll also get *Crown of Thorne* an exclusive FREE ebook bonus prologue to the Cass Leary Legal Thriller Series just for joining. Find out what really happened on Cass Leary's last day in Chicago.

Click to Sign Up

http://www.robinjamesbooks.com/newsletter/

About the Author

Robin James is an attorney and former law professor. She's worked on a wide range of civil, criminal and family law cases in her twenty-year legal career. She also spent over a decade as supervising attorney for a Michigan legal clinic assisting thousands of people who could not otherwise afford access to justice.

Robin now lives on a lake in southern Michigan with her husband, two children, and one lazy dog. Her favorite, pure Michigan writing spot is stretched out on the back of a pontoon watching the faster boats go by.

Sign up for Robin James's Legal Thriller Newsletter to get all the latest updates on her new releases and get a free digital bonus scene from Burden of Truth featuring Cass Leary's last day in Chicago. http://www.robinjamesbooks.com/newsletter/

Also by Robin James

Cass Leary Legal Thriller Series

Burden of Truth

Silent Witness

Devil's Bargain

Stolen Justice

Blood Evidence

With more to come...

Mara Brent Legal Thriller Series

Time of Justice

Made in United States
Orlando, FL
30 March 2024

45183606R00211